Other Books in the
Emmeline Kirby/Gregory Longdon Series

Lead Me Into Danger

Deadly Legacy

From Beyond The Grave

A Checkered Past

When Blood Runs Cold

Old Sins Never Die

Viper's Nest of Lies

A Mind To Murder

**Praise for the
Emmeline Kirby-Gregory Longdon Series**

"A new book with Emmeline and Gregory is like a visit with old friends - if the visit began with breakneck action and didn't let up until a totally unexpected ending. Sometimes old friends have the most surprising secrets of all."
—Tracy Grant, author of *The Seven Dials Affair*

"*In Betrayed by the Truth*, Bernett ramps up the excitement in a nonstop escapade that takes sleuthing duo Emmeline and Gregory from Spain to England and finally Switzerland for an unexpected twist that contradicts everything they thought they knew about the case."
—Alyssa Maxwell, author of *The Gilded Newport Mysteries* and *A Lady & Lady's Maid Mysteries*

"A fast-paced adventure of espionage and murder, with drama on every page. Husband and wife sleuths Emmeline and Gregory make a formidable team."
—Linda Stratmann, author of the *Early Casebook of Sherlock Holmes* series.

"Danger, political machinations, murders…Ms. Bernett is an author whose storytelling draws you in….There is a depth to the characters….[With] shocks and revelations to the end, [her] books [leave] me wanting more. If you like international mysteries that transport you to various locations, give her books a try."
—*Novels Alive*

"A brilliant novel of murder and suspense…that sets the blood boiling…. It is as if Ian Fleming colluded with Agatha Christie to create…beguiling twists, sparkling dialogue and sharp relationships while uncovering clue after clue…Everything a mystery reader wants and more."
—Humphrey Hawksley, former BBC Asia and World Affairs Correspondent and author of the best-selling *Dragon Strike* series and *Rake Ozenna* thrillers

"Packed with suspense, action and drama…[these] books grab you from the first page and never let go until the last sentence on the last page. Daniella Bernett is a brilliant storyteller who seamlessly combines a thrilling and unpredictable plot, with humour and fabulous characters…Bernett never disappoints with her books, they seem to go from strength to strength."
—*Bookliterati Book Reviews*

"Revenge and murder are served up at a cracking pace as Emmeline unites with Gregory in…Daniella Bernett's [intriguing] mystery series."
—Tessa Arlen, author of the *Woman of World War II* series

"Scintillating…theft, murder and general mayhem… styled to mirror the writing of classic Golden Age authors. With strong characterization…Daniella Bernett has enhanced a series which…has the potential to gain a strong following."
—*The Dorset Book Detective*

Betrayed By The Truth

An Emmeline Kirby/Gregory Longdon Mystery

By: Daniella Bernett

A Black Opal Books Publication

GENRE: ROMANCE/MURDER MYSTERY, INTERNATIONAL THRILLER, AMATEUR DETECTIVES

This is a work of fiction. Names, places, characters and incidents are either the product of the author's imagination or are used fictitiously, and any resemblance to any actual persons, living or dead, businesses, organizations, events or locales is entirely coincidental. All trademarks, service marks, registered trademarks, and registered service marks are the property of their respective owners and are used herein for identification purposes only. The publisher does not have any control over or assume any responsibility for author or third-party websites or their contents.

BETRAYED BY THE TRUTH
Copyright © 2023 by DANIELLA BERNETT
Cover Design by Transformational Concepts
All cover art copyright © 2022
All Rights Reserved
Print ISBN: 9781960050236

First Publication: OCTOBER 2023

All rights reserved under the International and Pan-American Copyright Conventions. No part of this book may be reproduced or transmitted in any form or by any means, electronic or mechanical, including photocopying, recording, or by any information storage and retrieval system, without permission in writing from the publisher.

WARNING: The unauthorized reproduction or distribution of this copyrighted work is illegal. Criminal copyright infringement, including infringement without monetary gain, is investigated by the FBI and is punishable by up to 5 years in federal prison and a fine of $250,000. Anyone pirating our ebooks will be prosecuted to the fullest extent of the law and may be liable for each individual download resulting therefrom.

ABOUT THE PRINT VERSION: If you purchased a print version of this book without a cover, you should be aware that the book is stolen property. It was reported as "unsold and destroyed" to the publisher, and neither the author nor the publisher has received any payment for this "stripped book."

IF YOU FIND AN EBOOK OR PRINT VERSION OF THIS BOOK BEING SOLD OR SHARED ILLEGALLY, PLEASE REPORT IT TO:
skh@blackopalbooks.com

Published by Black Opal Books **http://www.blackopalbooks.com**

*To my mother and my sister Vivian, with love.
I'm so lucky to have you.*

Acknowledgements

I would like to thank Editor Susan Humphreys, who gave my book the extra polish it needed and created the beautiful cover.

My continued gratitude to the International Thriller Writers, Mystery Writers of America New York Chapter and the Crime Writers Association for their support.

I would like to thank bestselling author Tracy Grant, who has been on this journey with me from the beginning. My deepest thanks also go to Humphrey Hawksley, former BBC Asia and World Affairs correspondent, who I met at ThrillerFest and have corresponded with ever since, and authors Alyssa Maxwell, Emma Jameson, Tessa Arlen and Kate Quinn, with whom I became friends via Facebook and exchange lively ideas about writing and life.

Prologue

Madrid, Spain December 2010

After the "incident" at the Palacio Real involving the Raven, an international assassin who had been planning a hit on a prominent British official, Emmeline and Gregory had decided to spend a well-deserved week's holiday in Madrid. They went to the Prado, strolled in El Retiro Park, and made a point of visiting the Plaza de Cibeles, where the fountain of the Greek goddess Cybele on a lion-drawn carriage resided. They also ventured to Plaza Mayor and Plaza de España. They found that the squares were much more pleasant since they were no longer being hounded by assassins and Russian spies. She also was able to relax because she knew that her half-brother Adam Royce was no longer implicated in any crimes.

Every evening after dinner, husband and wife took long walks along Grand Via, the main thoroughfare graced with Belle Epoque buildings, restaurants, and shops.

Now, Emmeline was feeling wistful because tomorrow

would be their last day.

"I wish we could stay longer. Madrid is beautiful."

Gregory threw his arm around her shoulders and kissed the top of her head. "We could return in the spring, if you like."

She tilted her head back to smile up at him. "Ooh, yes. I'll start making some plans when we get home."

Gregory chuckled and drew her closer to him.

"Excuse me, señor," a man called behind them.

They stopped and turned around. "Yes?" Gregory asked.

"You're English, are you not?"

Gregory's eyes narrowed in suspicion. "Why do you want to know?"

Beads of perspiration were sprinkled across the man's forehead and his breathing was coming in rasps. He fumbled in his pocket and drew out a black velvet pouch.

His hands trembled as he shoved it against Gregory's chest. "Please take these to London. Give them to Alexander Colefax."

His gaze seemed to dart in every direction at once. "Only to Colefax. It's very important."

"Look here—" Gregory began, but the fellow cut him off.

"They will kill me if they find them. Please help me," he begged.

He shot a glance over his shoulder. "*Madre di Dios*, it is too late."

The fellow scurried off, leaving Gregory staring down at the pouch in his hands. He slowly loosened the drawstrings. His heart stopped between beats when six luscious red diamonds tumbled into his palm. The tip of his tongue flicked over his lips. Red, the rarest variety of natural fancy-colored diamonds.

Emmeline gasped and her hand flew to her mouth. Gregory hastily stuffed the gems back inside.

He took her elbow. "Come on," he commanded. "Let's go back to the hotel."

A horrifying screech followed by a sickening *thud* shattered the peace. Chaos broke out as people scattered in different directions a couple of blocks ahead of them. Women started shrieking and men were shouting.

"What happened?" Gregory asked an older man, who was hustling away.

"A terrible accident, señor." The stranger crossed himself. "A young man was hit by a car."

Emmeline and Gregory traded a wary look, as the stranger bolted off.

Good sense dictated that they should go directly to the hotel. But curiosity drew them like a magnet to the scene of the accident.

An ambulance arrived and the paramedics were clearing a path to the victim.

It was too late.

The young man who had entrusted the diamonds into Gregory's care was dead.

Emmeline clutched his sleeve. "We have to find a policeman." Her tone was low and urgent.

Gregory's gaze skimmed the faces of the stunned onlookers huddled around the lifeless body in the road, their numb whispers clinging to the evening breeze. Only one man hovering at the outer edge of the human semi-circle exhibited no interest in the tragedy. His onyx gaze was locked on Gregory and his mouth curled into a menacing smirk. He began threading his way toward them.

Gregory caught Emmeline roughly by the arm. He could feel her muscles tense with apprehension, as her head whirled around.

Her dark eyes scoured his features. "What now?"

"Darling, Madrid has suddenly lost its charm." He offered her a tight smile. "We're leaving *tonight*. Right now, in fact."

One careful foot at a time, they backed away. They silently cursed the full moon for its insistence on drenching everything in pearlescent light. Every nerve in Gregory's body followed their unwanted admirer's progress. The man was only a few yards away. Any minute he'd be upon them.

Gregory drew out his wallet and pulled out a fistful of bills. He threw them up into the air and shouted, "*Euros*," as they fluttered back to the ground.

A cry went up and the crowd surged forward. The man was swallowed up and lost from view.

Gregory grabbed Emmeline by the wrist.

"*Run.*"

Chapter 1

The shrill peal of the telephone ripped Nigel Sanborn from the throes of a terrible nightmare. He sat bolt upright, his body slick with sweat and his heart hammering against his ribcage. For a moment, panic seized his chest and he didn't know where he was. Soon, his eyes adjusted to the gloom and his breathing slowed as he realized that he was in the bedroom of his Earl's Court flat in Nevern Square. He couldn't recall anything about the dream. But his nerves still tingled with a sense of doom.

As his hand snaked out to grab the phone, the ringing stopped. He slumped back against the rumpled pillows and dropped his chin to his chest. He took a couple of deep, cleansing breaths and then poured himself a glass of water from the pitcher on his night table. He downed it in two gulps. Just as he was about to pour another glass, the phone started to scream again.

"Hello," he barked, his voice thick with sleep and

confusion.

"Nigel, I'm sorry to wake you."

Nigel scraped a hand over his face. "Superintendent Burnell?" He flicked on the light and scooped up his watch. "It's three o'clock in the morning."

"Believe me, I'm well aware of the time," the detective replied tartly. "I'll be lucky if I see my bed at all."

"Sorry," Nigel mumbled. "I know you wouldn't have called if it wasn't important."

He heard Burnell exhale a weary sigh. "I'm afraid a man named Alexander Colefax was murdered tonight." He paused for a beat as if choosing his next words carefully. "We've arrested—"

Nigel threw off the bedclothes and leaped out of bed. "Good Lord. Don't tell me it's Gregory or Emmeline. I thought they were still in Madrid."

"Don't get your knickers in a twist. It isn't our meddlesome husband and wife. Thankfully they're not involved. This time."

Another thought struck Nigel. "It's not Brian, is it?" Blood thundered against his temples, as he waited for an answer.

"No, it isn't your brother either."

A wave of relief washed over Nigel. "Then, I don't understand."

"The chap we have in custody didn't have any identification on him. He claims he was mugged earlier in the evening and his wallet stolen. Rather convenient, if you ask me," Burnell grumbled. "He refuses to give his name, but he says he's a good friend of yours. Can you come down to the station? His mouth is clamped shut tighter than an oyster guarding a pearl. Maybe you can get him to talk."

Nigel's mind was reeling. He ran a hand distractedly through his sleep-tousled hair. Who was this chap? "I don't see what I can do. But of course, I'll come down if you think I can help. I'll get dressed and be there as quick as I can."

"Much appreciated. You're a gentleman, as always."

⌘

Sergeant Finch was waiting for Nigel, when he stepped out of the lift on the seventh floor of the steel-and-glass office tower that Scotland Yard called home. It was a stone's throw from St. James's Park.

The detective's cheeks were covered by a shadow of reddish-brown stubble and there were purple smudges beneath his eyes. However, he offered a cheerful smile. "Hello, Nigel. The guv sent me to meet you. Thanks for coming."

Nigel clasped his extended hand and gave it a brisk shake. "Anything for the Metropolitan Police," he replied as he fell into step beside Finch. "I hope Burnell's confidence in me is not unwarranted. I wracked by brain on the way over here and can't imagine who this mystery fellow could be."

The sergeant's jaw clenched in a grimace. "He still hasn't said a word."

"I take it the evidence against him is fairly strong." Nigel raised an eyebrow in askance. "And the victim? Alexander Colefax? I've never heard of him."

"We're only at the beginning of our inquiries," Finch offered circumspectly. "I'll leave it to the guv put you in the loop."

"Right. Of course."

Finch led him to Burnell's office. He rapped his knuckles on the door once and opened it without waiting for the superintendent to respond.

Burnell's head shot up at their entrance. He quickly rose to his feet. "Ah, Nigel. Thanks for coming."

"I just hope it isn't a waste of time," Nigel said after they had shaken hands. "Surely it would have made more sense for this chap to ask for his solicitor."

Burnell gave a resigned shrug. "A criminal's mind is like a dark labyrinth. Best not to go down that path, otherwise you're liable to sink into the mire of madness."

Nigel inclined his head. "I don't want to compromise your investigation, but is there anything I should know before I speak to him?"

"A witness picked out this chap in an identity parade without hesitation." Nigel pursed his lips and gave a glum nod. "But I want to assure you that you'll be perfectly safe. A constable is posted outside the door, and Finch and I will be nearby. All you have to do is knock, if he threatens you in any way."

"I wasn't really worried. Do you have any particular questions you'd like me to ask him?"

"To be brutally honest, I don't want you playing detective at all. Just get his name. Leave the rest to us."

"Understood. Well, I suppose that's it. I'm ready to see him."

❧❧❧

Nigel hesitated before the door to the interrogation room. He was uncertain what to expect. After a moment, he nodded to the constable, who turned the knob and stood aside to allow him to enter.

An involuntarily shudder coursed through his body, as the door closed behind him with an ominous *thud*. Shadows clung to the perimeter of the cramped, airless room. Only the plain, wooden table in the center was bathed in artificial light.

He staggered backward, when he saw the fellow sitting in one of the chairs.

The man's upper lip curled into a smirk and amusement danced in his brown eyes. "It's been a long time. Did you miss me?" He had the poor taste to chortle.

Nigel's chest clenched and all the air was sucked from his lungs. His skin prickled with goosebumps. This was *not* happening. It was a nightmare. Yes, that was it. He was still in his flat. All he had to do was wake up and it would all go away.

He blinked. A few seconds ticked by, but everything remained the same. Except the icy tendril of dread that curled around his heart.

"Da-mian." The name was snatched from his lips on a hoarse croak. He swallowed hard and drew his shoulders back.

He stood there transfixed, as he stared back into the past with loathing and contempt. He saw Damian for what he always had been—a man absorbed with himself and what he could get out of the world because he thought he deserved it. Nigel's younger self had been naïve enough to allow this man into his life.

When he had found his voice again, he asked, "Why?"

Damian's sensuous mouth curved into that smug, self-satisfied smile that Nigel remembered and despised.

"You don't seem happy to see your old friend," Damian drawled.

"Friend?" The word flew through the air like a missile honing in on a target.

Friends make the worst enemies because they know one's weaknesses and how to twist the knife to exploit them. With the familiar taste of bitterness on his tongue, Nigel cursed himself for ever trusting this man.

He strode toward the table and gripped the back of the chair. It was taking all his willpower not to reach out and curl his hands around the other man's throat. A rush of adrenaline coursed through his veins, as he imagined his fingers squeezing and squeezing until there was no life left in Damian. "You're the devil's spawn," he hissed through gritted teeth.

"I should be offended, but I'll put it down to the surprise of this unexpected reunion."

"What do you want?"

Damian motioned at the chair. "Please sit down. You look as if you could do with a rest."

Nigel, not a violent man by nature, was fast succumbing to primitive tendencies. He lifted the chair off the floor and dropped it in place. The rattling *boom* bounced off the walls.

The next second, the door flew open and the constable was looming before them. His wary gaze slithered from Damian to Nigel. "Are you all right, Mr. Sanborn?"

"You must forgive my friend, Constable," Damian droned. "He always gets a bit tetchy, when he doesn't get his beauty sleep."

The constable scowled at him and pressed, "Mr. Sanborn?"

Nigel's nostrils flared with anger. However, he drew in a deep draught of air as he sought to steady his racing pulse. He could march straight out of the room. After all, he had only promised to give Burnell the name of the man they had in custody. And, as much as he wished he had never laid eyes on Damian again, he now needed to know why he had been summoned.

"I'm fine," Nigel replied tersely. "I'm apologize for my outburst."

The constable's skeptical gaze raked his face, but with

a reluctant nod he withdrew from the room.

Nigel's head whirled round once the door closed. "What do you want?"

Damian slumped back in his chair and regarded him steadily. "My solicitor left yesterday on a skiing holiday and won't return until after the new year. As you can see, I'm in a spot of bother and need a lawyer."

Nigel huffed an incredulous laugh. "Everything is always about you. I haven't practiced criminal law for ten years."

"It will come back to you," Damian shot back tartly.

"I'm the corporate counsel for Sanborn Enterprises."

"Oh, yes, how could one forget? Dear old Dad snapped his fingers and you chucked everything for a cushy job in the family firm."

Nigel gripped the edge of the table and leaned forward. "The *only* reason I joined the company was because Brian needed me. Not Dad." He bristled with indignation. "He was an arrogant bastard, just like you."

"Oh, do sit down and stop glaring at me. I'm not impressed."

"Why should I help you?"

"Because no matter what you feel about me, I know you believe in the law." Damian paused for a moment. "And Barbara would have wanted you to."

Barbara.

Nigel drew a sharp breath and dropped heavily into the chair opposite Damian. "How dare you utter her name," he snarled, his hands curled into fists, "after what you did to her."

Damian threw his head back and barked with laughter. There was a cruel glint in his eye, when his gaze met Nigel's again. "I didn't do anything. Barbara made her own choice. I can't help it, if you didn't satisfy her."

"She was my wife and you deliberately set out to seduce

her. It was all a game to you."

"You're wrong. I did care about her. In my own way."

"Really? When she was diagnosed with cancer, you turned your back on her because suddenly it became too serious and you couldn't handle it. Barbara came back to me. I took care of her through those long, painful months before she died." This last word caught in his throat.

Damian's shoulders twitched in an indifferent shrug. "What can I say? I'm not good with complications."

"No," Nigel sneered, "of course not. When things get messy, you run in the other direction because you're selfish."

"Look, I could care less what your opinion of me is. I *need* a lawyer. That fat, plodding copper out there"—he waved a hand at the door—"thinks I murdered Alexander Colefax."

Nigel chortled. "Superintendent Burnell more than thinks that's the case. An eyewitness has identified you."

Damian slammed his open palm on the table and leaned forward. "Well, the witness is mistaken or was paid off to point the finger at me."

"For what reason?"

"I don't bloody know, do I? I swear to you I'm not guilty of killing Colefax. But things look pretty bleak at the moment. That detective is going to arrest me."

Cracks were beginning to form in Damian's cool, self-assured demeanor. Nigel could hear the tremor of desperation in his voice. However, his own emotions were churning in his chest and he held his tongue.

"No matter how much you despise me," Damian tried again, "you won't be able to live with yourself if I'm banged up for a crime I didn't commit." He regarded Nigel steadily. "At least represent me until I can find a lawyer who is willing to take on my case. That's fair, isn't it?

Everyone is entitled to representation under the law."

Nigel scraped a hand over his face and exhaled a weary sigh. "Do you have an alibi?"

Damian beamed at him. "I knew you wouldn't leave an old friend in the lurch."

Nigel raised a finger in admonishment. "Don't press your luck. Just answer the question."

The other man settled back and hooked an elbow around his chair. His usual smug smile slipped into place. "Of course, I have an alibi."

And then, he fell silent.

"This is no time to play coy. If you want my help, you'll have to tell me."

"As alibis go, it's rather good. I'm just not sure whether you're going to like it."

Nigel dropped his chin to his chest and groaned. When he reluctantly dragged his gaze back to look the other man in the eye, he commanded through gritted teeth, "Spit. It. Out."

"You're absolutely right. Best to have it out in the open. I was in Bayswater, in a flat in Westbourne Terrace murdering an actress named Julie Brentford."

Wave upon wave of blood thundered in Nigel's ears and the room began spinning. He couldn't have heard Damian properly.

"Can you…Would you please repeat that?" he stammered.

"Dear, oh dear," Damian clucked his tongue. "Only forty-seven and already your faculties are going." He raised his voice slightly. "I said I couldn't have killed Alexander Colefax because I was across town murdering Julie Brentford."

Bile rose in Nigel's throat. He was going to be sick.

He gripped the edge of the table with both hands to steady his shattered nerves. He forced himself to take deep gulps of air, while Damian studied him in bemusement.

A suffocating silence stretched out between them. In the space of a few minutes, Nigel's world had splintered into a million razor-sharp shards of glass. And he had been completely lacerated.

He surged to his feet, knocking over the chair. "You contemptible bastard. You've just made me an accessory after the fact," he spat savagely.

"Well, they say misery loves company," Damian replied philosophically. "What makes this situation even more delicious is the fact that your exaggerated sense of honor and your conscience won't allow you to breathe a word because, as my lawyer, whatever I tell you is privileged."

He chuckled at Nigel's evident distress and horror.

Thanks to Damian, Nigel's knowledge made him a criminal.

He was trapped between guilt and the law.

And there was no way out.

Chapter 2

It had taken Emmeline and Gregory twenty-three hours to reach London. Their hasty journey had started when they caught the 8:40 TGV from Puerta de Atrocha, Madrid's main railway station. They changed trains twice, at Barcelona and Paris, and at 6:40 the following evening their Eurostar pulled into St. Pancras International.

If husband and wife had managed to doze at all, it had only been for a few minutes. The adrenaline was beginning to wear off, as they clambered into the back of a taxi on Midland Road. They stared, bleary-eyed, out the window on the drive to Holland Park. The traffic had been lighter than usual and they arrived at their townhouse in twenty minutes.

Emmeline darted up the steps to unlock the door, while Gregory paid the fare and scooped up their bags. She was shrugging out of her jacket, when he shot the bolt into the lock.

He rested his back against the door and watched her slow movements. The curve of her cheek was stretched taut with tension and fatigue. "Emmy, say something," he implored.

Her head whipped round, her dark gaze impaling him. "We have to go to the police. We should have gone to the nearest police station straightaway in Madrid."

Gregory pushed himself away from the door and drew her into his embrace. She put up a half-hearted struggle for a moment and then surrendered. He cupped her chin and tilted it, forcing her to look at him. "Darling, if you'll recall that rather nasty-looking chap left us with very little choice."

She glared at him, but leaned into his body nevertheless. "All the more reason to go to the police," she grumbled. "Clearly, he was involved in that young man's death." She dropped her voice to barely above a whisper, although they were alone in the hall of their own home. "And now, we're fugitives from the law. And in possession of six rare, *stolen* diamonds"

Gregory threw his head back and a laugh erupted from his throat.

"There is nothing amusing about this situation," she reproached him.

He kissed the top of her head, inhaling the scent of lily of the valley mingled with her fury and horror. "We don't know that the diamonds are stolen. It's unseemly for the *Clarion*'s intrepid editorial director of investigative features to make such assumptions." He gave a disapproving shake of his head. "I'm surprised at you, darling. You must remain objective at all times."

Her quelling look lashed him to pieces. "You *know* that they are. The man in Madrid was terrorized because they— whoever they are—were hunting him down. That's why he foisted the gems onto you. Only it was too late. We must go to Superintendent Burnell. Make a clean breast of it. And let the law take its course."

A pensive expression crossed her husband's face. "When put like that, it makes tremendous sense. However, love of my life, you've forgotten one tiny point."

She raised an eyebrow in askance.

"Alexander Colefax is waiting for the diamonds. I think he'll be more than a bit miffed, when they fail to arrive on schedule."

She rolled her eyes at the ceiling. "I hope you're not saying that Superintendent Burnell and Sergeant Finch can't be trusted with the diamonds. Besides, Colefax could be the head of a criminal gang for all we know."

"We wouldn't want to burden old Oliver. He's far too busy with police work to undertake such a menial errand."

"Hmph," she grunted. "On the other hand, you, as chief investigator for the insurance firm Symington's, is eminently qualified to carry out the delicate task I suppose?"

"Haven't we been model guardians over the last twenty-four hours?" he countered. "And I know for a fact you're dying of curiosity to find out more about Colefax."

Oh, how well he knew her. Colefax was an enigma that she was eager to unravel. *Who was he?*

However, it wouldn't do to get into Burnell's bad books. He was none too pleased about their recent entanglement with the Raven and Verena Penrose's murder.

So pragmatism won and she punched her husband's arm. "Gregory, we have to turn over the diamonds to the police."

"Ouch." He rubbed the spot. "You may have crippled me for life. My arm is going numb." He rubbed more vigorously. "I have a good mind to start divorce proceedings."

A frustrated sigh escaped her lips. "You are incorrigible."

"But extremely lovable, you must admit." He arched an eyebrow suggestively. "Why don't we go upstairs and discuss this matter in depth in the privacy of our bedroom?"

"Seduction will not work," she sniffed and tossed her chin in the air. "I'm adamant about the diamonds."

"Oh, yes?" His lips left a trail of kisses from her earlobe down her neck. His mouth lingered at the hollow at the base of her throat.

"Mmm," she murmured. "This is not fair. You are a beast."

He chuckled, his warm breath tickling her skin. "Think of the fun you'll have trying to tame me."

❦

The next morning, Nigel sat in his office at Sanborn Enterprises, staring at the contract in front of him. This was his third attempt to review it. His eyes felt gritty and raw. The words blurred before him. He blinked a few times, but it was an exercise in futility. He couldn't concentrate on his work. He hadn't slept in over thirty-six hours. He couldn't eat. His mind was fixated on bloody Damian Rossiter.

I was in Bayswater, in a flat in Westbourne Terrace murdering an actress named Julie Brentford.

The confession taunted him.

Nigel clasped his hands together to stop them from trembling. What was he going to do? He couldn't allow Damian to get away scot-free. The man had exhibited no remorse. He was liable to kill again. It would be Nigel's fault, if that happened. He would never forgive himself. But *how* could he ensure that Damian was arrested for the crime? Did the police even know that Julie Brentford was lying dead in her flat? He didn't even know her precise address.

He certainly couldn't ask Burnell. The superintendent now considered him a leper because he had announced that he was Damian's lawyer. It didn't matter that it was a temporary situation. *Very temporary*. Only until Damian could find someone without scruples who was willing to defend him, despite the fact that he had taken a woman's life.

A sigh rumbled through Nigel's chest. At the moment, though, the prospect of turning over the reins of Damian's case seemed a long way off. He pushed himself to his feet. He supposed he had better go to Scotland Yard to ask to see the case file. He raked a hand through his hair. Never had he dreaded anything more.

But he had to go. He shrugged into his suit jacket and grabbed his coat. He would think of a way to inform Burnell about Julie Brentford, without violating his client's confidentiality.

⁂

Gregory peered through the glass door and saw police officers wandering back and forth or stopping briefly to exchange a word at the desk with the sergeant. He smoothed down the corners of his mustache and hesitated.

"Stop stalling." Emmeline nudged him in the ribs with her elbow. "We agreed last night that we have to inform Superintendent Burnell about the man in Madrid *and* turn over the diamonds."

The pouch with the precious red gems nestled against his heart, snug and safe. His mouth curved into a smile calculated to melt her heart. "Emmy, I don't recall agreeing to anything of the sort."

Her eyes narrowed and she poked him in the chest. "Inside," she commanded, jerking her chin at the door.

"Darling, there's no reason to resort to violence. Frankly, it's unbecoming."

She pushed the door open and stood aside waiting for him to enter the building.

He favored her with another smile and made a sweeping gesture with his arm. "Ladies first."

She returned his smile, but her hand clamped down on his forearm. "Thank you. Now, come along, dearest," she said as she dragged him over the threshold.

Her gaze darted to the desk, where she saw that Sergeant Trimble was on duty. He was sharing a joke with a fellow police officer, but he seemed to sense her scrutiny and looked up.

He raised a hand in a wave. "Good morning, Miss Kirby. Nice to see you." His brow furrowed when he saw Gregory by her side, although he inclined his head in greeting. "Mr. Longdon." His gaze slid back to Emmeline. "How can I help you?"

She smiled at him. "My husband and I need to see Superintendent Burnell. It's rather important."

Trimble's good humor evaporated, and his mouth compressed in a grim line. "I'm afraid he's rather busy. There was a murder last night."

Emmeline's journalistic antennae were always on the alert for a juicy lead. "Oh, yes? How interesting. Any details you can share?" Her lips curled into a smile that invited confidences.

Gregory coughed to cover up the laughter bubbling in his throat. He rubbed his chest with a hand. "Bit of a cold."

Emmeline gave a disapproving shake of her head, but she was smiling when she turned back to Trimble.

"Sorry, Miss Kirby. We're not releasing any information at this time."

She sniffed. "I see." Her voice was laced with disappointment. Never mind, she'd wheedle something out of Burnell about this new murder. Right now, the diamonds were the pressing issue. "Of course, I understand. Perhaps we'd be able to speak to Sergeant Finch?" she cajoled. "I promise we'll only be ten minutes, at most."

Gregory took her elbow. "Darling, we wouldn't want to waste police time." He smiled at the constable. "It's nothing urgent. We'll come back when it's more convenient."

Emmeline shook off his grasp. Her eyes shot daggers at him. "We—"

She never finished what she had intended to say because she spied Finch heading toward the lift. "Sergeant Finch," she called after him.

He spun around at the sound of his name. His eyes widened, and then narrowed, when he saw husband and wife standing by the desk. He strode toward them. "Emmeline, Longdon," he murmured. "I thought you were still in Madrid. What are you doing at the station?"

"Lovely, as always, to see you, Sergeant Finch," she gushed. "We had to cut our trip short. We returned last night." She lowered her voice. "We need to speak to you and Superintendent Burnell about a sensitive matter." She lifted her eyebrows and gave him a meaningful look to emphasize her point.

His warm brown gaze immediately flew to Gregory's face. "Oh, yes? What mess have you gotten yourself into this time?"

"I rather resent that you and Oliver immediately jump to the conclusion that I've done something illicit. I needn't have to remind you that I'm a law-abiding citizen,"

Gregory reproached him, but his cinnamon eyes danced with mischief.

Finch snorted, "Your wife is the only one who believes that."

"Ahem." Emmeline cleared her throat. "It happens to be true," she asserted with a touch of asperity.

Finch sighed and pinched the bridge of his nose between his thumb and forefinger. "I'm sorry, Emmeline. It's been a long night."

She took a step closer to him. "Yes, Sergeant Trimble mentioned that you and Superintendent Burnell are investigating a murder. Can you tell us anything?"

Finch met her gaze and smiled. "Yes."

"Oh, good." She fumbled in her handbag for her notebook and pen. When she'd flipped to a clean page, she prompted, "Please go ahead."

"At this time," he paused, unnecessarily stretching out the moment, "the Met has no comment."

A spasm of annoyance flitted across her features and she snapped her notebook closed. "Very droll."

"Right." He took each of them by the arm and propelled them toward the door. "The two of you had better shove off before the guv sees you. He's not in the best of moods this morning."

"Is old Oliver ever in a good mood?" Gregory queried innocently.

"Only when you're not around, Longdon." Burnell's gruff voice boomed from behind them.

The trio turned in unison to find the superintendent with his arms folded over his broad chest and a scowl darkening his haggard features.

"Oliver." Gregory beamed at the detective and proceeded to straighten his tie. "I know you're only teasing."

Burnell swatted his hand away and grunted, "It's *Superintendent Burnell* and I never joke, especially when it comes to you." He flicked a glance at Emmeline, who offered him a shy smile. "Emmeline," he mumbled, his tone softening slightly. Then to Gregory, he demanded, "Why are the two of you here?"

"Well, if you must know, it was Emmy's idea." She rolled her eyes toward the ceiling. "But we can see that you're busy." He placed a hand on her elbow again. "We'll come back another time."

"We will not," she declared. Addressing Burnell, she explained, "We wouldn't bother you, if it wasn't terribly important."

Burnell stroked his neatly trimmed white beard. He remained silent, his gaze flitting between husband and wife. Eagerness vied with anxiety in Emmeline's dark eyes.

He groaned. "I know I'm going to regret this, but I suppose you had better come up to my office. Otherwise, you'll make a nuisance of yourselves down here."

"Thank you," Emmeline mumbled, while Gregory remarked, "I knew you missed us."

"It would be a gift from heaven, if I wasn't tripping over you every five minutes, Longdon," Burnell muttered out of the corner of his mouth, as they made their way toward the bank of lifts. "I dream of the day when I never have to see your smug face again. Preferably the day I put you behind bars."

Without missing a beat, Gregory quipped, "So you dream about me?" He pressed a hand to his heart. "I'm truly touched, Oliver."

The detective glowered at him and jabbed the button to call the lift, silently giving vent to a stream of invectives.

Chapter 3

Burnell settled himself behind his desk with a heavy sigh and flapped a hand impatiently at the chairs opposite. "Right, get on with it," he ordered. "My ulcer is already telling me I'm not going to like whatever you're about to say."

Emmeline and Gregory quickly sat down, while Finch hitched a hip on the corner of the desk.

She took a deep breath and mentally organized the facts, before launching into an unvarnished account of their unsettling encounter in Madrid. "We were forced to cut our holiday short because two nights ago a stranger approached us on Gran Via. He was quite agitated and kept looking over his shoulder. He asked if we were English and before we had a chance to answer, he thrust a pouch at Gregory—"

One of Burnell's wispy, thin eyebrows arched upward. He fixed his blue stare on Gregory's face. "A pouch?"

Gregory gave a slight nod and smiled at the superintendent. "Black velvet, if you're curious."

Burnell glared at him, while Emmeline rushed on, "The

young man told us that 'they' were going to kill him. He asked us to take the pouch to London and give it to a man named Alexander Colefax."

"What?" The detective slammed his desk with his open palm. "Alexander Colefax. Are you sure?"

She shot a worried glance at her husband and then swallowed hard. "Ye-es, but there's more. Before we could gather our wits, the man ran off and…and five minutes later he was lying dead in the road. A car had struck him and sped off. It all happened in the blink of an eye." She paused, her gaze trailing from the superintendent to Finch. "The pouch contained six red diamonds." Burnell's eyes widened in disbelief. "A man in the crowd must have seen the dead chap hand over the pouch. This new fellow came after us, but we managed to give him the slip. That's why left Madrid a day earlier than planned. Gregory thought it would be best not to risk going to the airport, so we took the train home." She slumped back in her chair. "That's the long and short of it. We came straight here this morning."

Burnell stroked his beard meditatively, as his gaze snaked over to Gregory. "You expect me to believe that of all the people in Madrid, this stranger decided to entrust the diamonds to you. Why?"

Gregory smoothed down the corners of his mustache. "What can I say? I have the sort of face that inspires confidence," he replied silkily.

The detective snorted. "Pull the other one." He leaned forward and propped his elbows on the desk. "Where are the gems?"

Gregory held up one finger and with the flourish of a conjurer drew out the pouch from his inside breast pocket. He silently slid it across the desk.

The superintendent stared down warily at the pouch and then reluctantly picked it up. He pulled open the drawstrings, before giving it a gentle shake. The diamonds tumbled onto the desk in a shimmering cascade ranging from deep red to red-purple. An involuntary gasp escaped from Emmeline's lips, although she knew what to expect. The gems were even more impressive upon second viewing. Burnell and Finch were momentarily tongue-tied and utterly bewitched by the diamonds' charms.

Gregory broke the spell by gustily clearing his throat. "As I'm certain you chaps are aware, red diamonds are the rarest and most unique of the fancy-colored diamonds. That's why they are highly sought after by collectors. They can cost one million dollars a carat. Therefore, I'd say these beauties are worth one hundred twenty million dollars or about one hundred million pounds. That's an educated guess, you understand."

A low whistle escaped from Finch's lips, while Burnell slumped back in his chair and groaned. "I despise diamonds, especially fancy ones," he muttered.

Gregory continued with his lesson, as if the detective had not spoken. "Very few mines produce red diamonds. Africa, Australia, Brazil, and India are areas where they have been produced. However, the majority come from Australia, particularly the Argyle mine. Only twenty to thirty pure red diamonds are known to exist in the world. Their rarity means nearly all red diamonds are less than one carat." A faint smile touched his lips, as he reverently recalled, "The Moussaieff Red is the largest red diamond. It is a triangular brilliant cut, fancy red and internally flawless. It weighed 5.11 carats and sold for eight million dollars in 2001. The second-most famous of these beauties was the 5.05-carat Kazanjian Red Diamond, which was discovered in the Lichtenberg South Africa, in 1927. It was originally 35 carats." He shook his head and sighed. "But it was ultimately turned into an emerald-cut diamond. The

Kazanjian Red was once seized by Nazi soldiers from a home in the Netherlands. An American general later found it in a salt mine. He thought it was a ruby. Of course, I can't forget the DeYoung Red Diamond, the Hancock Red, the Graff Purplish-Red—"

"Enough," Burnell snapped, visibly cringing. "I don't want to hear any more about diamonds."

Gregory sniffed. "Really, Oliver. I'm rather surprised by your attitude. A policeman, let alone a senior detective, should be well-informed on all subjects. If you are well-rounded"—he flicked a mischievous glance at the superintendent's ample stomach—"it will help you to perform your job in a better, more efficient manner."

"*Longdon.*" Burnell's tone held a steely edge of warning.

One of Gregory's shoulders twitched in a casual shrug. "As you wish."

Emmeline took advantage of this momentary lull in their verbal duel to venture, "Superintendent Burnell, you had a strong reaction when I mentioned Alexander Colefax. I take it you know who he is."

A pained expression flitted across the detective's features. "In a manner of speaking." He paused for a beat. "He's lying in the morgue. He was murdered the other night."

Her jaw dropped at this unexpected, and tantalizing, morsel of news. She quickly regained her wits and plunged a hand into her handbag to draw out her notebook. "I see," she mumbled as she scooted to the edge of her chair.

Leaning forward, she held her pen aloft. "Who was Colefax? Where was his body found? Do you have any suspects?" She rattled off the questions without taking a breath.

Finch dropped his chin to his chest and shook his head, while Burnell's eyes narrowed. "No comment," he roared.

Emmeline would not be fobbed off. "Oh, come on, Superintendent," she wheedled. "You can't keep this quiet." She offered him a smile. "I'm on your side. The side of justice and the truth. You can trust me to be objective. If you told me something, you could control the narrative. You do see that, don't you?" When he remained silent, she pressed, "I would hate to have to go around you to find out the details."

Gregory choked back a laugh by turning it into a cough. This earned him a withering look from Burnell.

Emmeline held her breath, hoping she had broken through the detective's defenses.

Burnell shook his head at the eager expression etched into her features. He wagged a finger at her and Gregory. "I should have the pair of you barred from entering the station. Separately, you are a nuisance. Together, you are a menace to a simple policeman's sanity."

Emmeline silently crowed. Despite his bluster, she had won. Again. She would get her story. Out of the corner of her eye she saw Gregory's lips part to offer another teasing quip, but she swatted his arm before he could utter it. He had the good grace to incline his head and abandon the idea. At least for the moment.

Burnell sighed and folded his hands in front of him on the desk. "Right. Our investigation is in the preliminary stages." She gave a mute nod and held his gaze. "Alexander Colefax was one of the wealthiest men in the UK. His fortune was estimated at four hundred million pounds last year. He owned the Royalton Hotel in Mayfair, The Corbett in St. James's, the Belvedere Gardens Hotel in Park Lane, and the Heatherwood Grand in Knightsbridge, as well as hotels in Bath, Cheltenham, Dorset, Berkshire, and Aberdeenshire. He also had extensive property and farming holdings, including a ten-bedroom estate in Norfolk. Outside the UK, he owns hotels in Paris, Milan, and Hong Kong."

Glancing down at his notes, Finch picked up the thread. "We've learned that he made five trips over the past seven months to Moscow, where he wanted to build a hotel. Rumor has it Colefax wasn't terribly fussy about the company he kept. He waved his wealth about and landed *tête-à-têtes* with Kremlin elites, oligarchs, and Russian mafia bosses. In other words, anyone willing to grease the wheels to secure him the permits he required. If that wasn't ambitious enough, the fellow had aspirations for a luxury hotel in the heart of Beijing."

Emmeline's hand stilled and her gaze flickered between the two detectives. "How was he killed?" she asked, after digesting the information.

"He was savagely bludgeoned to death in the living room of his Chester Row townhouse in Belgravia." Burnell tapped a file at his elbow, presumably a preliminary report from Dr. Meadows, the medical examiner. "Colefax suffered blunt-force injuries to the head, neck, torso, and upper and lower extremities."

A shudder of revulsion rippled through her body, as Gregory murmured, "Rather excessive and messy."

A troubled expression flitted across his features. Violence was utterly revolting and frightfully distasteful. That's why he never carried a gun. After all, the bloody things leave holes in delicate parts of one's anatomy. But to beat someone to death? That was a chilling and gruesome matter altogether. "It seems to me that the murderer must have been consumed with rage, which fueled a desire to inflict as much pain as possible and to *punish*. Although a woman scorned is more than capable of killing in cold blood, the violence you describe makes me think that the culprit must be a man." He arched an eyebrow at Burnell. "What's your theory, Oliver? Could it have been a business rival who decided to clear the playing field? Or perhaps a cuckolded husband?"

"Well," the superintendent hedged. "We're still exploring a range of possibilities."

Emmeline cocked her head to one side and frowned. Her ear caught the ring of something evasive in his answer. "The diamonds must be the motive." She bit her lip. "Colefax returned home unexpectedly and surprised the murderer." She paused, puzzling out her theory. "At this stage, it's quite obvious the diamonds were stolen and the young man in Madrid was the courier." She gave a dissatisfied shake of her head. "But why the devil would a rich man like Colefax steal the diamonds? He could have written a check for any amount without batting an eye. Moreover, his accountant could have used some creative maneuvers and declared it as a business investment."

"Mmm" was Burnell's noncommittal response.

A light tapping on the door jarred them from their troubled thoughts.

A spark of annoyance kindled in the blue depths of the superintendent's eyes. "Come in."

Nigel's head popped round the door. "Hello, Superintendent Burnell. I was wondering whether you were going to release my client…" His sentence trailed off, when his gaze landed on Emmeline and Gregory.

Some of the blood drained from his cheeks. "Ah." His lips compressed into a thin line, as he stepped into the office. His attention returned to Burnell, but he could feel Emmeline's probing questions boring into his body. "Right. My client has been detained for over twelve hours. If you're not going to charge him, then you must release him."

The skin beneath the detective's neatly trimmed white beard flushed pink. "I can hold your client for forty-eight hours. You know that."

"But the evidence is circumstantial," Nigel protested.

"He had a violent row with the victim earlier in the evening. He made threats against the victim."

"Oh, come now. Each of us has said things in the heat of the moment that we regret later and never meant in the first place."

Burnell folded his hands on the desk and gripped them hard to keep a rein on his temper. "Your client has scratches on his face and neck, as well as cuts on his knuckles. We also found a shirt with blood on the cuffs stuffed in the back of a drawer. And let's not forget that a man fitting his description was seen leaving the victim's house."

"That's a complete fabrication. He didn't kill Colefax because—" Nigel broke off abruptly.

Burnell raised an eyebrow. "Because *why*? If you have evidence to the contrary—" he spread his hands wide— "by all means share it with us. We're keen to hear it."

Nigel moistened his lips with the tip of his tongue. His hazel eyes clouded with a mixture of repugnance and helpless fury.

Colefax? Emmeline's ears perked up.

"What client?" she demanded, unable to remain silent a moment longer. Her words hung upon the air, already crackling with tension. "What does Alexander Colefax's murder have to do with Sanborn Enterprises?"

"Nothing," Nigel muttered out of the corner of his mouth.

"Then why are you involved?" Gregory challenged. "You don't practice criminal law."

Nigel raked a hand through his hair and sighed. "I did for ten years," he explained, "before chucking it because Brian needed help with the company. And with Dad. But thankfully Dad's no longer a concern."

"Mmm," Gregory murmured, his shrewd gaze searching his cousin's face. "How does Brian feel about you representing a murder suspect?"

"I haven't told him yet," Nigel snapped. "Now, stop interrogating me." Gregory and Emmeline exchanged a startled look. "Both of you."

Far from being chastened, his words only served to bolster Emmeline's determination to get answers. "Is this chap a friend of yours?"

"*No*," Nigel retorted acidly. "Damian's only friend is the devil."

"If that's the case, I'm at a loss to understand. It's obvious you despise this man and yet—"

He cut across her. "Damian didn't do it. That's why. You, of all people, should appreciate the desire to see that justice is served. Every man is entitled to a proper defense. I can't sit idly by and allow an innocent man to be charged with a crime he didn't commit."

"My years of experience tell me that Damian Rossiter doesn't have a single innocent bone in his body," Burnell commented derisively.

"If Rossiter is as unscrupulous as you suggest, his objective was to get the diamonds by any means," Emmeline tossed into the fray. "Perhaps he and Colefax were partners. The situation came to a boil. One thing led to another and then Colefax was dead. Obviously, a bit more digging is needed to determine whether Rossiter was the one who carried out the dirty deed himself or he hired someone to do it."

Four pairs of male eyes stared at her.

"Don't gawp at me like that. It's a perfectly reasonable theory."

Nigel's forehead puckered in confusion. "What diamonds?"

"Never mind," the superintendent snapped, his features contorted into a dark scowl.

Nigel blinked at Emmeline, before reluctantly dragging his gaze back to Burnell. "Right. Are you going to release my client?"

A gurgling sound rumbled at the back of the detective's throat. "Not at the present time," he replied tersely.

Nigel's jaw was set in a stubborn line. "I see." His tone was clipped. "For the record, the Metropolitan Police is wasting valuable time, not to mention resources, by focusing on my client."

Burnell pursed his lips. "That is a matter of opinion." His nostrils flared, as he sought to remain calm. "We'll know more when the results of the analysis on his shirt come back."

Nigel placed his palms on the desk and leaned toward the detective. "I pity you, Superintendent. The real killer has slipped through your fingers. My client is not guilty of *this* crime. And yet, you already seem to have convicted him."

"No," Burnell replied slowly. "I'm a humble policeman. I merely gather the evidence. A jury makes the ultimate decision about whether to convict and a judge metes out the punishment. That's how the law works in a free society. Your client has emerged as our prime suspect. I have to follow the trail where it takes me."

Nigel blinked a couple of times and exhaled a ragged breath. To everyone's bafflement, he rambled on undeterred, "I suppose that means you're going to badger his mates and his *girlfriend* and…and others." His sentence trailed off lamely.

"We don't 'badger,'" the superintendent intoned with gravitas. "We are only concerned in getting to the truth. We have to understand the nature of the relationship between the victim and your client, as well as to establish the timeline of events." His eyes narrowed as he regarded Nigel speculatively. "You're a lawyer. I shouldn't have to explain that to you. Thus far, your client has been uncooperative. If he's innocent"—he held up a plump hand to forestall the protest about to burst from Nigel's lips—"as you claim, it's in his interest to answer our questions. The fact that he's lost his ability to speak, except with you, sets my mind to wondering what he has to hide."

"I agree with Superintendent Burnell," Emmeline interjected, as she bestowed a smile on the detective, "I haven't met your client yet—"

"Nor will you, if I can help it," Burnell muttered under his breath.

Emmeline sniffed and tapped the desk with one finger for emphasis. "Once again, I must remind you that there is a free press in this country."

Burnell grunted in disapproval. "A free press, yes. But interference with a murder inquiry is another matter altogether."

She pretended not to have heard this word of caution and instead spoke to Nigel, "I haven't even met your client, but his behavior makes me think he's covering up a crime or crimes."

Oh, Emmeline, if you only knew the sordid details, you'd run as fast as possible in the opposite direction, Nigel lamented in silent chagrin. He straightened his spine as another thought struck him. *No, you wouldn't. You'd dig and dig because you're like a dog with a bone. And no one would find it curious, since it's a journalist's job to ask questions.*

She shot him a quizzical look, as the ghost of a smile curled around his lips.

He cleared his throat and changed tack. "In recent months, there have been a series of stabbings all over the streets of London, not to mention other terrible crimes. Are you insinuating that my client is responsible for all of them?" He breezed ahead without giving her a chance to respond. "If a murder is reported in Bayswater tomorrow, for example, I *hope* you're not going accuse my client."

She rolled her eyes at the ceiling. "You're being ridiculous," she scolded.

"Am I?"

He had thrown down the gauntlet and could see that she was eager to accept the challenge. He congratulated himself for planting a seed in her mind about Damian without violating his oath as a lawyer.

Or had he merely been a clever fool?

He felt the weight of Gregory's wary gaze upon him and a flutter of dread stirred in the pit of his stomach. Nigel cursed himself because he was quite certain that he had just placed Emmeline in harm's way. And that was the last thing he ever intended.

His breath caught in his throat. If something happened to her…

Not even the cold cocoon of his grave would be able to assuage the torment of guilt.

Chapter 4

The unexpected peal of the telephone shattered the quiet tension that had descended upon the office.

The superintendent snatched up the receiver. "Burnell," he barked.

"Really, Superintendent Burnell, when are you going to deport yourself with a modicum of professionalism?" a female voice reprimanded, her tone laced with contempt. "How do you expect the public to have confidence in the Force, if you behave in such a boorish manner?"

Sally bloody Harper, Assistant Commissioner Cruickshank's supercilious secretary.

Burnell glowered at the mouthpiece as if it were Medusa's head of writhing snakes. He knew Sally dared to take such liberties because she had made herself indispensable to Cruickshank and he would never sack her. Burnell wondered whether she made similar snide remarks to any of his colleagues or if she saved her barbed *bon mots* only for him. In any event, he wasn't outraged since he despised Sally as much, if not more, than she loathed him.

He swallowed down his vexation and prepared a verbal

assault of his own. "Ah, the melodious forked tongue of the viper. Therefore, it must be Sally," he replied with faux heartiness. "As always, you've brightened my day with your caustic niceties. What can I do for you?"

His fingers drummed on the desk, although they itched to wrap themselves around her throat.

He experienced a small stab of joy at her gasp. "My greatest wish is that I never lay eyes on you ever again."

"If wishes were horses, beggars would ride, as the saying goes," he quipped. He leaned back in his chair and smiled at Finch and the others, as he waited for the tiresome woman to get on with it.

"Insufferable beast," she muttered in his ear. Then in clipped tones, she said, "Assistant Commissioner Cruickshank wants to see you straightaway."

His smile faded and he squeezed his eyes shut. An audience with the Boy Wonder was the last thing he was in the mood for at the moment.

He opened his eyes and sat up wearily. "Finch and I are rather busy with the Colefax murder. I'm afraid—"

She cut across him. "Were you born insubordinate? Your *commanding* officer wants to see you *at once*. Stop shirking your duty."

Finch, sensing that he was about to give vent to his temper, clamped a hand on his shoulder to steady him. Burnell shot him a grateful look.

"The assistant commissioner expects you in his office in the next five minutes," Sally snarled. She rang off without waiting for his reply.

The superintendent pressed his tongue against his cheek and replaced the receiver in its cradle.

His gaze trailed from Emmeline to Gregory, before settling on Nigel's face. He flapped a hand and jerked his chin at the door. "All of you out. I can't deal with you now. The Boy Wonder has issued a summons. Lord knows what he wants."

Gregory's hand shot out to scoop up the diamonds, but Burnell was quicker and gave his knuckles a hard rap. "Ah, ah. Not so fast, Longdon. The diamonds *stay*."

The corners of Gregory's eyes crinkled in amusement. "You have far too much on your plate, Oliver. As a good friend, who always has your best interests at heart, I was merely attempting to ease your burden."

A harsh bark of laughter erupted from Burnell's lips. "*Friend*? You and I never have been, nor will ever be, friends. The diamonds are now evidence in the Colefax murder. They will be logged in and sent to the evidence store. A property clerk will take charge of them. As far as you're concerned, they never existed."

Gregory's smile only grew wider. "If I didn't know better, Oliver, I'd think you didn't trust me."

"Very perceptive. Now, everyone *out* before Cruickshank lets Sally loose from her lair to hunt me down."

Gregory cast a last longing glance at the pouch with the diamonds and reluctantly rose to his feet. He took Emmeline by the elbow. "Come along, darling."

Nigel cleared his throat. "May I speak with my client, Superintendent?"

Burnell's jaw clenched. "If you must," he replied grudgingly and turned to Finch. "Bring Rossiter to one of the interrogation rooms." He wagged an admonitory finger at Nigel. "Only half an hour."

Nigel gave a curt nod and hurried after the sergeant, who had left to make the arrangements. Emmeline was close on Nigel's heels, calling out questions to his retreating back.

Only Gregory lingered behind, one shoulder casually resting against the doorframe.

"Why are you still cluttering up my office?" Burnell demanded.

"I was marveling at your air of commanding authority," Gregory observed with a cheeky wink.

And then he was gone. At last.

Burnell threw a pencil at the closed door and steeled himself for his audience with the Boy Wonder.

Into the valley of death, he lamented to himself with a sigh. *The sacrifice one makes for the job.*

ೞ

Nigel was pacing outside an interrogation room, when Emmeline cornered him. "May I join you? I'd like to interview your client."

Nigel spun on his heel, when she gently laid a hand on his arm. The last thing he wanted was Emmeline anywhere near Damian. "Out of the question," he replied gruffly. "Conversations between lawyer and client are privileged. It's similar to the relationship between a journalist and her source." He arched an eyebrow pointedly.

"I'm surprised by your attitude. If Mr. Rossiter is innocent he would welcome the opportunity to tell his side of the story. Why don't you let him decide?" Her mouth curled into a cajoling smile.

"It's not—" He broke off, when he saw Finch approaching with Damian in tow.

"Ah, Nigel, it's about time. I hope you've come to get me out of this stinking place."

Damian's face was covered by a night's growth of beard and his sandy hair was tousled. His tie was missing and his shirt collar gaped open at the hollow of his throat, adding to his general air of dishevelment. His bloodshot eyes were clouded by exhaustion, but a spark kindled in their brown depths when his gaze fell upon Emmeline.

He appraised her from head to toe. "Well, well, well. And who is this sexy creature? I'd gladly spend another night in jail, if this is the prize that awaits me in the morning."

Emmeline's back stiffened at his lecherous affrontery. The scowl that creased her features failed to make an impression. Damian's grin only grew wider.

Nigel took a step forward and placed himself between her and Damian. "Apologize for your rudeness," he demanded through gritted teeth.

"Oh, come off it. Every woman enjoys being the object of men's desire. Isn't that right, love?" Damian asked.

Emmeline curled her fists at her sides and spat back, "Mr. Rossiter, I am here in a purely professional capacity. Otherwise, I would have nothing to do with you. We've been acquainted for only a few minutes and already I find you quite revolting."

He scraped a hand over his jaw, as he regarded her. "I'd love to know what profession you practice?" One eyebrow arched up suggestively.

She drew in a sharp breath at the lascivious innuendo behind his words. She took a half-step backward.

"Shut your gob," Finch snapped. Then, he jerked his chin in the direction of the bank of lifts. "You'd better go, Emmeline."

"Emmeline, is it? The name melts on the tongue like sugar," Damian cooed.

"If you continue to insult my wife, I'll be left with no choice but to rip your tongue out and to feed it to you."

The smile on Gregory's lips warred with the steely glare in his eyes. When he reached Emmeline's side, he slipped an arm around her waist.

Damian's eyes widened for a second and then his

arrogant grin slipped back into place. "Married? Well, I don't hold that against you, love. I realize you're full of pent-up frustration in search of an outlet. Married women intrigue me"—he cast a sideways glance at Nigel. "Just ask Nigel."

Two ugly crimson stains crept up Nigel's cheeks. Emmeline could feel the anger radiating from every sinew in his body. It made her question yet again why he had agreed to defend such a detestable man.

"Apologize to my cousin and his wife or else I'll walk out of the station *now*." His voice was hoarse, but the threat lanced the air.

"Cousin? A family affair. How utterly," Damian paused, seemingly to choose his words, "charming." He pressed a hand to his chest and dipped his head. "I apologize, if I've offended you in any way, *Emmeline*. I assure you I'm quite a likeable chap once you get to know me."

"I rather doubt it," Gregory quipped.

"Right, I'm putting an end to this circus," Finch announced. He gripped Damian roughly by the arm. "Rossiter, your behavior has earned you a trip back to your cell." Then, he inclined his head toward Emmeline and Gregory. "It would be best if the two of you left."

Gregory gave a mute nod, while Emmeline continued to glower at Damian.

"That's not cricket," Damian complained. "I haven't had a chance to consult with my lawyer. I have rights. Tell him, Nigel. Do your job."

"Alexander Colefax had a right to breathe and walk on this earth, but you snuffed out his life," Finch countered.

Damian wagged a finger at him. "Careful, Sergeant. Your bias is showing. I believe the correct legal parlance is *alleged*. I didn't murder Colefax. The only way a jury will convict me is if you and that tub of lard manufacture evidence. You read about dirty coppers all the time in the papers."

As someone cursed with a short temper and impatience, Emmeline admired Finch's cool demeanor. It must have taken a supreme effort to remain calm and not rise to Rossiter's bait.

She watched as Rossiter, flanked by Finch and Nigel, disappeared into the interrogation room. He may not be guilty of this murder—although her instincts told her he wouldn't bat an eye at taking a life—but beneath that bravado he was definitely hiding something.

She was determined to find out what it was.

At the same time, the mysterious diamonds gnawed at her brain as she and Gregory walked toward the lift. Whatever illegal game Colefax was involved in, someone was willing to go to great lengths to possess the gems.

An icy tendril of dread slithered down her spine and her gait faltered. Her gaze flickered toward her husband's profile.

And now that someone knew Gregory had the diamonds. Was it a matter of being in the wrong place at the wrong time? Or was he intentionally targeted as retribution for something in his past?

She drew in a ragged breath. Either way, her husband was tiptoeing blindfolded through a minefield.

Chapter 5

"Bloody marvelous. What is he doing here?" Gregory muttered under his breath.

His voice tore Emmeline from the worry that was swelling in her chest. "Hmm. Who is it?"

Gregory gestured with his chin toward the lift.

She followed his gaze and saw Laurence Villiers, the deputy director of MI5, duck into the lift. She pursed her lips. Only something extremely dire could have compelled Villiers to leave his office at Thames House, MI5's headquarters on the north bank of the river near Lambeth Bridge.

"Villiers," Gregory called out in an exaggerated hiss and increased his pace.

Villiers pretended not to hear as he jabbed the button with his forefinger. The doors slid closed just as Gregory reached the lift.

"Bloody hell," he swore, his features pinched in a scowl.

To say that his feelings toward Villiers were complicated would be the embodiment of British understatement. Years ago, the deputy director had appealed to Gregory's sense of Queen and country and recruited him to do "little jobs" for MI5. What Villiers had neglected to mention was that he was Gregory's father. He had abandoned a woman who was his wife in every sense, except a legal one, and their three-year-old son. The truth had come to light recently. If it had been up to Villiers, the secret would have remained locked away forever.

Emmeline touched her husband's arm lightly. "Don't let him upset you."

Gregory took her hand and laced his fingers through hers. Some of the tension eased in his muscles. "Wise woman that you are, I know you're right." He continued to stare at the lift. "There's no doubt Villiers saw us. Has he taken to following us now?"

"I think we just witnessed an example of see no evil, hear no evil."

"Hmph," he grunted, as the doors opened again. They stood aside to allow two constables to step out of the car.

"Whatever the reason Villiers came down to the station, it can't have been good," she murmured as they entered the lift. "It sets the mind to wondering all sorts of things."

Could his presence have anything to do with the Colefax murder? Or was it another matter entirely?

She sighed and added another item to her growing list of mental notes.

☙❧

Burnell came to a halt before Sally's desk. Her head was bent in concentration over a sheet of paper, so he cleared his throat noisily.

It was several more seconds before her scornful brown

gaze raked over his face. "It is unnecessary for you to make such noise. You give off a disturbing aura. I could feel your presence from a hundred feet away. Quite an unsettling experience, I can tell you."

The superintendent plastered a grin on his lips. "Unsettling, really? That must mean you miss me terribly when I'm not around."

He froze and his smile faded. *Good Lord, I'm beginning to sound like Longdon*, he thought. A shudder of horror rippled through his body. *For the sake of my sanity, I must see to it that the man is barred from setting foot in the station.*

"Huh," Sally snorted. "A case of delusions of grandeur, if I ever saw one." She reached for her phone. "I'll inform Assistant Commissioner Cruickshank that you've *finally* deigned to stir yourself."

His fists curled at his sides, as he waited. After a brief exchange, Sally replaced the receiver and nodded toward her boss's office. "You may go in." She paused and then offered, "It wouldn't hurt to admit your shortcomings and show a little humility. The assistant commissioner is a compassionate man."

Compassionate? Burnell choked in silent fury. *Was the woman talking about the same Cruickshank? A man who was a pompous prat.*

"He realizes no one is perfect. You merely have more flaws than the rest of us." She oozed reptilian spite.

"Sally, I'm sure you're familiar with the expression: What goes around, comes around." He wagged his finger at her. "I'm ticking off the days until your day of reckoning arrives. I'm not a religious man. But if the Lord has any pity for mankind, I hope what He's planned for you is a thousand times worse than Pandora's plagues."

He turned his back and left her with her mouth gaping open, struggling to formulate a blistering response. With a flick of his wrist, he opened the door to the Boy Wonder's office and steeled himself for the irksome audience.

"Sir," he said, hovering on the threshold.

Cruickshank waved at him. "There you are. At last."

Burnell swallowed down his resentment, as he lowered himself into one of the chairs opposite his commanding officer.

The Boy Wonder holding court in all his glory, he grumbled to himself as he studied the bane of his existence. *What a cruel joke. The fellow is around forty. Despite his chiseled physique and custom-made suit, he's barely out of nappies.*

For millionth time since Cruickshank had assumed command six months ago, Burnell speculated how those in the upper echelons could ever have considered it a brilliant idea to inflict him on the hard-working men and women of the Metropolitan Police.

The superintendent placed his hands on his knees, arranged his features in a bland expression, and waited for the Boy Wonder to impart whatever passed for pearls of wisdom in his mind.

Cruickshank folded his hands on the desk and leaned forward. Earnestness and dissatisfaction vied with one another in his brown eyes. A mirror image of a toddler about to have a tantrum.

"Burnell, you are one of my most senior officers. And yet, you're the one who has the most trouble toeing the line. Why is that?"

The superintendent dug his fingers into his knees and gripped hard. He opened his mouth to speak, but Cruickshank didn't give him a chance to respond.

The assistant commissioner sighed and shook his head. "I blame myself. I must have failed you on some level."

Burnell choked on the bile rising in his throat. In a

strangled voice, he managed to say, "Sir, respectively, could you please get to the point. I'm quite busy with the Colefax murder."

"No, you're not."

"I beg your pardon."

Cruickshank's brow furrowed in displeasure. "The case is no longer your concern."

Burnell blinked. "But, sir, you can't give it to another—"

The assistant commissioner held up a hand. "Laurence Villiers paid me a visit a short while ago. MI5 is now taking the lead. You will turn over whatever evidence you have collected to MI5 *immediately*. I rang Dr. Meadows. He will send the postmortem directly to me and I will pass it on. Obviously, this is bigger than we initially believed. And we wouldn't want to interfere. Is that understood?"

Villiers and MI5? Burnell's ulcer churned with revulsion. Not again.

જ⁄જ⁄

Nigel's bones were heavy with fatigue, as he slumped down into the uncomfortable metallic chair. He pinched the bridge of his nose between his thumb and forefinger. His brain was a jumble of disturbing questions.

When he heard the soft click of the door closing behind Finch, he reluctantly opened his eyes again and regarded "his client."

"You look dreadful." Damian's upper lip curled with distaste. "Couldn't you have smartened yourself up a bit? You are my lawyer, a direct reflection upon me. What are people going to think?"

"Stuff it. I want the truth."

Damian slouched back in his chair and folded his arms over his chest. "I told you the truth."

"I very much doubt it. At least not all of it. Let's start with your row with Colefax. Why did the two of you come to blows?"

A blue vein throbbed beneath the stubble along Damian's jawline. "The bastard tried to renege on his promise to open one of my restaurants in his hotels around the world. He also said that he would make me an equal partner in his business empire." He tapped a finger on the table. "It was simply not on. He owed me."

Nigel lifted an eyebrow. "You had a contract?"

"We had a verbal agreement. The deal was as good as sealed."

Nigel snorted and permitted himself an ironic smile. "I'm surprised you were that naïve. A deal is *never* final until both parties sign on the dotted line."

Damian swatted at the air with an impatient hand. "I can do without your holier-than-thou sanctimony. You have that in common with Colefax. Only he was a hypocrite. He showed one face to the world, but underneath he was as dirty as they come."

"Meaning?"

"Colefax collected people. He cultivated leaders in business, politics, finance, science, the arts, film, and the media. It was an incestuous sort of relationship. Everyone was out for himself or herself. Alexander liked to provoke a reaction. I'm certain that he was the instrument of his own demise."

"Charming." Nigel pursed his lips. "Now, tell me how the diamonds fit into this sordid affair?"

A spasm of surprise rippled across Damian's pinched features before it was quickly replaced by a blank mask. However, he failed to entirely extinguish the guilt that flared in his eyes.

He scraped a hand over his chin and with forced

casualness asked, "Diamonds? I have no idea what you're on about."

Nigel pounded his open palm on the table. "Liar." He wagged his forefinger in the other man's face. "I need very little excuse to walk out that door. In fact, I'd like nothing more than to see you rot in jail for your multitude of sins."

Damian grabbed his forearm and drew Nigel toward him. Their faces were only inches apart. "I'll ruin you if you breathe a word about Julie. I'll see to it that you're disbarred, and I'll go to the press. By the time I'm finished, you'll be begging in the gutter and Sanborn Enterprises will be bankrupt. And for my *pièce de resistance*"—he rubbed his hands together, as his mouth quivered with malicious glee—"I'll take your cousin's pretty little wife away from him. She looks like she'll be amusing for a few months. How would your precious conscience feel then?" He paused, his words hanging upon the air. "So, don't you dare threaten me. I have nothing to lose, but you do."

Nigel shook off his grasp. His voice dropped to a dangerous hiss. "I have no fears where Emmeline is concerned. She's immune to your oily charm. She would slice you to pieces in a heartbeat. But let's get one thing straight. My family and the company are off limits. This dirty bargain is between us alone."

"Then do your job and defend me. That fat copper is frothing at the mouth."

"I can't help you unless I know everything. Therefore, tell me about the diamonds. Is that what you and Colefax were really arguing about?"

Damian clasped his hands before him on the table. The skin was stretched taut and white across his bony knuckles. Nigel could read in his eyes that he was warring with himself, weighing how much to disclose.

At last, he exhaled a harsh breath. "Oh, all right. Yes. We argued about the diamonds. Where are they, by the way?"

"Superintendent Burnell has them."

"What?" Nigel delighted in watching the other man's cheeks flame with annoyance. "That interfering copper again. He's beginning to get on my nerves. Half of the diamonds are mine." He pointed at the door. "Go blind him with some legal jargon and get them back. Go on."

"I'm not your servant. Where did the diamonds come from?"

"Does it really matter? They're *my* property."

"Oh, now *all* the diamonds are yours. A moment ago, you said half of them belonged to you. Which is it?

"Well, naturally they're all mine now that Alexander is dead. We were partners."

"Partners in your mind alone. Unless Colefax left a will naming you as his beneficiary, I'm afraid you have nothing."

Damian's fingers clamped down on Nigel's forearm, biting into his bone like a vice. "I'm not walking away empty-handed. If I hadn't agreed to act as his intermediary, to be the face of some of his—shall we say less *salubrious*?—deals, he would never have been able to amass half the riches he has squirreled away in Switzerland, the Cayman Islands and God knows what other corners of the globe. He needed someone the authorities wouldn't suspect." He jabbed his thumb against his chest. "Alexander needed *me*. And the diamonds were the reward for my assistance and silence."

"What were Colefax's business dealings?"

Damian stiffened and his gaze slid away. "It wasn't safe for Alexander to tell me all the details. The fact that he's dead seems to indicate that he wasn't careful enough."

Nigel huffed a laugh. "You mean he didn't trust you. Obviously, Colefax was a discerning judge of character or lack thereof in your case."

Damian tossed his chin in the air and sniffed. "If you think you're going to shame me with your disdain, you're mistaken. Now, what else do you want to know?"

"You've barely scratched the surface of this sordid mess. What possessed Colefax to ever turn to you for 'assistance'?"

Damian hooked an elbow around the back of his chair. "He dined at Rossiter's in Mayfair one evening four months ago. He enjoyed his meal tremendously and sent for Pascal, my chef, to pay his compliments personally. Then, he offered Pascal a great deal of money to come work at The Corbett in St. James's. One of the waiters overheard and came to tell me." He shook his head at the memory. "Can you imagine the nerve? Alexander tried to pinch my chef from right under my nose, but I suppose being ruthless is the only way to get ahead in business.

"I walked over to the table and broke up the *tête-à-tête*. Pascal went scurrying back to the kitchen, while I sat down and gave Alexander a piece of my mind. I must admit that he was a master charmer. Without batting an eye at the cost, he ordered a bottle of Château Cheval-Blanc as an apology and then proceeded to talk business. He said that a mutual acquaintance—the bloke's name is an unimportant since you don't run in the same circles—suggested that I might be interested in joining a syndicate that was looking to buy Morning Glory, a thoroughbred." Damian's mouth curved into a smile at the memory and his tone softened. "He's a beautiful two-year-old bay colt that was bred in Ireland. He was from the first crop of foals sired by Heavens Above who won the Poule d'Essai des Poulains and Prix de la Forêt in 2008."

Nigel shot him a skeptical look. "Since when do you have enough money to acquire a share in a racehorse? For that matter, I always wondered how you were able to raise the capital to open your restaurants."

Damian examined his nails. "My business affairs are none of your concern. I have diversified interests and many contacts. Let's leave it at that."

Translation, you have your thumb in a number of illicit pies. The law simply hasn't caught up with you. Yet.

Although this revelation came as no surprise, the dagger of hot fury plunged itself even deeper into Nigel's chest.

Damian didn't seem to notice. "We're planning to race him at Ascot next year. He can't lose. If you're smart, you'll put a wager on Morning Glory."

"Never mind the bloody horse. I very much doubt it has anything to do with Colefax's murder and the diamonds."

Damian tapped the side of his nose with his finger and smirked. "Oh, but you're wrong. It was a means to an end. You can't imagine how many lucrative deals are negotiated every day in plain sight at the races and no one is any the wiser.

"At the first race I attended as a newly-minted member of the syndicate, I noticed Alexander slip away from the box just as Morning Glory burst from the gate. I was torn about whether to watch the race or follow him. Curiosity won out. I caught up with him in the bar. Although he ordered a beer, he just sat there rolling the glass between his hands. His gaze kept roaming around, as if he was waiting for someone. A quarter of an hour ticked by, but no one joined him. I was getting bored and about to return to the box, when this stunner jostled him. After murmuring an embarrassed apology, she wandered off on unsteady feet. The whole incident was over in seconds. It was cleverly orchestrated. I nearly missed her pressing a piece of paper into Alexander's palm. As soon as he read the note, he tossed a handful of bills on the bar and slunk off to a private box, where a rather severe chap clapped him on the shoulder. 'Ah, you came,' he said. Alexander shook off the man's hand. 'You left me with no choice in the matter. I don't like spying on my friends.' The other fellow chuckled. 'Spying is a relative term. I'm sure you'll see things differently after a glass of bubbly and some caviar.'

"That's all I heard before the door closed. I had no idea who the fellow was. He looked as if he stepped off the pages of a Burberry advert. Fortyish, classic good looks, Savile Row suit, went to a posh public school followed by either Oxford or Cambridge. He could have been anything from an investment banker to an oil magnate. But I smelled a government type." Damian gave a smug nod. "At that point, I didn't know Alexander well but I sensed something big was in the offing. Therefore, I made a few discreet inquiries and found out the stranger works for MI6. His name is Matthew Honeysett. Who could have dreamed of a more perfect name for a spy?"

Nigel's eyebrows shot up to his hair line. "MI6? How could you possibly have discovered all of this?"

"It pays to have impeccable sources."

"Just when I thought the situation couldn't get any worse. That means Colefax's death could have security ramifications."

Damian smirked. "I see you still have a negative outlook on life. From my perspective, that brief encounter led to new opportunities to make pots of money."

Nigel snorted and couldn't help rubbing salt in the wound. "I hate to point out the obvious, but if the two of you had never crossed paths you wouldn't find yourself accused of Colefax's murder." One eyebrow quirked upward. "Perhaps, it's Fate punishing you for all your sins at last?"

A dark scowl rippled across the other man's features. His jaw clenched. "I didn't kill him. It was probably Peter

Zorkin. It's Pyotr really, but that's too foreign for business purposes. Therefore, it's Peter to his friends. He and Alexander were at university together. If it wasn't Zorkin, then one of his Russian associates did the dirty deed. Definitely dodgy, one and all." His shoulders twitched in a careless shrug. "But I kept my opinions to myself and happily accepted the outrageous fee Alexander offered me to have my private dining room at his permanent disposal. He said he wanted a quiet place, away from prying eyes at his hotels, to meet with Zorkin and other friends to play chess and relax over a bottle or two of vodka. Who was I to question how he chose to spend his money?

"Around that time, Alexander also asked me to act as his intermediary. To be the face of certain negotiations. I was flattered because he seemed to admire my business acumen." He huffed a bitter laugh. "In hindsight, I see that he was maneuvering from the outset to have me take the fall in the event his grand schemes collapsed. That way he and Zorkin would have time to disappear." His upper lip curled in a sneer. "Only it didn't work out that way, did it?"

L'homme propose, mais Dieu dispose. Isn't that always the case?

The ominous refrain rattled around Nigel's brain, making him wonder what else was in store. *Russians, MI6 and a cache of diamonds.*

Thus far, it had been a lethal cocktail.

Chapter 6

Burnell swore with impunity, hurling curses through the ether at the Boy Wonder and Villiers in equal measure.

"Why?" he fumed, as he barreled down the corridor toward his office. He resented MI5's cavalier manner. Whatever happened to interagency cooperation and mutual respect? A little professional courtesy and trust would go a long way. He wouldn't like it, although he would understand, if it was a matter of security. But instead, he had been shunted aside and left to molder in the dark like a mushroom.

"*Oof.* Steady on, Oliver," Dr. Meadows said after the superintendent collided into him.

"What? Sorry, John. My mind was miles away." He touched his friend's arm. "Are you all right?"

The medical examiner's slate-gray eyes glittered with amusement. "I'll live. I take it your foul mood has to do with Cruickshank's order to turn over the Colefax murder to MI5."

Burnell grunted.

"I knew it would drive you mad. On the positive side, it's one less case on your desk."

"I'm not afraid of hard work," the superintendent groused. "What galls me is being dismissed without an explanation."

Darting a glance to his right and left, Meadows dropped an arm across Burnell's shoulders and pitched his voice lower. "That's why I took the scenic route. I thought you might like to review the postmortem on Colefax *before* I delivered it to our illustrious assistant commissioner." He pressed a folder against Burnell's chest. "It would be unforgivable if I allowed you to die of ignorance, now wouldn't it?"

A broad smile broke out across the superintendent's features. "A man could not have asked for a better friend. You're a prince among men."

"Then the pints are on you." He lifted an eyebrow. "Usual time on Friday?"

"Of course. The only thing that would prevent me from meeting you is if I'm arrested in the meantime for strangling the Boy Wonder."

Meadows chuckled. "Why waste your energy? Just get on with your job. In the end, keeping the criminals behind bars and the public safe is why we're here. We can't escape the politics. We simply have to rise above it and do the best we can in spite of it."

Burnell gave a weary sigh. His annoyance had dissipated. "You're right, of course." He patted the file. "Thanks for this."

"My assistant will come to collect it in the morning. I'll have her deliver it to Cruickshank."

They shook hands and parted ways.

Burnell spent the next half-hour sifting through the

postmortem's findings. Unfortunately, it didn't elicit any surprises. Colefax was beaten severely about the head, neck, torso, and upper and lower extremities with some sort of metal pipe or more likely a crowbar. The fatal blow was to the back of the head, which cracked the victim's skull.

The superintendent sighed gustily and flipped opened the lab analysis on Rossiter's shirt. The blood was O positive, a match for Colefax and the most common type. This placed Rossiter at the scene of the crime.

Ha. Blood will out. Why is it that criminals think that they can outsmart science and the police? the superintendent observed to himself.

However, his moment for self-congratulation was short-lived. His brows knit together when his eye fell on John's notes indicating that the tests also revealed traces of AB negative. Burnell's gaze scanned down the page. Rossiter was A positive.

He slumped back in his chair and stroked his beard meditatively. Someone else had been there. A witness who managed to escape?

We haven't received reports from any of the hospitals, nor has anyone come forward, he mused. *Or it could have been an accomplice who was injured in the struggle and scarpered, leaving Rossiter to face the music alone. Damn. The accomplice could have fled the country by now.*

The forensic evidence revealed that Colefax fought back, until he was rendered insensible. It could have been two culprits.

Bloody marvelous. His faculties were failing him. How could he have missed the telltale clues that a second person had been at the house? They had no inkling who it could be or where to start searching.

Burnell reached for his phone. He and Finch would take another look at the crime scene.

But he slammed the receiver back down in the cradle almost as soon as he had picked it up again. "Damn and blast," he swore aloud. They couldn't go back to conduct another sweep of Colefax's house because MI5 was now in charge.

"Ah, I see you've heard the bad news, sir," Finch said, closing the door behind him.

"Villiers and MI5," Burnell grumbled, as the sergeant settled into one of the chairs opposite him. "All condescension as they trespass on the Met's patch."

"Why would MI5 be interested in a multimillionaire hotelier? Granted, I had barely started digging into Colefax's life, but nothing struck me as unusual. No security flags. He was floating in money. No debts. He appeared as clean as the proverbial whistle."

Burnell grunted. "If MI5 is so keen to shut us out of the loop, then you can count on it being a particularly nasty business."

Finch nodded. "Mmm. Surely if it was a matter of security, Colefax's name would have come up before now."

"Perhaps it has and MI5 in all its superior wisdom chose not to share the information with us lowly coppers."

"More than likely." A sly smile curled around the sergeant's lips. "So how do we proceed, sir? Because over the years I've soaked up a great deal of knowledge in your shadow. Enough to know that you have no intention of turning your back on the case."

Burnell returned his smile. "Clever chap." He slid the two files across the desk. "John popped by earlier. He thought we might like to preview the postmortem and the test results on Rossiter's shirt."

One of Finch's eyebrows quirked upward, but he reserved comment until he had finished scanning both reports.

"Good and bad news," he commented, as he folded his hands on the desk. "We have sufficient proof to officially charge Rossiter with murder."

The superintendent wagged a finger at him. "In an ideal world, yes. But MI5's involvement puts a different complexion on the murder."

"They wouldn't set him free, would they? Why?"

Burnell threw his hands in the air. "Who knows what their agenda is. At the moment, Colefax's life is a blank canvas. We know nothing about him, his business, his associates, any ex-wives, current and former lovers. Only one person can tell us what really happened that night and he or she has vanished. And we don't have even a whisper of suspicion about whether he or she is one of the baddies or merely an innocent bystander who had the misfortune to be there by chance. Either way, Colefax's house is the only place that could have provided a clue and now it's off limits."

"Sir, as far as I know, MI5 hasn't sent any agents to collect Rossiter yet. We could interview him again."

Burnell pushed himself to his feet and grinned. "Oh, yes, let's do that. He's ruined the last twenty-four hours, so it's only fair if we return the favor."

❦

"The bastard tried to cheat me," Damian spat back at Nigel. He glanced down at the scabs forming over the cuts on his knuckles. "That's why I hit him. I wanted to wipe that arrogant smile off his face. He had the gall to laugh at me. He called me a common thug, without an ounce of brains or imagination." His nostrils flared on an indrawn breath. "He said that I was merely a means to an end and I had served my purpose." He tapped the table with his forefinger. "If it hadn't been for me, Zorkin wouldn't have been able to—" He broke off abruptly and pressed his lips together in a tight line.

"Zorkin wouldn't be able to what?" Nigel prodded.

Damian folded his arms across his chest and the corners of his mouth curled down in a pout. "Never mind."

A harsh bark of laughter erupted from Nigel. "Oh, no. You gave up the right to privacy, when you were arrested and dragged me into your sordid mess. If you'd like to take your chances with the law, then by all means keep mum."

Although daggers flew from Damian's eyes, Nigel caught a flicker of fear in their depths. "All right. I haven't told you everything."

"Why am I not surprised?"

Damian took a deep breath. "Zorkin is the son of Ilya Zorkin, who started out as a private banker before moving into the energy sector. Ilya is a metals and mining magnate whose close ties to high-ranking Kremlin officials propelled him in 1999 into the role of chairman of RosGrid Energy, the country's largest transmission grid company. In 2003, he seized control of NovoEnergy, which at the time was the largest builder of electricity grids and thermoelectric plants in Russia. To keep from getting bored, he also started a construction company, which no surprise, has managed to win some of the most prestigious government contracts. He hasn't looked back, gaining interests in all sorts of companies over the years. However, Ilya is a banker at heart. To keep his hand in the game, he launched a private bank for an exclusive clientele, who coveted secrecy. These include fellow oligarchs, Russian mafia, and a string of disreputable chaps. They all have one thing in common. Their business practices are highly dubious and definitely illegal. For these dregs of society,

Zorkin offers a specialized laundering service. The dirtiest money flows into the bank's coffers and after a thorough sanitizing and bleaching, out it goes again miraculously transformed for the most part into assorted luxury real estate, diamonds, art, and antiques. As a layman, I'm certain you are unaware that diamonds are extremely desirable because they are an unregulated form of investment."

Nigel opened his mouth to say something, but words failed to coalesce on his tongue. What was especially unnerving was Damian's apathetic depiction of the underworld.

How could someone be so utterly without scruples?

Heedless of Nigel's silent censure, Damian breezed on, "Ilya's fortune is estimated in the region of twelve billion pounds. He owns property all over the world, two superyachts, and a private jet. I could go on, but it would only make you ill. Over the years, Ilya bestowed his largesse on his two sons, Sergei and Pyotr. Both were sent abroad for their education. Sergei, the dutiful, serious heir, studied hard and entered the family business. Ilya installed him as the head of the construction company, although he is the one who makes all the important decisions behind the scenes.

"Pyotr had a more relaxed attitude toward life. He was sent to Cambridge, where he was a mediocre student but not from a lack of mental prowess. He read economics because he had a brilliant head for numbers. He takes after his father in that regard. But university life didn't offer any challenges. Being a playboy was more appealing. And why not, when daddy was footing all the bills? He met Alexander at Cambridge and they'd been thick as thieves ever since.

"Pyotr—what a mouthful. I always think of him as Peter—doesn't have any of his own money. Ilya retains iron control over all the purse strings, so that his son's exploits don't embarrass him with the boys in the Kremlin."

"Get to the point," Nigel interrupted. "Thus far, nothing you've said about this Russian oligarch and his sons helps your case in any way."

Damian's replied through clenched teeth, "You're the one who demanded to know *everything* and now you have the nerve to complain? Patience is a virtue, after all." These last words were infused with some of his usual arrogance.

Nigel grunted and waved a hand for him to continue.

"Now, where was I? Oh, yes. Peter was beginning to suffocate under Ilya's overbearing presence. He felt as though he was in a prison with invisible bars. He desperately wanted to sever the paternal umbilical cord. But to live the comfortable life he had envisioned, he needed money. A great deal of it. He turned for advice to the only person he could trust, Alexander. Coincidentally, his bosom mate had a proposal that could solve all his problems. This is where the mysterious Mr. Honeysett of MI6 enters the picture. Honeysett also knew Alexander from Cambridge. I gather they didn't share confidences, but their relations were sufficiently close that they kept in touch after they left university. They would meet occasionally for drinks or dinner.

"I subsequently learned that day at the races, Honeysett asked Alexander, who had many projects lined up in Moscow, to provide general details about his contacts, the business atmosphere for foreigners and anything else he considered relevant. He would be helping Her Majesty's government get an insider's view of what was happening on the ground. Alexander wouldn't be on MI6's payroll, Honeysett explained, rather he'd be more of an informant.

By now, you may have guessed that one of the people MI6 was most interested in was Ilya Zorkin, his family, his Kremlin connections, and his shadowy business empire. Honeysett suggested that Alexander, because of his cozy ties with Peter, could easily maneuver to get a foot in Ilya's world. I gather Alexander balked at the idea of using his friend in such a manner. In the end, he and Peter put their heads together and came up with a way to turn the situation to their advantage.

"Alexander went back to Honeysett and agreed to inveigle himself through Peter into Ilya's sphere of influence. Peter promised to get any information Honeysett wanted on condition that MI6 helped him to disappear because when his father inevitably found out he would be a marked man. The codicil to this demand was that MI6 provide a hefty bank account in the Cayman Islands or Switzerland. He also had a fancy for a villa on Lake Como. It was a one-time offer. Take it or leave it.

"After years of unsuccessful attempts, MI6 was salivating at the prospect of finally having a crack at Ilya. Alexander and Peter were given carte blanche. From that point on, Honeysett told Alexander to contact him only in an emergency. He gave him the name of a chap, a former MI6 agent who now runs a consultancy that advises foreign businesses trying to invest in Moscow and other parts of Russia. When in Moscow, Alexander could pass messages through this chap or someone at the embassy.

"If it were me, no matter how much Honeysett appealed to my sense of patriotism, I would never have agreed to any of it. Russians can't be trusted. Peter is living proof. He provided a trickle of information to keep MI6 happy, while he plotted to play both sides against the middle. He accepted whatever MI6 was willing to give him. But in the end, blood was still thicker than water and Peter chafed at turning over Ilya's dirtiest secrets to the West. Mind you, that didn't stop him from setting out to systematically embezzle from his father's accounts, as well as his vast art collection, to build up his own nest egg with an obscene bottom line that would last him ten lifetimes. At heart, though, he was a cautious fellow and made sure that part of this fortune was in diamonds in the event of unforeseen occurrences.

"His conscience—I'm being generous calling it that— must have bothered him. Or he was simply tired and wanted to be left alone. Whatever his motive, he decided to serve up on a silver platter a deep-cover Russian spy who had managed to infiltrate high society and government circles right here in London. Apparently, Peter was childhood friends with this spy. By a quirk of fate, their paths crossed again about a month ago. Honeysett was over the moon when Alexander came to him with this juicy news. Peter also reckoned this move would divert MI6's attention from dear old Dad. He was right on that score. Alexander was busy as a bee the past two weeks shuttling between Peter and Honeysett. To thank him for his intervention, the red diamonds were Peter's parting gift. As Alexander's partner, half of the gems are mine by right." He jerked his thumb against his chest. "I wouldn't have taken the risks I did, if there wasn't a reward waiting for me. The fact that I'm in this stinking place is proof of the dangers I was up against and continue to face."

Nigel snorted. "Poor Damian, always persecuted, aren't you?" He leaned toward him and hissed, "You're here because you *did* commit murder."

Damian flapped a hand at him. "Forget about Julie. She was nothing. A second-rate little actress with fantasies of becoming the next Judi Dench. She was gorgeous, otherwise I wouldn't have looked twice at her. She was amusing. Great for a tumble between the sheets. No one will miss her. I assure you."

Nigel was outraged on the dead woman's behalf at the irritation echoing in Damian's tone. "Why did you kill her, you bastard?"

"I didn't plan it, if that's what you're asking. It just…sort of…happened. She told me she was pregnant and expected me to be overjoyed by the news. She wanted me to marry her." He shook his head and grunted at the memory. "Can you believe her nerve? I told her that I was not the marrying kind and to get rid of the brat as soon as possible. That's when the crying and screaming began. I do so hate it when women become emotional." He shook his head in disgust. "Such an undignified fuss. Julie flung herself at me and began pummeling my chest with her fists. And she did this." He gestured at the scratches on his face and neck. "On and on she went crying. I put my hand over her mouth and shook her to shut her up. But she wouldn't. Then I gave her a slap across the face. She lost her footing and fell backward, hitting her head on the night table. That was it. A pathetic end to her sad little life." His shoulders twitched in a dismissive shrug. "Fortunately, no one saw me leave her flat."

Nigel's jaw dropped. But before he could offer a coherent response to such a callous account, there was a rap on the door. The next instant, Burnell and Finch filled the doorway.

"Mr. Rossiter, you are officially under arrest for the murder of Alexander Colefax."

Chapter 7

With a kiss and a promise to exchange notes at home that evening, Emmeline and Gregory parted ways on the pavement outside Scotland Yard. Husband and wife were both on the hunt for answers. She bolted to the St. James's Underground station, impatient to get back to the *Clarion* to start sifting through the secrets that bound Damian Rossiter to Alexander Colefax in life and death. From the tissue of lies, the truth would emerge. It always did. She merely had to be persistent and follow up every lead. But then, that was second nature to her. She never gave up. The truth and justice were too important.

Meanwhile, Gregory had set himself the unenviable task of confronting Villiers and teasing out what the devil the man was up to this time. Nothing good. He knew that for certain. Gregory was intent on preventing his dear Papa's convoluted schemes from ensnaring Emmy and putting her life at risk as they had done on several occasions in the past.

ℯↄℯↄ

"Oh, no," Damian bellowed, pounding his closed fist on the table as he surged to his feet. His chair toppled backward and landed with a shuddering *thud* against the cold floor. "Like hell will I play the role of scapegoat in your bloody conspiracy."

"Sit down, Mr. Rossiter," Burnell commanded, his tone edged with steel. His blue stare was devoid of any sympathy for the other man's untenable predicament. "I suggest you calm down, Mr. Rossiter. You'll only make things more difficult for yourself otherwise."

Damian's upper lip curled into a sneer. "How can the situation get any worse?"

The superintendent ignored his question and turned to Nigel, who had risen as well. "I suggest you advise your client to cooperate. He's in a good deal of trouble."

Damian's helpless gaze darted from the stone-faced detective to Nigel. "Don't just stand there sucking the air from the room. They want to charge me with murder. Do something."

Nigel gave a curt nod. "Right. Sit down and answer their questions."

"Wh-what? Is that it? You're going to let them bury me."

"The law doesn't work that way," Burnell countered. "All we want is the truth."

"Whose truth? The truth you concocted." Damian's voice dripped with contempt.

"Evidence doesn't lie." Burnell pressed his palms on the table and leaned toward Rossiter. "I know you're hiding something," he said through clenched teeth. "I can smell the fear on you. Contrary to popular belief, silence is *not* golden when it comes to murder. Now, pick up your chair, place your bum on it and start talking."

Nigel wordlessly walked around the table and lowered himself into the chair next to Damian. He folded his hands in front of him on the table and gave his client a pointed look.

After several seconds, Rossiter scooped up the chair and set it upright. Then, he plonked down and crossed his arms over his chest, a mutinous expression made the scratches on his haggard features stand out.

Burnell pressed the button on the tape machine to start recording their interview. Finch took out his notebook, waiting with pen poised as the superintendent identified everyone present as well as the date and time.

Burnell leveled his gaze at Damian. "Mr. Rossiter, the victim's blood was found on your shirt cuffs and—"

Damian interrupted, "I already explained that Alexander and I had a heated argument earlier in the evening. I admitted that I hit him." He raised a finger. "But just the once. In the nose."

Burnell went on as if the other man had not spoken. "—and we have a witness that places you at the scene of the crime about two hours before Mr. Colefax's body was discovered."

"It's a lie," Damian grumbled.

Nigel gave a disapproving shake of his head and then to Burnell he said, "Please go on, Superintendent."

"That means we've established probable cause. If that wasn't enough, the lab tests found traces of a second blood type on your clothing." He paused to allow these words to sink in. "This leads us to conclude that either you had an accomplice or there was a witness and you disposed of the body."

Damian flicked the tip of his tongue over his lips.

Burnell caught the sideways glance he shot at Nigel, whose features were ashen and pinched with strain. The lawyer's chin was tucked against his chest and he studiously avoided meeting the superintendent's eyes.

Hmm. Nigel, if I didn't know better, I'd think you had a guilty conscience, Burnell ruminated. He frowned. *What are* you *hiding?*

Instead, he prodded, "So which is it, Mr. Rossiter? We like clarity."

"I—I have nothing more to say."

"That's your prerogative, of course. We have enough to charge you." He hit the button to halt the recording. Both he and Finch stood. At the door, Burnell tossed over his shoulder, "A sergeant will be along shortly to book you." Before he swept out of the room, he couldn't help adding, "Don't go anywhere."

ফ৩ফ৩

Villiers head shot up when the door burst open. His eyes narrowed when he saw Gregory looming on the threshold.

"What the devil do you want?"

Dorothy, his secretary, cast a withering glance at Gregory as she stepped around him and sought to regain a measure of official decorum. "I'm sorry, Mr. Villiers." The words tumbled out in a breathless rush. "I tried to stop him, but Mr. Longdon barged in. Shall I have him escorted out?"

A wry smile tugged at the corners of Gregory's mouth. His eyes locked on his father's. "I wouldn't recommend it." He paused for a moment. "Mind you, these musty corridors could do with a bit of rattling to shake off all the cloak-and-dagger cobwebs."

Villiers snatched his glasses off his nose and tossed them onto his desk. He leaned back in his chair and exhaled a long breath. "I have no doubt you'd derive no end of pleasure in making a spectacle. You have that in common with your interfering little wife."

The smirk vanished from Gregory's lips. "Leave Emmy out of this."

Villiers huffed a bitter laugh. "I'd like nothing better, but she keeps turning up uninvited at the most inconvenient moments." He tapped his finger on the desk. "And of course, one can be certain she'll be brandishing a long list of indiscreet questions as a weapon. She's at the peak of her abilities, when she's making a nuisance of herself."

Out of the corner of his eye, Gregory saw Dorothy nod and repress a smile at this salvo. He peered down at her. "Surely you must have some work to be getting on with?" His tone was clipped.

The secretary shot a questioning glance at her boss. "It's all right, Dorothy," Villiers said. "Despite his bluster, he doesn't pose a threat to life and limb."

The secretary sniffed as she swept out of the office, closing the door with a soft *click*.

Gregory crossed to the desk and draped his tall frame into one of the chairs opposite Villiers. He hadn't bother to take off his coat because he was hoping to make this audience as short as possible.

Without preamble, he plunged in. "Why are you following Emmy and me? And don't bother to deny it. I saw you at the station."

Villiers threw his head back and laughed. "Don't flatter yourself. I have better things to do with my time than to skulk after you and your wife. You're not that interesting. On the other hand, the pair of you appear to be cursed with a restless energy in perpetual need of an outlet. I don't know which one of you is worse. Frankly, I'm surprised she's not with you." He paused for a moment, his gaze raking Gregory's face. "One day, your wife's incessant curiosity is going to get you killed."

"A bit late in life to start playing the role of doting *papa*," Gregory snarled. "We both know that you don't have a paternal bone in your body."

Villiers's features were a mask of inscrutability. He straightened some papers on his desk, reached for his glasses and then set them down again, before lifting his eyes to meet Gregory's hostile glare once again. "Does that soothe a long-held childhood wound? Because I'm not interested in your opinion of me. I never claimed to be perfect."

"Ha." Gregory's bark of laughter grated on the ears. "A truer word was never spoken."

Villiers waved his hand impatiently. "We all make choices in life. For instance, that mustache makes you look ridiculous. Why don't you shave it off?"

Gregory smoothed down the corners of his mustache. "If you think you can distract me with criticism about my personal grooming, you can forget it. Since you claim that you weren't spying on Emmy and me, what were you doing at the station? Does it have something to do with Alexander Colefax's murder?"

Villiers propped his elbows on his armrests and steepled his fingers over his stomach. His lips compressed into a thin line. Not a muscle in his face quivered. Only a barely discernible flutter of his eyelashes betrayed the wily spymaster's displeasure. In the cinnamon depths of his eyes, Gregory saw an internal war raging about whether to offer an unequivocal denial or to concede the point. Knowledge was a premium commodity. Elaborate chess maneuvers were second nature to Villiers. Trust was like an expensive wine. Imbibe too much and one risked losing control. Therefore, he trusted no one.

A heavy, tense silence closed in around them. The

minutes ticked by as they stared at one another without blinking.

Gregory finally lost his patience. "Let's drop the pretense, shall we? Admit that I'm right and tell me about Colefax. What is MI5's interest in him?"

Villiers threw his hands in the air. "Oh, very well. I don't know why I should shield MI6. It's their great cock-up and now it's my bloody headache." He leaned forward and wagged a finger at Gregory. "What I should do is leak the details to your wife and set her loose to teach MI6 a lesson." He gave a weary grunt, his mouth curving into a grim smile. "However, I haven't taken leave of my senses."

"I thought I made it clear that the subject of Emmy was off limits."

Villiers flapped a hand dismissively. "Don't get prickly." Then, another thought struck him and his eyes narrowed. "How are you and your wife involved in the Colefax debacle?" he asked suspiciously.

"It's not by choice," Gregory replied and went on to give an account of how the red diamonds came into their possession; the dead courier; their hurried departure from Madrid; and their visit to Burnell that morning.

Villiers shook his head. "How do the two of you always manage to be at the wrong place at the wrong time?"

Gregory offered him a tight smile. "It's a talent."

Villiers didn't acknowledge this glib response. He sat there, his brow puckered and unease deepening the lines bracketing either side of his nose. At last, he said, "I don't like it."

"Murder is always distasteful."

Villiers levelled his stare on Gregory's face. "Why you of all people? Why give the diamonds to you?"

"I suppose it's because the courier overheard us

speaking English and was relieved to find a way to get the gems off his hands. Obviously, he wasn't careful enough and paid for it with his life."

"Hmph," Villiers grunted. "That's a load of rubbish. You're not naïve. It doesn't smell right. You were deliberately targeted. You *know* that, even if you don't want to admit it to your wife."

Gregory inclined his head in reluctant agreement.

"Why?" Villiers demanded, as he tapped his pen on his desk. "What's your connection to Colefax?"

"There isn't any. The first and only time I heard the man's name was the other night."

"And now not only has Colefax been bludgeoned to death, but the courier was murdered too. Think," Villiers commanded.

"I'm not impressed when Oliver fixes his Gorgon stare on me, so as a tactic it's quite useless to get me to unburden my soul. I never met Alexander Colefax."

"Did you ever steal anything from him?"

Gregory threw his head back and laughed. "You seem to be under the same misconception as Oliver. I've never stolen anything in my life. I'm a law-abiding citizen."

"You may be able to run rings around that Metropolitan Police superintendent, but I know everything about you. You can't lie to me."

Gregory arched an eyebrow. "Everything, *Papa*? No one can know everything about another person."

"Oh, Toby, I wish you would stop saying that. It's beginning to grate on my nerves."

"Once again, I must remind you that my name is Gregory Longdon. Toby Crenshaw doesn't exist anymore. As for the rest of it, unfortunately we can't change the fact that we're bound by blood. However, hard I try to forget."

Villiers gave a disapproving shake of his head and slumped back in his chair. "Colefax," he muttered through gritted teeth in an attempt to steer the conversation back to safer ground. Murder was certainly a safer landscape than family ties and repressed hostility. "There must be a connection between the two of you. Otherwise, you've crossed someone else during your illustrious career as a jewel thief and they're trying to exact revenge. But how? For the life of me, it doesn't make sense. We're missing a great deal of the puzzle."

"You mentioned MI6. More than likely Colefax was killed because of his involvement with them. Was he an undercover agent? Oliver said that he was a hotel magnet."

"I haven't seen the file yet. This disaster fell into my lap this morning. MI6 is sending over one of its minions to brief me."

❦

Damian ran a trembling hand through his sandy hair. "This is a nightmare. How can you allow them to charge me?" he demanded.

"It's out my hands," Nigel replied phlegmatically. "Apparently, Superintendent Burnell feels he has sufficient evidence."

"But I didn't kill Alexander." His voice thrummed with a mixture of frustration and fear. "Of course, you can stand there all calm superiority. It's not your life hanging in the balance."

"Don't be so melodramatic. A jury of your peers will decide your fate. You must place your trust in the system. After all, justice is blind."

Nigel couldn't help the stab of glee at the other man's apprehension.

"Juries can be bought," Damian spat back.

"You've been watching too many detective dramas on television."

"You're happy, aren't you? I can see it in your eyes." Damian's tone was laced with aggrieved accusation. "Well, you're not off the hook. You're my lawyer. You'll have to defend me, when it comes to a trial. And you had better do a bloody brilliant job to get me off. Because I'd never survive in prison."

"You should have thought of that before you murdered Julie Brentford," Nigel snarled. "Her blood *is* on your hands."

"But you can't breathe a word on that score, so you had better start thinking up my defense." He had the temerity to smile. "If that fat copper starts sniffing in my direction where Julie's death is concerned, I'll know who whispered the poison in his ear. I promise I'll take you down and enjoy doing it."

"You're the Devil's spawn. Why have you placed me in this position? From what you say, you have money. You could have hired any number of high-profile lawyers who wouldn't have batted an eye at your confession. Why me?"

Damian's smile only grew wider. "Because you're too honest for your own good. Someone had to take you down a peg or two. To make you human like the rest of us. Despite what I've been through the past few hours, it was worth it just to watch you squirm."

Nigel's jaw dropped. With the exception of his own father, he had never confronted such venal viciousness.

"Don't gape at me like a dumb sheep. Run along home and work on my defense." Then, he added casually, "Before you go, though, you can do one more thing for me. I need to make a phone call."

Nigel blinked at him and shook his head, as if to physically rid himself of the fog that was clouding his brain. "You've already used up your one call when you rang me.”

Damian scolded with an admonishing finger. “Ah, ah. Technically, I didn’t. That tub of lard rang you. Therefore, I am entitled to one call. Now, off you go and arrange it.”

After a good deal of grousing, Burnell acquiesced to Rossiter’s request. Once he was certain that no one was eavesdropping, Damian called the number that he had seen scribbled in Colefax’s diary. It was a gamble. But then, life was rather dull without the occasional flutter.

He held his breath as various scenarios raced across his mind. On the third ring, his call was answered. His mouth broke into a broad grin when he heard the voice at the other end of the line.

“I thought it would be you.” He lowered his voice. “This is Damian Rossiter. I was Alexander’s associate. I *know* you killed him. There’s no use denying it. No, I wouldn’t hang up. You’ll regret it if you do because I can ruin you, although I would hate to do so. I’m not calling out of sentiment or a desire for revenge. Frankly, it takes too much energy. Alexander and I weren’t close. We both know he wasn’t a particularly nice fellow. By contrast, I’m rather easy-going. Truly. My motto is live and let live. This is purely a business transaction.

“Now, listen closely. I’ve been arrested and the police are about to charge me. There’s no way in hell that I’m going to pay for *your* crime. I don’t care what strings you have to pull. Use your connections to make these charges disappear. Otherwise”—he let the word float in the air ominously—“I will do my civic duty and divulge all the sordid details about Alexander and Zorkin. By the way, the police haven’t mentioned a certain long-lost Russian treasure. That means you stole it from Alexander’s house the night of the murder.” He held the phone away from his ear. “Swear at me all you like. I have a thick skin. Just get cracking. Your first task is to see to it that I walk out of here a free man with my impeccable reputation intact. Then, we can talk money. I like large, round figures. And I want the diamonds. In the grand scheme of things, it's a small price to pay to keep your secrets."

Chapter 8

Emmeline spent the morning digging up information to gain greater insight into the lives of Alexander Colefax and his alleged murderer Damian Rossiter. It seemed that Colefax was a well-known figure in social and political circles. He served on the board of several charities and donated to the arts. He was always seen at the best parties with a gorgeous woman on his arm. He and his ex-wife had parted on good terms five years ago. Emmeline's eyes bulged at the generous settlement that the ex-wife received. It was no wonder that they had remained friends. The ex-wife now resided in New York, which meant it was highly unlikely that she could have been involved in Colefax's death. On the other hand, she could have hired someone to kill him. But she didn't have a motive. Therefore, Emmeline surmised Colefax's murder must have something to do with his business. He appeared to have a golden touch in this arena. The Colefax Hotels Group had been a modestly successful family company, when he was thrust unexpectedly into the role of managing director after the tragic death of his cousin in a skiing accident in Switzerland. His uncle, who stayed on as chairman, completely devastated by the loss of his son, came to rely heavily on young Alexander. Sadly, the uncle died a few months later and never saw how Alexander transformed the company into a multibillion-pound empire.

Emmeline leaned back in her chair and tilted her head to stare up at the ceiling. Superintendent Burnell had said that Colefax wanted to build a hotel in Moscow and was willing to deal with anyone—and grease as many palms as necessary—to make his dream a reality. Kremlin elites, oligarchs, and Russian mafia bosses.

"Hmm," she wondered aloud. "Could Colefax's approach have been too aggressive for someone's taste? Was he encroaching on someone else's patch?"

That was the only thing that remotely made any sense. An irate rival could have sought to do away with the competition. Envy and greed made lethal bedfellows. Her instincts told her she was on the right track with these suppositions.

How did the diamonds come into play? She shook her head in frustration. The gems seemed to be a payoff. For what? Colefax was an extremely wealthy man. What could he possibly have that was worth a king's ransom?

Six little diamonds. Gregory estimated that they could be worth £100 million. It boggled the mind. To the unscrupulous, it was a seductive prize indeed. But Colefax had been killed *before* the gems came into his possession. That means something else was involved. At the moment, the answer eluded her. Perhaps with a bit of cajoling, Burnell would allow her to visit the crime scene. She doubted it, but it never hurt to ask.

She sat up and frowned as she turned her attention to the notes she had made on Rossiter. His high-end restaurants were all Michelin-starred and attracted the filthy rich and infamous. As soon as he made any money, it poured through his fingers. His weaknesses were women and horses. However, it was unclear from where he had raised the capital to start his restaurants. She came across unsubstantiated rumors that he was "owned" by some nasty underworld figures, but she couldn't find concrete links to anyone specific. She exhaled a heavy sigh. Naturally, there wouldn't be. The police were convinced that Rossiter was the murderer. All the evidence pointed to him. Burnell abided by the law. He would never knowingly charge an innocent man. If Rossiter ran around with criminals, something was bound to rub off. She had despised him on sight. But journalistic tenets dictated that she view the situation objectively. Simply because the man was repulsive and of questionable morals didn't make him a murderer. He continued to proclaim his innocence. As did Nigel.

She groaned at the thought of Nigel. He was the odd piece in this vexing puzzle. Why was Nigel defending a man he obviously loathed? He claimed that everyone was entitled to the best defense possible and innocent until proven guilty. That was all well and good. But Nigel hadn't practiced criminal law in ten years. He was more than up for the task. And yet…A flutter in the pit of her stomach told her something was wrong, aside from the fact that two men lay stone-cold dead.

She had come full circle back to the diamonds. Rossiter admitted that he had a violent row with Colefax. Could they have come to blows over the diamonds? She sat bolt upright in her chair. That was a plausible assumption. She allowed her mind to run with this supposition. Rossiter was seen leaving Colefax's house, but he swore it was two hours earlier. Where was he at the time of the murder? If he had a concrete alibi, as he claimed, why had he refused to provide it when questioned by the police? Had she been in his shoes, she would have shouted it at the top of her lungs to anyone who would listen. The only answer she could come up with to explain his silence is that he was shielding someone. Could Rossiter's alibi be a married woman?

She gave a dissatisfied shake of her head. Rossiter didn't strike her as having a chivalrous bone in his body. Then again, a woman could very well be at the heart of the matter. It was vitally important that she discover evidence that someone else had committed the crime. Aside from ensuring that the real culprit was apprehended, it was the only way to get Nigel to sever his ties with Rossiter.

To get to the truth, she required more background on Colefax. She must speak to someone who knew him well. She'd call the ex-wife to sketch in some of the details, but she didn't think it would yield anything useful since the woman was in New York. Then, she recalled that Colefax had one other relative, a goddaughter, who fortunately lived in London. Emmeline had no idea whether the two had been close. It was worth a try, though. She flipped through her notes and found the woman's name. She frowned as she did a search for the address and phone number.

Something niggled in the back of her mind as she punched in the number, but she couldn't place her finger on what bothered her. The line rang and rang. Damn. The woman was out. When the answerphone picked up, she left a message identifying herself and explaining that she was doing a story for the *Clarion* on Colefax's murder. She requested an interview and promised not to take up too much of the woman's time. It could either be over the phone or she was willing to meet the woman wherever she liked. Emmeline left her mobile number and asked the woman to call her back at her earliest convenience. She scowled at the receiver as she replaced it in the cradle. She hoped the goddaughter wasn't one of those people who had a low opinion of the press and therefore ignored her call. Oh, well, it wouldn't be the first time. It didn't deter her at all. It just made things a bit strained and meant that she had to be even more persistent. The truth demanded persistence.

Right. There were always many angles to flesh out to get a complete and balanced picture. She would start at the scene of the crime. She was about to ring Burnell and prepared a speech in her head, when she spied Nigel crossing the newsroom. She quickly replaced the receiver and leaped up. She yanked opened her office door and called out, "Nigel, could you spare a moment? I need your legal review of a story."

He stopped short and his head whipped around. His guarded gaze darted to his left and right, as if he were seeking an escape route. All the while, the voices of correspondents and editors, and the sound of fingers tapping furiously on keyboards mingled in the air.

He tried to fob her off with a watery smile and a wave of his hand. "Sorry, must dash. I have a lot on my plate. I'll look at it later."

She had no intention of letting him off the hook. "I'm afraid it can't wait. We're on deadline."

Nigel's chin drooped to his chest and he sighed in resignation. "Deadline, of course," he mumbled.

Only a condemned man on his way to the gallows could have walked more slowly than Nigel wending his way across the newsroom. He avoided meeting her gaze when he stepped into her office.

She pursed her lips and pressed the door closed, leaning her back against it for a moment as she watched him lower himself into a chair.

"It's just us now," she said. Her voice soft, inviting confidences. "You can tell me what's really going on."

His torso stiffened and his fingers dug into his knees, as if he were clinging to a lifebuoy in a vast and lonely ocean.

"I have no idea what you're on about." He cast a deliberate glance at her desk. "I thought you wanted me to look over some copy."

"Stop pretending, Nigel," she reproached as she stalked over to her desk in three strides, dropping heavily into her chair. "I'm not blind, and neither are Gregory and Superintendent Burnell. We can all see that something is troubling you." She paused, her eyes scouring his face for answers. "We were friends before I married Gregory and became part of the family. Why won't you trust me?"

His lips twisted in a grimace. "I'm afraid you've trained yourself to look for conspiracies under every bush. I suppose it's a trap any journalist can easily fall into, if he or she is not careful."

"That's a load of rubbish. I'm not gullible and you know it," she snapped. "Why are you defending a man for whom you clearly have no respect?" He opened his mouth, but she held up a hand. "And please don't trot out the trite observation again that everyone deserves the best defense possible."

"It's the truth," he shot back mulishly.

She surged out of her chair. "That's precisely what's missing from this unholy mess. *The truth.* It's obvious to me that Damian Rossiter learned to lie before he started to crawl."

Nigel was on his feet now too. "I thought journalists prided themselves on their objectivity."

"You *know* my stories are always balanced and fair."

"In this instance, I think you're allowing your personal bias to cloud your judgment."

Her eyes narrowed as she studied his face. The hostile

silence stretched out for several excruciating minutes. When her temper had cooled to merely simmering, she cleared her throat. "Fine. Set me straight." She scooped up her notebook and a pen. "The police contend that they have irrefutable evidence against Rossiter."

"Burnell has the wrong end of the stick. He should look elsewhere for the killer."

She clenched her teeth and gripped her pen harder. "Where? I'm willing to listen to Rossiter's side. Give me a statement. Better yet, allow the public to hear it in his own words. Let me interview him. Just give me *something*."

"It would be irresponsible of me as his lawyer to agree to an interview."

Emmeline tossed her notebook and pen on the desk. "I can't believe you've resorted to legal double talk. You still look like Nigel Sanborn, but I'm staring at a stranger." She drew in a ragged breath. "The truth will out. One way or another."

"I have no doubt you'll find the answer. You're more than capable of doing it without my help. I've said all that I can."

"I resent the fact that you're waving the privileged excuse in my face. As a journalist, I value every little crumb my sources whisper in my ear and protect their anonymity—"

"Therefore, you should understand the position I'm in."

"This situation is different. You appear less than enthusiastic. Either you're committed to taking on Rossiter's defense or walk away."

"I can't do that," Nigel snapped. "I'm bound by a code of conduct."

She regarded him steadily. "Yes, because you're an honorable man. That's why your behavior is so baffling."

"You're the second person in the last twenty-four hours who has condemned me for my honesty. If I were truly honorable, I'd—" He broke off abruptly.

She raised an eyebrow and held her breath. *Come on, Nigel,* she silently urged. *Get it off your chest.*

His lips pressed into a thin line. They were as good as sealed with a lock. She sighed.

"I see you're determined to go ahead with this charade. However—" She paused for a beat. "As Rossiter's lawyer, you are permitted access to the crime scene. In fact, it's in your client's interest to visit the *locus in quo.* Since you're unwilling to speak to me on the record, the least you can do is to get me into Colefax's house. I can take it from there."

His eyes bulged in disbelief. "You're crackers. Burnell will never agree to it. He'll flip his lid, if he catches sight of you."

She offered him a silky smile. "Nothing is impossible, when one puts one's mind to it." She leaned toward him, her voice soft and smooth. "The day of reckoning has arrived. Get me a peek at the crime scene or tell me what you're hiding."

૭၁૭૩

"I rather enjoyed our *tête-à-tête* with Rossiter," Burnell chortled as he sank into his chair. "It's fascinating to watch the transformation from arrogant bastard to quivering bowl of jelly."

Finch sighed and took the seat opposite his boss. "The only question is what do we do now?"

"We charge him, of course. We have means, motive and opportunity all tied up with a neat little bow." Burnell enumerated on his fingers. "Rossiter argued with the victim; he was seen leaving the scene of the crime; and the victim's blood was on his shirt."

"Sir, you know it's not that cut and dried. We can't ignore the elephant in the room. Is it wise to antagonize MI5? Villiers's feathers are going to be more than a bit ruffled, when he learns that we've charged Rossiter. Not to mention the fact that Cruickshank will hit the roof."

The superintendent flapped a hand at him. "Bah. The Boy Wonder is useless." He tapped his desk with his forefinger. "This is about making sure a murderer is locked away."

"Only a jury can find him guilty," Finch pointed out, taking on the role of devil's advocate.

"To get to that stage, we have to charge Rossiter and present our irrefutable evidence in a court of law."

"Sorry, chaps," a male voice intoned lugubriously.

Both detectives turned their heads in unison at this interruption. A tall, blond man in his thirties loomed a few paces from the desk. They had been so intent on their conversation that they hadn't noticed when he slipped into the office.

Burnell's chair groaned as he leaned back and surveyed the fellow. "And you are?"

The man offered him a haughty smile, as he casually reached into his inside breast pocket and drew out his identification. He flashed it at the superintendent and Finch. "Gilmour, MI5. I've come for Rossiter."

Burnell's eyes narrowed, as he stroked his beard. "We have enough to charge him."

Gilmour tucked his identification back in his pocket. "He's no longer your concern." He turned to Finch. "Sergeant, run along and get Rossiter."

Finch didn't move a muscle. Instead, he shot a glance at Burnell and raised an eyebrow.

"Come on." Gilmour clapped his hands. "Chop, chop. I don't have all day."

"This is a routine murder case. Why is MI5 interested in Rossiter?" Burnell asked.

"I'm afraid it's above your pay grade. Security of realm and all that. I'm sure you understand," Gilmour sneered in a clipped tone. "Now unless you'd like me to report to Deputy Director Villiers and your superior that you're being obstructive, I suggest that the sergeant stir himself off his bum and get the prisoner."

Burnell pushed himself to his feet and took a step toward Gilmour. There was barely a hairs breadth between them. The MI5 man stood a couple of inches taller and he had a lean and muscular frame but what the superintendent lacked in athletic prowess he made up for in sheer physical presence. At this moment, he oozed menace.

"I don't appreciate MI5 swanning in here and barking orders all lord-of-the-manor."

A mocking gleam danced in the younger man's brown eyes. "I suggest you see a psychiatrist about your inferiority complex."

Finch surged to his feet and caught Gilmour by the arm, pulling him toward the door. "You can wait in the squad room. I'll bring Rossiter to you."

Gilmour tossed over his shoulder. "Glad to see that the spirit of interagency cooperation is alive and well at Scotland Yard."

Chapter 9

"Surely the fact that Scotland Yard has captured the murderer makes the situation easier," Gregory observed. "You can grill Damian Rossiter before he's charged."

"Don't worry." Villiers gripped his armrests until the papery skin across his knuckles turned white. "I intend to squeeze the smarmy weasel until there's nothing left." His lips drew back into a lupine leer. "I can't wait to get my hands on him. Then we'll see—"

He broke off at the sound of light tapping. The next instant, Dorothy popped into the office.

Before she could utter a word, Villiers exploded when he saw the dark-haired man in his early forties close on his secretary's heels. "Honeysett? Just marvelous." He threw his hands in the air. The laugh that escaped his lips was devoid of mirth. "I didn't think this day could get any worse." His eyes impaled Dorothy. He motioned with his chin toward the door. "You may leave us. However unless the PM has been kidnapped or assassinated, I don't want any more interruptions."

"Yes, Mr. Villiers. You won't be disturbed again," the secretary murmured and withdrew.

Honeysett took a step forward and gave a crisp nod to Villiers. "Laurence, it's been a while." His curious gaze snaked to Gregory, who rose to his feet.

Villiers waved a hand at Gregory. "This is Gregory Longdon, chief investigator at Symington's. He's consulting on a case."

One of Gregory's eyebrows quirked up in surprise. Villiers usually took great pains to distance himself. This case must have irked the spymaster in more ways than one.

Villiers gave a gusty sigh, as his glance fell on the unexpected visitor once more. "And this is Matthew Honeysett, MI6."

Ah, MI6. That explains the added layer of tension and rivalry in the air, Gregory thought.

This should be fun.

He clasped Honeysett's outstretched hand. The frosty expression in the agent's green-gray eyes was infused with wariness and annoyance.

"Laurence, we need to talk." He shot a pointed look at Gregory. "Alone."

Villiers leaned forward and folded his hands in front of him on his desk. "Longdon stays."

Gregory removed his coat and resumed his seat. He was right. The day had just perked up. He settled back in his chair and casually crossed one leg over the other. He inclined his head to Honeysett. "Carry on. Don't mind me."

"But I *do* mind," the MI6 man bristled in outrage. Then to Villiers, he said, "It's a matter of a sensitive and urgent nature. For your ears only."

"Longdon has been vetted and signed the Official Secrets Act. He has assisted MI5 on several occasions. He stays. Now, get on with it or leave. You've already wasted far too much of my time."

Daggers flew from Honeysett's eyes, but Gregory's roguish grin batted them away effortlessly.

The agent clenched his hands into fists. "Fine," he replied. He dropped heavily into the chair beside Gregory.

"I'm waiting," Villiers prodded with a touch of asperity.

Honeysett's back stiffened. Gregory saw the blue vein in his jaw pulse beneath his skin. "For the record, this is highly irregular," Honeysett observed.

"My patch, my rules," Villiers countered. "You're welcome to trot back to Vauxhall Cross. No one is holding you hostage."

Honeysett gritted his teeth. "Right. It's about the Alexander Colefax murder. I've been informed that MI5 is taking over the case and Damian Rossiter is being transferred to your custody." When Villiers remained silent, he went on, "I can't allow that."

The spymaster's mouth curved into a smile that did not reach his eyes. "You have no authority in this matter."

"Authority?" The word flew across the air like a bullet seeking a target. Honeysett jabbed his thumb against his chest. "Colefax was working for me."

Villiers arched an eyebrow. "He was an asset?"

"Let's just say that he was an informal source," Honeysett responded grudgingly.

"What precisely was the substance of his intelligence?"

"I can't get into all the details. Need to know. I'm sure you understand."

Villiers leaned back in his chair and chuckled. "It appears to have slipped your mind that MI6 is prohibited from operating on UK soil. Colefax was killed in London. His death falls under my purview. Either you read me in or I go straight to the PM and the press, and tell them what a naughty boy you've been. Your career will be in tatters. Like father, like son."

"You wouldn't dare. You have no right to throw Dad in my face like that. He was your friend."

"He was." Villiers nodded. "A good friend. Until he betrayed his country and his wife. He walked straight into a Russian honey trap that a new recruit would have spotted a mile away. His pillow talk led to the deaths of five agents, good *loyal* men. It took us years to undo the damage your father inflicted on the country and the security services."

"Dad paid dearly for his mistake," Honeysett asserted. "After Mum left him, he drowned himself in a bottle. He lost his mind and died in a prison cell."

"I have no sympathy. He was a trained agent. He paid the consequences for the path he chose willingly. I can't help it if it still stings. That's the cross you have to bear, not me."

Honeyesett swallowed hard. "I've spent years working myself to the bone, simply to prove that I'm a patriot."

"Like the blood on Lady Macbeth's hand, the taint of treason lingers," Villiers commented phlegmatically. "MI5 and MI6 have long memories."

"Are you saying that I'll never be trusted?" The younger man's fists curled into tight balls. "No matter the sacrifices I've made and continue to make for the job?" His voice dropped to a whisper. A glazed, faraway look entered his eyes as memories assailed him. "My wife and son…"

Villiers cleared his throat. "Ahem. I was sorry to hear about your family," he said gruffly.

The tension in the room eased, but Gregory felt it was tactful to remain quiet. He witnessed the spasm of raw pain that rippled across Honeysett's features.

"What?" The MI6 agent blinked twice, as he dragged

his mind back to the present. "Laurence, I never thanked you for your thoughtful note at the time." His voice was still thick with emotion. "I'm afraid those days were all a blur."

"Perfectly understandable," Villiers murmured.

They fell silent. After Honeysett had regained his composure, Villiers ventured tentatively, "I hear you've remarried."

The other man nodded. A corner of his mouth twitched up in a crooked smile. "Yes. About eight months ago. I was lost for so long and suddenly she entered my life. Hmph"—he broke off, his brow furrowing into an oddly thoughtful expression—"Everything happens for a reason. Yes, I see that now."

Villiers winced at this confession. Emotions were messy things to be avoided at all costs.

Honeysett didn't seem to notice his discomfort and went on, "My wife's a wedding planner. She's gaining quite a reputation in high society circles."

"Oh, really. How…nice."

Gregory bit back a smile because he could almost hear Villiers cringing inwardly.

Villiers reached for a pen and began tapping it on his desk. "To get back to the matter at hand, I want to know every minute detail about your arrangement with Colefax and why it was flawed."

Honeysett's chin jutted into the air. "Who said that it was flawed?"

"Your informal source is dead, isn't he? It may be different at MI6—although I doubt it—but here at MI5 we like our assets roaming around in the flesh. We find that it facilitates the flow of information." Villiers held up a hand to prevent the protest rising to the other man's lips. "Spare me your excuses. Plain facts so that I can determine how extensive a salvage operation I have to set into motion."

Honeysett hesitated, his gaze flitting between Villiers and Gregory. Then, he shrugged his shoulders and sighed. "What Colefax was assisting with was rather delicate. It could have serious ramifications for our already rocky relations with the Russians."

A cold tendril of dread clutched at Gregory's chest. *Not the bloody Russians again.* He and Emmy had been sucked into too many of their sordid machinations in the last few months.

"Colefax had vast dealings all over the world. His latest dream was to build a hotel in Moscow."

"Thus far, I don't see why the man's ambitions—however foolhardy—should be of interest to Her Majesty's government," Villiers remarked tartly.

A spark of smugness kindled in Honeysett's eyes. "Because Colefax's close friendship with Pyotr Zorkin gave us an entrée to Ilya Zorkin, unofficial dirty banker to Kremlin elite, the *crème de la crème* of the Russian underworld and other assorted baddies.

"Colefax and I were at Cambridge together. As was Pyotr, although I had never met him at the time. I approached Colefax quietly and appealed to his sense of Queen and country. Initially, he resisted. Despite being a cunning entrepreneur, he chafed at the idea of using his friend—or so he claimed. Ultimately, he agreed to pass on general information about his contacts, the business atmosphere for foreigners and anything else he considered relevant. However, the main objective was for Pyotr to get something that we could use to compromise his father."

"Ilya Zorkin." Villiers gave a low whistle and settled back in his chair. He nodded appreciatively. "A coup, indeed." His next comment lanced Honeysett's bubble, though. "If it had succeeded…which it obviously did not. Like Icarus, you didn't heed the warnings and flew too close to the sun."

"Not even you could have foreseen the drastic changes on the horizon," Honeysett snapped.

"A good agent goes over every angle of a mission and anticipates at least a hundred ways it could go wrong, and then comes up with contingencies to address them all as well a dozen others. Your plan was amateurish and slapdash."

A pink flush spread across Honeysett's cheeks. He was perched on the edge of his seat, his body rigid. His nostrils flared with anger, while naked hatred darkened his green-gray eyes.

Villiers had no patience for petty resentment and demanded, "Where's the son?"

Honeysett dropped his chin to his chest and shook his head. "He's in the wind," he admitted reluctantly.

Villiers chuffed a bitter laugh. "Marvelous. He had you chasing your tail."

The MI6 man's scowl clashed with Villiers's flinty gaze. "He can't get far. He has no money of his own. Everything comes from his father. Pyotr was feeling the pinch because our sanctions have frozen all of dear old dad's UK assets. That's why he agreed to help us. He wanted to disappear and live like a king."

"Bully for him," Villiers quipped. "What did he give you on his father?"

"Nothing," Honeysett replied through gritted teeth. "In the end, he had an attack of conscience. He said he wouldn't be able to forgive himself, if he crossed his father."

Villiers snorted. "More likely, he came face-to-face with the cold reality that he was the progeny of a den of wolves and his father would put a target on his back."

"In his defense, Pyotr did offer to give us someone else

instead."

"How magnanimous. Who was the subject of this shell game?"

"A deep-cover SVR operative code-named Snowdrop, who has been funneling a steady stream of intelligence on MI6's European networks to the Kremlin over the last year. Apparently, Pyotr ran into Snowdrop here in London about a month ago. Imagine the coincidence. He and Snowdrop were childhood playmates back in Moscow."

"I despise coincidences." Villiers wrinkled his nose. "There's something inherently capricious about them. This Snowdrop certainly sounds dodgy. Even his code name is ridiculous. I don't like this sleight-of-hand at the last moment. I'm afraid the apple doesn't fall far from the tree. Zorkin pulled the wool over your eyes yet again."

Honeysett pounded his clenched fist on the desk. "No." The word hurtled around the office.

"You're deluded if you think otherwise."

"The lead was solid. It confirmed MI6's suspicions. I was tasked with finding the source of the leak. For months, Snowdrop has been one step ahead of us. I couldn't dismiss this lead out of hand. Everything was planned. Pyotr was going to deliver the material on Snowdrop to Colefax, who would pass it on to me. Only he never had the chance."

"Once Colefax had made the initial contact with Zorkin and he supposedly agreed to provide information on his father, why didn't you deal with him directly? It was sheer lunacy to have Colefax continue to play intermediary. Too many risks arise when a civilian is in the mix. They're notoriously unpredictable and get ideas into their heads."

Villiers cast a sideways glance at Gregory as he uttered these last words. Clearly, he was thinking of Emmeline. But this was not the time nor the place to embark on one of their ongoing arguments.

"Life is one big risk," Honeysett spat back, his tone dripping with scorn. "I felt it was prudent to remain in the background. Easier to maneuver that way."

Gregory pursed his lips and frowned. He deemed this explanation nonsense. A spy's mission was no different from a jewel heist. Each required meticulous planning. The only way to ensure success was to be involved in every facet of the job.

"You're a virtuoso at running around in circles," Villiers scoffed. "All you have to show for your troubles is a trail of blood."

"It's not as bleak as all that."

"Really?" Villiers enumerated on his fingers. "Nothing on Ilya Zorkin. No Snowdrop. Pyotr has vanished. And for the *pièce de résistance*, MI6 is leaking like a sieve. I'm at a loss to see the silver lining."

"We have Rossiter. I gather he doesn't bat an eye at flouting the law. Thus far, he's managed to stay just under the radar. Colefax had been worried lately that Rossiter was snooping into things that were none of his concern. I've seen a copy of the police report. It indicates that a witness saw him leaving Colefax's house the night of the murder. Perhaps, Rossiter broke in and concealed himself somewhere. When Pyotr left, he confronted Colefax. They came to blows. After Colefax was dead, Rossiter stole the Snowdrop material. His object is blackmail."

Gregory was even more uneasy now than when he had entered Villiers's office half an hour earlier. The blood in his veins had turned to ice at the thought of the lethal scenarios that lay in store. It was only a matter of time before Emmy picked up the scent of Pyotr Zorkin and the Russian spy Snowdrop.

"Setting aside the fact that MI6 has wasted taxpayer money with this fiasco," he interrupted, "how are the diamonds involved?"

Honeysett's dark brows knit together. "Diamonds? What diamonds?" he asked guardedly.

Gregory caught Villiers's eye. A curt nod granted him permission to relate the saga of the diamonds for the third time that day.

He had always had a penchant for diamonds. However, his recent exploits with the Blue Angel, Pink Courtesan and now the red diamonds, had set him to wondering whether the seductive gems were his destiny or a curse. He sighed. That was a philosophical debate he would have to leave for another time.

"The bastard," Honeysett swore. "He went behind my back."

"Meaning what?" Villiers prompted.

"Before Pyotr had a change of heart about cracking open the door on his father's illicit business ventures and even more dubious cronies, he had no qualms about embezzling from his father's various bank accounts to amass his own fortune. He also took a jaunt to Switzerland and rummaged through the art treasures his father had squirreled away in a bank that prided itself on its discretion. Sanctions from all sides had put a halt to Pyotr's clandestine maneuvers.

"It will come as no surprise that papa Zorkin acquired many of the pieces in his collection through illegitimate channels. If a certain object took his fancy, he would arrange to have it stolen, whether it belonged to a friend or an archrival. He took particular pleasure when it came to the latter. There are whispers that Zorkin had the Galleon Egg stolen from Bogdan Kozlov."

Gregory's widened in disbelief. "Kozlov? The boss of bosses in Russian mafia circles."

Honeysett allowed himself a wry smile. "Got it in one. They've been bitter enemies for years. Kozlov has vowed to kill Zorkin. The Galleon Egg was his pride and joy. A status symbol. He has political ambitions and set his sights on becoming a statesman. But Zorkin couldn't have a common street thug muscling in on his patch. So he decided to teach Kozlov a lesson by stealing the egg.

"It was one of the fifty Easter eggs that Tsar Alexander III and Nicholas II commissioned from the House of Fabergé between 1885 and 1917. The eggs are crafted in gold, covered in layers of enamel and decorated with precious gems. Each has a unique design and conceals a surprise, ranging from a miniature of the Imperial family's palace and a replica of an eighteenth-century coach to a gold hen and enamel rose.

"The House of Fabergé was dissolved during the Bolshevik revolution. As part of his 'Treasures to Tractors' order to raise foreign money to feed the country, Stalin sold fourteen Fabergé eggs and masterpieces from the Hermitage. Only forty-three of the Imperial eggs are believed to exist today. Some went missing in the ensuing decades. The Galleon Egg is the most expensive of the lost pieces. The shell is drenched in diamonds, emeralds, rubies, sapphires, and pearls. It contains a gold pirate ship with a diamond treasure chest that pops out from the hull. Inside is an openwork, lace pattern necklace in 18-karat white gold featuring emerald flowers and diamond buds and a companion miniature diadem tiara with a swirling foliage design."

Gregory was salivating at the vivid description of these exquisite pieces, which had been lovingly made by artisans.

"Is there a point to this history lesson on Fabergé?" Villiers asked peevishly.

"Colefax joked that it would teach Zorkin a lesson, if MI6 stole the Galleon Egg. The Russian would never dare to report the theft. Colefax pointed out that the agency could use the egg as leverage to turn Zorkin. He'd be a gold mine for years to come, if we succeeded." Honeysett ran a hand distractedly through his dark hair. "I think Colefax hired someone to steal the egg. Either he offered it directly to Kozlov or put it up for sale to the highest bidder. The red diamonds seem to indicate that he found a buyer." His brow puckered in a frown, as his searching gaze raked Gregory's face. "It's funny how you ended up with the gems."

Villiers waved a hand vaguely. "Jewels happen to be Longdon's area of expertise. That's why I called him in."

Honeysett nodded. "Is it?" His eyes narrowed as he scrutinized Gregory even more closely. "Curiouser still," he murmured.

"I hate to point out the obvious," Gregory interjected in the hopes of stopping him from pursuing this line of thinking, "but even if Colefax had planned to sell the Galleon Egg, he never received the diamonds. The police didn't find the egg in his house. So what happened to it?"

"Rossiter probably took it when he killed Colefax. That's the only thing that makes sense." Honeysett turned to Villiers. "Look, Laurence"—he offered him a deferential smile and leaned forward—"I know this is MI5's jurisdiction, but I'd like you to turn over Rossiter to me. This was my case. I want to see it through. I owe that much to Colefax."

"Colefax was a double-dealing scoundrel. It's no wonder he was murdered," Gregory sneered.

"Zorkin is the bigger fish in the grand scheme of things," Honeysett pointed out. "There's still a possibility, slim though it may be, that we can turn him. But it's vital that we break Rossiter, before he's thrown into solitary confinement for the rest of his miserable life. We also have to find Pyotr."

"I've always found professional courtesy to be a slippery slope," Villiers observed dryly. "After all, once it begins where does it end? Thank you for the enlightening briefing. If MI5 has any further questions about Colefax or Rossiter, we'll be in touch."

Honeysett leaped to his feet. He pressed his palms on the desk and leaned toward Villiers, his eyes ablaze with menace. "How dare you dismiss me as if I were some wayward child? You're not bloody God. This is my case. Not yours or this"—he flapped a hand at Gregory—"bumbling amateur."

Villiers regarded him with icy disdain. "*Was* your case. My advice to MI6 is to get its house in order. If Snowdrop isn't neutralized, you will be solely responsible for bringing down the agency in flames." He paused for a beat. "Mind you, that would burnish your family's treacherous legacy in perpetuity."

Honeysett's sharp intake of breath set Gregory's nerves tingling with unease. The man appeared poised to pummel Villiers with his bare hands. Only the desk stood in his way.

Instead, Honeysett spun around on his heel and stalked out of the office. The door rattled on its hinges in his wake.

"You have such a way with words and people, *Papa*," Gregory quipped.

Chapter 10

Nigel drew up to the curb halfway down the block from Colefax's townhouse on the highly desirable Chester Row, which was mere steps from Sloane Square in Belgravia. He turned off the ignition and cast a glance at Emmeline in the passenger seat beside him. Her dark eyes glittered with excitement. Her fingers were already curved around the door handle.

A sigh rumbled through his chest. "This is ill-advised," he asserted.

The door was open and she had one foot on the pavement, but she turned to face him. "You've made your feelings perfectly plain on that point. However, I'm not doing anything illegal. If it makes you feel better, think of me as your assistant. I'm merely here to observe and take notes."

"Hmph," he grunted. "And butter won't melt in your mouth." He pointed at the uniformed police constable rocking back and forth on the balls of his feet in front of Colefax's door. "There will be hell to pay, if he recognizes you and reports your presence to Burnell."

She craned her neck and squinted at the windscreen. A smile spread over her face and she patted him on the shoulder. "Not to worry. I don't know him, so we're all right. Shall we?"

She was out of the car and slamming the door, before he had a chance to answer.

Nothing was all right. Would it ever be again?

He cursed Damian Rossiter to perdition. It didn't change matters, but it helped to have a target for his frustration.

Nigel had to hurry to catch up to Emmeline. Although she was petite, her feet had wings. "Listen," he ordered when he had fallen into step beside her, "let me do the talking. And do not, under any circumstances, start peppering the constable with questions. Observe in silence."

She mimed locking her lips with a key and tossing it over her shoulder. The action did not inspire confidence, quite the contrary in fact.

The constable held up a hand and barred their way into the house. "I'm sorry, sir, miss," he asserted politely. "I'm going to have to ask you to move along. This is a crime scene."

That was stating the obvious. A blue-and-white tape that screamed POLICE DO NOT CROSS was stretched across the shiny black door behind him.

Nigel drew out his wallet to produce his identification. "It's all right, constable. I'm Nigel Sanborn. I represent Damian Rossiter. As his lawyer, I have a right to view the crime scene."

The constable wrinkled his nose as he glanced at the driver's license. His mouth curled into a grimace. Clearly, he had formed a low opinion of Rossiter and any of his associates.

The officer returned the driver's license, as his gaze landed on Emmeline. Her lips parted, but Nigel spoke briskly before she could utter a word, "This is my assistant. She…takes notes for me."

Emmeline offered the constable a smile and brandished her notebook in the air.

His brows knit together. "Hmm. I'd better check with the station. Procedures."

"Of course, go ahead," Nigel replied. He tried to make his tone as casual as possible. He didn't dare glance at Emmeline. However, he could feel her gaze boring into him. "But I feel it only right to tell you"—he peered at the name badge on the officer's uniform—"P.C. Wilmot, that Superintendent Burnell was in a foul mood when I left the station an hour ago. I wouldn't want you to get on his bad side."

The constable's Adam's apple worked up and down, as he contemplated whether to incur Burnell's wrath.

"Well if the superintendent authorized it, then I suppose it's all right. There's no need to bother him." He cleared his throat, as he assumed an air of authority. "You have half an hour. I will escort you." Emmeline scowled at this prospect, but he was intent on issuing instructions and didn't notice. "Forensics has dusted and taken photos. Do not remove anything from the premises. I will have my eye on you the entire time."

Nigel dipped his head deferentially. "I would expect nothing less." He pressed a hand to the small of Emmeline's back in warning.

Satisfied, Wilmot turned and opened the door. He stood aside to allow them to enter the hall ahead of him. An awkward silence pressed in around them, as they watched him carefully close the door.

The house had a rustic ambiance, blending classic style and contemporary architecture. It appeared to be arranged over two floors. Even on this murky, gray December afternoon the long, narrow hall was flooded with light from the row of windows that overlooked the private interior courtyard below. Not a speck of dust or dirt clung to the highly polished hardwood floor. Emmeline slowed her pace, as her gaze roamed over the eggshell white walls covered in photos. The majority were of snow-capped mountains and glistening Alpine lakes, but there were some more exotic locations too. The images were so crisp, she felt as if she could step into them.

The constable caught her eye. "They make you long to take a holiday, don't they?"

She nodded. "Indeed, they do."

"It seems the victim loved to travel and was something of an amateur photographer." He motioned at the wall. "He took all of these photos. I believe he won some awards."

"I'm not surprised."

"Now then, where would you like to start?"

The officer directed his question to Nigel, but Emmeline was the one who answered. "The room where Colefax was murdered, of course. Then, we can take a peek at the other rooms." She touched Nigel's sleeve and offered him a sweet smile. "Just to be thorough, isn't that right?"

At Nigel's nod, the constable led them toward a curving staircase at the end of the hall. Wilmot halted and placed one hand on the banister, barring their way. His angular face was pinched with concern. "Perhaps it would be better if the young lady remains up here."

"Why?" she demanded. "It will be impossible to take notes, if I don't view the scene."

"It's not pleasant, miss. Mr. Colefax was bludgeoned to death. There was an awful lot of blood."

"P.C. Wilmot has a point," Nigel concurred. "There's

no need to upset yourself."

She rolled her eyes at the ceiling. "You're both very considerate, but my sensibilities are made of sterner stuff."

Nigel and the officer exchanged a dubious look.

"Oh, for heaven's sake." She pushed past them and descended the stairs.

When she reached the bottom step, the cloying, coppery tang of blood assaulted her nostrils. She cringed inwardly but arranged her features in a bland expression at the sound of the men's voices behind her. She would not give them the satisfaction of saying "I told you so." She walked briskly into the heart of Colefax's cinema/media room. A glass door opened onto the interior courtyard. She spied a sunken seating area, where a charcoal sofa and marble table were nestled next to a water fountain, which was dry and likely turned on only in the warmer months. Ivy crept up one wall and there were bushes on the other side. Two charcoal wicker chairs with matching cushions and a marble bench completed the scene. A number of pots were ranged around the perimeter of the terrace. No doubt in the summer they were overflowing with flowers or plants. The courtyard would be the perfect spot to while away an afternoon with a good book and a cup of tea.

Alas, she tore herself from these daydreams and turned her attention back to the media room. Dark, forest green cabinets covered the wall to her left. A tray with several decanters of various spirits and crystal tumblers rested on a shelf in the corner. An L-shaped sofa upholstered in a heavy mustard velvet stood in the center of the room opposite a wall dominated by a film screen.

She scribbled a few notes, as she walked deeper into the room. The bitter taste of bile rose to her tongue, when her gaze fell on the ugly brown stains smeared across the sofa and carpet. There were even some dried splotches on the glass coffee table.

A shudder rippled through her body at the fury that could have provoked such violence.

So much blood.

Her stomach roiled in revulsion and horror. A wave of nausea threatened to overpower her. She put a hand to her lips and bolted toward the courtyard.

"Emmeline," Nigel called after her.

She collapsed into one of the wicker chairs and dropped her head between her knees. She took greedy gulps of the nippy winter air.

She felt a gentle hand between her shoulder blades.

"Are you all right?" Nigel asked softly.

For a moment, she couldn't trust herself to speak and squeezed her eyes shut. After the wave of nausea had subsided, she drew herself upright.

She placed her hands on Nigel's forearms to steady herself. Concern was reflected in the depths of his hazel eyes.

"I'm fine now." Her voice was a hoarse whisper. She cleared her throat and tried again. "Honestly. I'm fine." She cast a glance out of the corner of her eye at the open glass door. "I just...didn't expect it to be so..." Her sentence trailed off.

"It's my fault, miss," Wilmot said. "It went against my better judgment to allow you in there."

She gave him a watery smile and waved off his apology. "Nonsense." She took a last cleansing breath and rose to her feet. "It was a shock. That's all. As you can see, I'm all right. I'm ready to see the rest of the house."

"No, we're leaving at once," Nigel commanded. He seized her by the elbow.

She shook off his grasp. "Don't be silly. We're here now. We must go over every inch of the house. It's vital to Mr. Rossiter's defense."

And my story. But of course, she couldn't say that.

"Damian can go to the devil," he growled. "I can't have you making yourself ill. Gregory would never forgive me."

"You make it sound as if I did battle with a gang of criminals. I became a little nauseous. It passed. I'm fine. Let's just get on with the task we came here to do."

Crime scenes were a repository of so many secrets begging to be discovered. She was not going to waste this opportunity to explore Colefax's house.

Although her stomach still churned, she squared her shoulders and tossed her chin in the air. Without waiting for the two men, she crossed the flagstones to some stone steps leading into the house via a different door. She couldn't bear to enter the media room again. At least for today.

P.C. Wilmot hurried after her. "Hold on a moment, miss. You can't wander about alone," he reprimanded.

She stopped on the top step. "I wouldn't dare." She flashed a smile and obediently waited for him to open the door. Wilmot returned her smile and ushered her inside. By contrast, an expression of disapproval was etched into the planes and angles of Nigel's face as he brought up the rear.

You only have yourself to blame, she reproached him silently. *If only you'd tell me what you know, we wouldn't have to embark on this scavenger hunt.*

"I think it would be extremely helpful to see Colefax's study. Don't you agree, Nigel?" she asked once they were in the drawing room.

He exhaled a long breath and nodded.

"Right. It's down the hall next to the living room," Wilmot said.

As they trailed after the officer, Emmeline kept peppering him with questions about Colefax, which he answered without hesitation. Nigel bit back a smile. She had a way of drawing people out. Before they realized it, they were chatting and telling her things that they never intended.

The study was a masculine refuge. There had to be a clue here, Emmeline reasoned.

The room was all clean, crisp lines. It overlooked the courtyard. Although the study was filled with natural light, it lacked warmth. She frowned as she wandered around. Granted, everyone is riddled with contradictions. Colefax was not a hermit. He enjoyed the company of beautiful women and was a gourmand. He was part owner of a thoroughbred racehorse and frequented casinos. His art collection was envied by rivals around the world. But as she halted before the fireplace and cocked her head to one side to scrutinize the painting above the mantelpiece of two prosperous men in rich Renaissance attire, she wondered who was the real Colefax. Was he the darling of society circles or the shrewd businessman who retreated to this inner sanctum to plot his next big venture?

A frisson slithered down her spine. Instinct told her that he had been self-centered and arrogant, and only his enemies saw his darker side. The brutal manner of his death seemed to suggest that the killer was seeking to punish him, to teach him a lesson. She shuddered as the sofa and carpet covered in dried blood flashed before her eyes.

She shook her head and swallowed hard, as a rumbling the pit of her stomach threatened again. Dwelling on the violence would only cloud her thoughts.

Her gaze snaked over to Nigel, who leaned one shoulder against the wall as he pored over the papers in the small safe in the corner. Wilmot was glued to his side to make sure nothing went missing. As if it would, she sniffed.

She went to the mahogany desk, which was positioned at a right angle to the window so that light could spill across it. The laptop was closed, so that wasn't going to be of much help since she didn't have Colefax's password. Instead, she opened the center drawer and began sifting through papers. They yielded nothing. She turned to the top right-hand drawer and let her fingers roam through the labeled files. She pulled one or two out and skimmed the contents. Most dealt with routine hotel matters and therefore were useless since she knew Colefax's business empire was thriving.

She sighed and plopped down onto the chair. A pad embossed with Colefax's name in bold calligraphy caught her eye. Just two words were scrawled on the top sheet.

Ring Kozlov.

She propped her elbows on the desk and stared at the paper. Who was Kozlov?

Colefax wanted to build a hotel in Moscow. Could this Kozlov be a government official or a local intermediary? Or…

A little voice in the back of her head whispered, *Wouldn't it be interesting if it's Bogdan Kozlov, the Russian mafia boss? Is it possible that Colefax had been contemplating a silent partnership with Kozlov to make his hotel a reality no matter the cost?*

As she made a mental note to follow up on this lead, her gaze fell on the handful of photos clustered on the desk. This was the only room that had photos of people in them. Obviously, they were important to Colefax. One was at a black-tie event, where he was accepting an award. Another was at what appeared to be the opening of a hotel. And there were several with him and a young woman with thick chestnut hair. She squinted at the photos. They ranged from when the woman was a child to a teenager and as an adult.

"P.C. Wilmot, who is this woman in the photos with Colefax?" she asked.

He craned his neck around and glanced at the photos she indicated. "I believe someone said it was his niece. I think he was quite fond of her."

Her ears perked up. "Niece? Could it be his goddaughter Julie Brentford?"

The officer nodded. "Come to think of it, I believe you're right."

Nigel dropped the document he had been reviewing. Papers fanned out all over the floor.

"Mr. Sanborn, you must be careful," Wilmot reproached. "The sergeant will have my guts for garters, if anything goes astray. Let me help you gather up the papers and then I must insist that both of you leave. You've been here far too long as it is."

Emmeline watched Nigel squat down on his haunches and hastily pull sheets toward him. He stuffed them back into the file. "Sorry. Clumsy of me," he mumbled.

"You are one of the most meticulous men I know," she observed. "Could it be nerves? After all, you haven't practiced criminal law in many years. Or is it something else?"

His head snapped up. She rested her chin on her hand and met his glare with a sweet smile.

"I have absolutely no idea what you're insinuating. This is a particularly complex case."

"I agree. It seems Alexander Colefax was a man of contradictions and secrets. He's not the only one, though. We came here in the hope of finding answers to help your client, but I have even more questions. I left a message earlier for Miss Brentford. She hasn't returned my call. Perhaps she can shed some light on her beloved godfather. What's your opinion?"

Nigel placed his hands on his knees and pushed himself to his feet. "You're the jour—" He broke off and slid a sideways glance at Wilmot. He had been about to say journalist. "As you're always reminding me, your job is to ask questions. Follow your instincts. Some people are loath to talk to a stranger on the phone. I've always found a face-to-face meeting to be more meaningful. If I were you, I'd hop on the Tube to Bayswater and pay a visit to her flat in Westbourne Terrace. I'm certain that familiar surroundings will help to loosen her tongue."

The blood began to race through her veins. *How do you know Julie Brentford lives in Westbourne Terrace?*

But a loud pounding on the front door prevented her from grilling her cousin by marriage.

Chapter 11

Gregory strolled along Millbank, after leaving Villiers's office in Thames House. He shrugged deeper into his overcoat and thrust his hands into his pockets, ignoring the drizzle that had begun to seep from the clouds. The chilly air was precisely what he needed to clear the cobwebs.

The revelations about Colefax, Zorkin, and the Fabergé egg left him in a pensive mood. A notorious Russian mafia boss and a MI6 mole with the seemingly innocuous name of Snowdrop. Which one paid Rossiter to murder Colefax? Because Rossiter was far too lazy and lacked the imagination to come up with the idea on his own. Although he had to concede that none of us knew what we were capable of until we were plunged into a situation.

Gregory grimaced at one certainty in this world. Emmy would rub her hands together in glee the instant word trickled into her ear that Kozlov or the spy Snowdrop were vying for the unsavory role of prime suspect. She lived for the thrill of the chase. By contrast, it made his stomach coil into increasingly tighter knots. He both admired and cursed her dedication to shine light on the truth. Often, it blinded her to the dangers trailing in her shadow. Asking a probing question of the wrong person could provoke a lethal reaction. And that was his greatest fear every time she set foot outside the house.

The purring of his mobile jarred him from these disturbing ruminations. He drew it out of his inside pocket. Damn and blast. It was one of Symington's junior investigators, an arrogant bloke who was keen to climb up the ladder no doubt by trying to oust Gregory from the top job. He was one of those people who smiled to your face and all the while held a knife at the ready to plunge between your shoulder blades. It was an old game and grated on Gregory's nerves. He had successfully avoided the man's calls all morning. He sighed and answered it now. He dealt with the matter quickly.

Then, he rang his boss and told him that he was working on an important case. He may have given the impression that it involved one of the firm's oldest clients and MI5. The mere mention of the latter was enough to prevent his boss from seeking more information. He took Gregory at his word. As chief investigator, Gregory had earned his complete trust. He prided himself on doing a good job. He had saved the firm from making hefty payouts on several suspicious claims. The problem was that legitimate employment didn't challenge him. It didn't have the same élan as planning—and carrying out—a heist. Nothing could compare to holding an exquisite diamond, ruby, emerald or sapphire in his hand. Cool and smooth to the touch. Glimmering facets catching the light. This jolt of adrenaline kept his senses sharp and nimble. Neither Emmy nor Symington's would understand. He strove to be a considerate gentleman, therefore it was only right that he didn't burden them with his secret.

Diamonds.

In the blink of an eye, his reverie melted into the murky reality of the present.

He quickened his pace. He was going to pop in to see an old friend who had "retired" five years ago, but still dabbled in a bit of fencing from time to time. His friend always kept his ears open. One never knew when an interesting nugget of gossip could bear fruit. There must have been some chatter about the Galleon Egg.

The hairs on the back of Gregory's neck suddenly prickled. Above the rumbling of midday traffic, he heard footsteps echoing loudly on the slick pavement behind him. His ears strained to listen. Two men. Now, it was a free country. They could be two friends out for lunch. Or more likely, two MPs or other sundry officials hurrying back to Parliament, which was a few hundred yards ahead. He could be jaded, but instinct told Gregory that these chaps had a more sinister agenda.

His reflexes were a fraction too slow. Before he could spin around and confront his new admirers, a hand grabbed him roughly by the arm and a gun was jabbed into his ribs. A second hand clamped down on his other arm, twisting it behind his back.

A man's warm breath tickled his ear, as he hissed, "Easy, Longdon. Just so that there are no misunderstandings, I have no qualms about shooting you. In fact, it would brighten my day no end. But business before pleasure. Isn't that always the way?"

"It seems our definitions of pleasure are vastly different."

This earned him a punch in the kidneys that sent a thousand stabbing needles of pain radiating through his body. The two men propped up his body between them before he crumpled to the ground.

"Feeling a bit peaky, are you?" one asked sarcastically.

"Perhaps you need to sit down."

Without waiting for a response—not that he was capable of uttering a word at that moment—they dragged him into Victoria Tower Gardens, across the lawn, and finally dumped him unceremoniously on a bench along the parapet overlooking the Thames. The sibilant murmur of the wind made the bare branches of the London Plane trees shiver, as the river traffic continued to flow past. For several long seconds, he struggled to draw air into his lungs.

At last, he lifted his head and looked into the faces of his tormenters. Two of the ugliest sods he had ever seen. Mind you, one couldn't have conjured up two more perfect specimens of the modern-day thug. Both were in their thirties. One was lean and fair with icy blue eyes. The other was only a shade shorter, but he was dark and beefy. His lips curled back, revealing crooked teeth. Gregory supposed that was what passed for a smile. He was certain he had this Neanderthal to thank for the pain roaming over his body. The bloke probably left imprints of his fists on Gregory's lower back as a souvenir.

"Now then"—the taller one placed one foot on the bench and rested his forearm on his thigh, his face looming over Gregory—"I'm only going to ask you this once. Lying to me would be an act of bad faith. Therefore, I advise you to think carefully before you speak."

"I hate to disillusion you chaps, but I don't have a religious bone in my body. If you're in desperate need of spiritual guidance, a member of the clergy is far more qualified to offer you succor."

The man threw his head back and laughed. "Do you hear that?" he asked his colleague. "We have a comedian."

Without warning, he bent his head close and snatched the lapels of Gregory's coat in his fists. "I'm not a patient man." He gave Gregory a shake that made his teeth rattle.

"No more jokes. I'm the only thing standing between you and my friend. A nod from me and he will rearrange all your bones, religious or otherwise."

The Neanderthal grunted in anticipated pleasure.

Gregory couldn't help himself. "Positively primitive."

The man lunged toward him, but his colleague placed a hand on his chest.

"You're pushing your luck, Longdon."

The pain had subsided to a dull throbbing, so Gregory stretched one arm casually along the back of the bench. "Impossible. I attract luck like bees to honey." He offered the chap a roguish grin. "It's a gift."

It delighted him no end to see two crimson patches stain the man's pale cheeks.

"No more games," he growled. "We know you have the diamonds. Our employer wants the egg."

"Hmph. Is that what this about?" The two men held their breath. He was relishing stretching out the moment. "If your employer is feeling peckish, I suggest that he pops into the nearest Tesco's and buys a dozen eggs."

He anticipated the fist and ducked his head to the left seconds before it came flying toward his face. The Neanderthal howled as several bones crunched, when his hand made contact with the sturdy wooden slats of the bench.

Gregory scrambled to his feet. "I was happy to resolve your little dilemma. No need to feel embarrassed. We all need help from time to time." He shot his cuff and glanced at his watch. "As much as I enjoyed this interlude, I'm afraid I must dash."

He vaulted over the bench and was halfway across the lawn in two strides. They stared at him, their jaws agape, for several suspended seconds. Then, their wits returned. He gave them a hearty wave over his shoulder, as they bounded after him.

Fortune was indeed smiling down upon him. When he was back on the pavement on Millbank, a constable was ambling toward him.

He raised a hand and greeted this most welcome representative of the law. "Constable, this is my first time to London," he babbled on breathlessly, as if he were a tourist, "and I'm afraid I'm lost. I wonder if you can give me directions to Trafalgar Square. My wife and her mother went shopping. I promised to meet them half an hour ago. My mother-in-law is an ogre. She never approved of me. She's probably shredding my character to bits and pushing my wife to hire a divorce lawyer."

Sometimes he surprised himself at how easily his tongue could improvise on the fly.

The constable took pity on a fellow male and was only too happy to provide assistance. He had a friendly disposition. Gregory kept him chatting as he surreptitiously guided him toward the corner. The two men who had waylaid him were forced to abandon their mission and hailed the first taxi that trundled by.

As the cab passed the spot where he was standing, Gregory sketched a cheeky salute at his stone-faced antagonists. However, this was merely an uneasy truce. They would be back.

The question was who was their employer: Kozlov or Snowdrop? Neither option was palatable.

Chapter 12

Emmeline's antennae had tingled with excitement, when P.C. Wilmot opened the door to find two hulking giants from MI5 looming on the threshold. The agents brusquely informed the constable that Scotland Yard was off the case and Rossiter had been transferred to MI5's custody. It was sheer torture not to remain behind at Colefax's house. Alas, too many complications would have arisen, when they discovered she was a member of the press. She had no qualms about confronting Villiers, but she had to choose her battles. It was no use poking the bear unnecessarily. Therefore, she left Wilmot and Nigel to sort it and she scurried off to the Sloane Square Underground station, where she caught a Circle Line train to Notting Hill Gate and switched to the Central line.

Sleet was mingling with the raindrops when she emerged from Paddington Station in Bayswater. The chill began seeping into her bones. She was happy it was only a five-minute walk to Westbourne Terrace. The tree-lined avenue runs between Westbourne Bridge in the north and the junction of Westbourne Crescent and Sussex Gardens in the south. Julie Brentford's flat was located in the four-story, Grade II listed stucco terraced house at the corner with Chilworth Street, only a stone's throw from Hyde Park.

She climbed the slick marble steps and raised her hand to grasp the brass knocker, when the black door was flung open and a woman in her fifties nearly collided with her.

"Oh dear." She pressed a hand to her chest and took a half-step backward. "You did give me a start." Her gaze narrowed. "Can I help you?" she asked suspiciously.

Emmeline offered her a smile to put her at ease. "I'm terribly sorry." She rooted around in her handbag and produced her press badge. "My name is Emmeline Kirby. I'm a journalist with the *Clarion*. I've been trying to reach Julie Brentford"—she gestured with her chin at the door—"one of your neighbors. I'd like to ask her a few questions regarding a story I'm working on. However, she hasn't returned any of my calls so I thought I'd pop along to speak to her in person. Do you know Miss Brentford?"

"Yes, I know Julie." Her mouth curved into a smile. "She's a lovely, friendly young woman. Very polite. Always ready to help me with my shopping. She's an actress. Only minor roles so far, but she has big dreams. I have no doubt she'll succeed. She often invites me to her flat for a nice cuppa and a chat. When the weather is mild, we go out onto her roof terrace."

The expression in her pale blue eyes suddenly clouded and she bit her lip.

"Has something happened to Miss Brentford?"

She fixed a level stare on Emmeline's face. It appeared as if she were carrying on an internal debate about whether to trust her. In the end, the need to confide in someone won out over her cautious reserve.

She nodded. Her fingers clutched Emmeline's wrist lightly and her voice dropped to a whisper. "I've been worried. I'm afraid something has happened to Julie."

Emmeline's back stiffened. "What makes you say that?"

"Julie is a quiet girl. No wild parties. Few visitors. Two nights ago, I heard her arguing with a man. She was doing most of the shouting. I opened my door and popped my head into the corridor. I couldn't hear what was said. However, Julie was crying something fierce. It broke my heart. And then…it all stopped. I listened for a few minutes longer, but all was quiet. I bolted my door, made myself a cup of cocoa and settled down with a John Le Carré. It was one of those books I couldn't put down. I didn't get to bed until nearly two in the morning."

"And you didn't hear anything else from Miss Brentford's flat?"

The woman gave a sad shake of her head. "Not a peep." There was a tremor in her voice. "I haven't seen Julie since. I went to check on her. I knocked on her door several times, but there's been no response. I was contemplating whether to ring the police. I wouldn't want Julie to feel that I was prying into her business."

"Of course not." Emmeline patted her arm reassuringly. "Mind you, from what you've said there is serious cause for concern. I think it would be wise to ring the police." She hesitated a moment. "I…I know Superintendent Oliver Burnell at Scotland Yard. He's thorough and will get to the heart of the matter. He's also discreet."

"I don't know."

She took the woman by the elbow. "Ms.—I'm sorry I don't know your name."

"Thorpe. Agnes Thorpe. I'm divorced, but I kept my married name. It was easier that way."

Emmeline nodded. "Mrs. Thorpe, I know you have no reason to trust me. I'm a stranger after all. However, I assure you my only interest is to find out the truth. I will call Superintendent Burnell. Before I do, why don't we go up together and knock on Ms. Brentford's door? There may be a perfectly simple explanation for her absence. Perhaps, she went away for a few days."

These words were uttered with more confidence than she felt. The hairs prickling on the back of her neck told her that Julie Brentford had been the victim of foul play. It couldn't be a coincidence that the disturbance in her flat occurred on the same night Alexander Colefax was killed.

They took the lift to the first floor. The carpeting muted their footfalls as Mrs. Thorpe led the way to the flat.

They stood side by side in front of Julie Brentford's door. Emmeline pressed the bell. It echoed hollowly inside. She tried again. When still no one answered, she rapped sharply on the door. Silence reined. She cleared her throat and said, "Miss Brentford, it's Mrs. Thorpe and Emmeline Kirby from the *Clarion*. We'd like to speak with you."

The door remained firmly closed in their faces. It didn't bode well.

Emmeline sighed. She reached into her handbag and drew out her mobile. "Right, we have no choice. I'll ring Superintendent Burnell. Just one thing"—she pulled out the photo of Colefax and Julie Brentford that she had surreptitiously taken from his house when the MI5 agents had arrived on the scene—"is this the man you heard arguing with Ms. Brentford?"

Mrs. Thorpe shook her head. "Heavens no, that's her Uncle Alexander. He dotes on Julie and visits often. I would have recognized his voice. He's a charming gentleman. Always has time to exchange a few words." She frowned. "I haven't seen him in at least two weeks, though."

"I see," Emmeline murmured as she punched in

Burnell's number in her mobile.

"Burnell," he boomed into her ear. There was a hard edge to his tone. Oh, dear. He was likely fuming over MI5 swooping in and taking over the case. She couldn't blame him. She'd want to strangle someone too, if she were in his shoes.

She pasted a smile on her lips, although he couldn't see her face. "Hello, Superintendent Burnell. It's Emmeline. I'm glad I caught you."

"Emmeline? Whatever the question is, the answer is no comment."

She sniffed, but let it pass. "Actually, I want to report a"—she flicked a sideways glance at Mrs. Thorpe, whose features were pinched with strain, and decided against saying *crime*—"a potential situation."

Without embellishments, she told him about Julie Brentford's disappearance. "Her neighbor is concerned that something might have happened to her. As am I." She paused, choosing her next words carefully. "It seems Miss Brentford is Alexander Colefax's goddaughter."

Burnell groaned. "Bloody marvelous. Don't go haring off. Finch and I will be there as quick as we can. I want to speak to the neighbor."

"Yes, of course, Superintendent. She's eager to speak with you." Mrs. Thorpe nodded vigorously and mouthed that the detectives should come directly to her flat.

As soon as Emmeline gave Burnell the address and rang off, Mrs. Thorpe offered to make a cup of tea.

Ah yes, tea to soothe nerves stretched taut by dread.

એન્ડ

When the two detectives arrived half an hour later, Mrs.

Thorpe was ringing her hands. She had been pacing back and forth in her cozy living room. Her tea had remained untouched on the coffee table. Emmeline could say nothing to assuage the older woman's anxiety. It was the not knowing that was unbearable.

Mrs. Thorpe nodded as she motioned for Burnell to sit on the sofa. Finch settled into a wing chair. He unobtrusively took out his notebook and flipped it open to a clean page, his pen poised above it. He had a way of melting into the background, which allowed witnesses and suspects to talk without feeling self-conscious.

Mrs. Thorpe sat bolt upright on the edge of the sofa next to Burnell. He seemed to sense her agitation and offered her a smile. He spoke in a gentle tone. "Please relax, Mrs. Thorpe. There is no reason to feel nervous."

Her restless fingers continued to pleat her woolen skirt. "I'll never forgive myself, if something horrid has happened to Julie."

"Let's not start imagining the worst. Why don't you take your time and tell us what you overheard?" He gestured with his chin at Emmeline, who flanked her other side. "Miss Kirby briefly told me over the phone, but I'd like to hear it in your own words. All right?"

Mrs. Thorpe drew in air through her nostrils and plunged in. Her gaze never left the superintendent's face, as she related the events of the other night. When she was finished, Burnell asked a few questions.

"Did Miss Brentford have many gentlemen friends?" He saw the spark of anger in the woman's eyes and held up a hand. "I'm not trying to impugn her reputation. But we need to know everyone with whom she came into contact. You must see that."

The tension in Mrs. Thorpe's shoulders eased and she inclined her head. "Yes, I'm sorry. Julie's such a sweet woman. Very steady. She didn't run around. No drugs, either. She had been seeing a man over the past three months. It was quite serious. Julie was head over heels. I've never seen her so happy. She was certain he would ask her to marry him in the very near future."

"I see," Burnell murmured. He exchanged a fleeting glance with Finch and then returned his attention to Mrs. Thorpe. "Right. Thank you." He placed his hands on his knees and pushed himself to his feet. "I think it's time that Finch and I paid a visit on Miss Brentford."

Mrs. Thorpe half-rose, but the superintendent waved her back. "No, I must insist that you remain here with Miss Kirby."

He gave Emmeline a pointed look and she immediately rose. "Your tea has gone cold, Mrs. Thorpe. I think you could do with something warm inside you. Shall I make us another pot?"

The woman shook her head and scooped up the pot. "No, no. I'll go put the kettle on. It'll give me something to do."

Mrs. Thorpe bustled off to the kitchen and the detectives slipped out of the flat.

Emmeline's gaze was fixed longingly on the door. All the answers lay on the other side.

ℭℐℭℐ

It wasn't long before Emmeline heard a door slam, followed by muffled male voices in the corridor. This was too much. She had to find out what was going on. She shot a glance at the kitchen and then tiptoed to the door. She opened it a crack and held her breath. Burnell was speaking rapidly into his mobile.

"I want a team out here at once," she heard him say.

"The landlady will show you up to the first floor." He listened for a few seconds and then severed the connection.

Burnell and Finch had their heads bent together and were talking hushed tones, when she sidled up to them.

"What did you discover?" she asked in a whisper.

The detectives' heads snapped up.

Burnell glared at her. "Emmeline, I told you to stay in Mrs. Thorpe's flat."

"I did…while you and Sergeant Finch went to check on Miss Brentford. You've done that. What did she say?"

The superintendent's lips clamped into a tight line.

"She'll find out anyway, sir," Finch pointed out.

Burnell exhaled a weary sigh. "Unfortunately." His gaze raked Emmeline's face. "Miss Brentford didn't say much. She's dead."

"Poor woman. I suspected as much." She nodded sadly as questions chased themselves through her mind. "Obviously, Julie was murdered because of her connection to Colefax."

She arched an eyebrow at the detectives, but they stubbornly refused to offer an opinion.

She shrugged and continued to puzzle it out aloud. "Was she Colefax's intermediary in his secret dealings with Bogdan Kozlov and therefore a loose end that had to be eliminated? Or was Julie killed because Colefax double-crossed Kozlov? As punishment to make Colefax toe the line. Surely, it would have made more sense to kidnap her and use her as leverage. Meanwhile if Kozlov murdered Colefax, he would never get—what? The diamonds?" Emmeline frowned. "That can't be right. The diamonds were a payoff *to* Colefax. So what was he selling to the Russian that is worth one hundred million pounds and where is it?" She gave a dissatisfied shake of her head. "It seems unlikely that a shrewd businessman would seek advice from his goddaughter, let alone involve her in his affairs. In fact, he would do everything in his power to keep Julie as far away from Kozlov as possible. And another thing, why would Kozlov hire a conniving schemer like Rossiter? Wouldn't the Russian have ordered his own thugs to carry out the dirty deed to ensure that no trace was left? I haven't had time to work out that connection yet.

"All the blood at Colefax's house points to a killer driven by primal fury, not cold calculation. Kozlov would have done things quietly, especially when it came to Julie. I can see his lackeys hiding in her flat and taking her by surprise. A broken neck would have ended things neatly and swiftly. Very little, if any, blood. But the yelling Mrs. Thorpe described seems to indicate that Julie had a heated row with someone she knew well. The boyfriend would be the most likely suspect. If it was a crime of passion, her death had nothing to do with Colefax. That seems to suggest that there are two killers. Because if Rossiter murdered Colefax, it was impossible for him to have been in Julie's flat at the same time. That's pure common sense. Wouldn't you agree?"

The detectives stared at her without blinking. Her rambling speculations had stunned them into silence.

"Any theories?" she prompted impatiently as her gaze flitted between them.

Burnell was the first to recover his wits. His fists curled into balls at his sides. "When precisely were you in Colefax's house?" he demanded in clipped tones.

She felt the blood drain from her cheeks. *Brilliant, Emmeline*, she scolded herself. *A masterful example of allowing your mouth to run wild.*

"Ah," she stammered and offered him a watery smile hoping to douse his smoldering ire.

Burnell folded his arms over his broad chest and arched

a wispy white eyebrow. "That is *not* an answer. I wonder if you would find it more conducive to talk at the station."

She moistened her lips with the tip of her tongue and swallowed hard. "That will not be necessary," she replied primly.

"I'm delighted to hear it." But the dour expression darkening his features suggested that delight was the farthest thing from his present frame of mind.

"You see," she began haltingly, "having had the opportunity, no the *privilege*"—she smiled again—"to observe first-hand the professional manner in which you conduct an investigation, I know that crime scenes provide a wealth of information. As you and Sergeant Finch were extremely busy, I didn't want to bother you by formally asking to visit Colefax's house."

Burnell's smile did not touch his eyes. "Did you hear that, Finch? How considerate."

"Indeed, sir. What impeccable manners."

She inclined her head. "Honed at Gran's knee."

"Emmeline." The superintendent's voice thrummed with a warning.

"Sorry. Since I didn't want to tear you away from your important work—"

"And you knew, I would never agree to your request."

"That too. I asked Nigel to take me to Colefax's house. As Rossiter's lawyer, he has a right to view the crime scene."

Finch snorted. "You mean you badgered Nigel into taking you along."

She tossed her chin in the air and sniffed. "I never realized you were a cynic. You make me sound manipulative."

Some of Burnell's ill-humor ebbed and the corners of his mouth quivered into a smile. "You're only infuriating half of the time. How did Nigel explain your presence to

P.C. Wilmot?"

She grinned. "I posed as Nigel's assistant. I was there to take notes. Which was true. So you see, it was merely a teeny white lie without any malicious intentions."

"Hmm. I'll have to drill proper procedures into Wilmot, if he ever hopes to rise through the ranks. But let's leave that for the moment. How do you know that Colefax had formed an unholy alliance with Kozlov, one of the most ruthless Russian mafia bosses?"

She went on to tell him about the scrawled note she had come across on Colefax's desk and the photos of Julie Brentford.

"I already knew Colefax had a goddaughter. In fact, I had left her several messages this morning because I wanted to interview her. I thought she could provide some background on him. Well, we now know why she didn't return my calls." She paused for a beat. "However, it was very odd."

Finch's brows knit together. "What was odd?"

"Of course, I didn't know what Julie looked like. When I commented on the photos, P.C. Wilmot said she was Colefax's niece. I asked if he meant goddaughter and the constable agreed. At the mention of her name, Nigel went pale and dropped the documents he was reviewing. Then, he insisted that I pay Julie a visit. He pointed out that she might be more willing to talk in person, rather than over the phone. This seemed reasonable. But what disturbed me was that he said that it wouldn't do to allow a lead to go cold, therefore I should go to her flat in Westbourne Terrace right away." Her eyes met Burnell's. "How did Nigel know Julie lived in Westbourne Terrace? I never told him her address."

The superintendent pursed his lips and traded a glance with Finch.

Emmeline clutched Burnell's sleeve. "You can't possibly think that Nigel could have murdered her. Julie Brentford was a stranger." She heard the tremor of desperation in her voice and cursed herself. She persevered, though. "It's ludicrous. You *know* Nigel. He's a good, decent man. He doesn't have a corrupt bone in his body."

Burnell patted her hand. "I can't allow personal feelings to color the investigation," he observed gently. "I must be guided by the evidence." She opened her mouth, but he held up a hand to silence her. "You must admit that Nigel's behavior has been entirely out of character the past few days. He has a great deal of explaining to do. And the sooner he does so, the better."

Before she could offer an argument, the forensics team and a contingent of uniformed police officers were bearing down on them.

Burnell took Emmeline's elbow and drew her aside. He clapped Dr. Meadows on the shoulder as he shuffled past. "John, Miss Brentford's flat is the one at the end of the corridor."

Meadows waved without stopping. The low murmur of voices reverberated off the walls and mingled together, as his team prepared itself for the grim task of cataloguing and gathering evidence.

Emmeline glanced at her watch. "Is that the time? Goodness. I must be off. Deadlines are hard task masters. I'll just say goodbye to Mrs. Thorpe and fetch my coat and handbag." She smiled at the two detectives and started to walk away.

"I don't like that gleam in your eye," Burnell called after her.

She pivoted on her heel to face him again. "I'm sure I don't know what you mean," she replied innocently.

"Hmph. I don't want the leader in tomorrow's *Clarion*

to be brimming with innuendo intended to lure out into the open the murderer—"

She wagged her forefinger at him. "Or murderers. Remember we agreed that we could have two killers on our hands."

The superintendent scowled. "*We* agreed on nothing of the sort. In fact, *you* are not part of the investigation."

One shoulder twitched up in a shrug. "Didn't we? In any event, I have more than enough to be getting on with. A successful hotelier who was involved with a notorious Russian mafia boss is found bludgeoned to death in his home and his goddaughter killed the same night. A fortune in rare diamonds. Those are the facts. Absolutely riveting stuff. I'm itching to get to my keyboard to inform our readers about this intriguing tangle of crimes. Would Scotland Yard care to provide a comment to give my article an air of gravitas?"

Burnell's cheeks flushed pink beneath his beard. "No," he growled.

She gave a curt nod and flashed a smile that would have made Gregory proud. "Right. I won't keep you from your work. I'll ring you in the morning to see if there are any new developments." She wiggled her fingers in the air in a little wave. "Toodle-oo."

Chapter 13

Emmeline knocked out her article with twenty minutes to spare before tomorrow's paper went to press. Her stomach rumbled in protest because she had missed lunch. Of course, now she was ravenous. Her mouth curled into a smile. If Gran were here, she would have received a scolding. Since she was a little girl, Gran had drilled into her the ills of skipping meals. However, the Colefax story and its surprising new twists were too important to take even a five-minute break for something as mundane as lunch.

She gathered up her handbag and slipped into her coat. As she hurried across the newsroom to the lift, her mind was already going over the angles she intended to follow up on tomorrow. She was eager to get home to find out whether Gregory had gleaned any insight from Villiers. More than likely, the deputy director of MI5 had adopted his usual obstructionist hauteur. She sighed and shook her head. She would have to interview Villiers. He would probably refuse to grant her an audience. But it was her job to cover all aspects of the story, particularly now that MI5 was playing a central role. Meanwhile, she was bursting to tell Gregory about Colefax's connection to Kozlov; the murder of Julie Brentford; and the possibility that there are two killers. She would have to tone down her enthusiasm because her dear husband wouldn't find these revelations as gripping as she did. In fact, he would probably try to discourage her from pursuing the story further. He should know that his entreaties will fall on deaf ears.

Ah, men, you had to love their need to play protector, she thought indulgently. She squared her shoulders and straightened her spine. *I'm perfectly capable of taking care of myself. Thank you very much.*

A frosty gust coming off the churning waters of the Thames slapped her in the face as she stepped out of the Sanborn Enterprises building. Tower Bridge, dotted with twinkling lights, stood out against the indigo evening sky. However, Emmeline didn't linger over the familiar view. She tucked her chin to her chest and shrugged deeper into her coat, as she struggled against the wind that pushed her along like a giant hand. Pellets of sleet stung her cheeks and sent a frisson down her spine. The pavement was slick and she had to be careful not to slip. She hoped that it wasn't going to snow.

When she turned a corner down a side street, she exhaled a long breath. It was only a short walk to the London Bridge Underground station, where she would catch the Jubilee line. She would have to switch to the Circle line at Westminster. Barring any problems, she would be home in Holland Park in about half an hour. She was trying to decide what to make for dinner, when two men unexpectedly blocked her path. She collided with the taller of the two, whose fair hair gleamed like a halo against the darkness.

"Oof," the word escaped from her lips. She lifted her

gaze to his face. The expression in his icy blue eyes sent a shudder through her body. She took a few paces backward, putting space between them. "Watch where you're going," she mumbled and tried step around him.

He blocked her path. His stocky companion grabbed her arm, pulling it behind her back. She was effectively sandwiched between the two men.

"Hey. Let me go." She tried to shake off his grasp, but his beefy fingers only clamped down harder. "You're hurting me. I'll scream."

She opened her mouth to put her threat into action. But before her lungs could unleash a blood-curdling cry, his colleague advised, "I wouldn't do that if I were you, Emmeline. Unless you want a good many more things to hurt. Like your husband, for example."

Her body went still. Only her mind raced. Was Gregory all right? Who were these men?

"Wh-hat do you want?" Her voice was a hoarse croak.

The tall one's upper lip curled into a snarl. "I know questions are a force of habit, but curiosity can be dangerous." He dipped his head toward her. "Especially for Jews." His warm breath ruffled her hair as his sinister hiss echoed in her ear. "You would do well to remember that."

That was the wrong thing to say. Anti-Semitism made her blood boil. She channeled her fury—and that of her fellow Jews—into a vicious kick to his shin. Then, she stomped on her tormentor's foot with the heel of her boot. He howled and let her arm drop. Both men gave vent to a string of curses.

She broke into a run, her gaze darting around wildly for a constable or anyone who could come to her aid. She didn't dare cast a glance over her shoulder for fear of tripping. Her breath was coming in gulps. Their irate grunts told her that they were catching up. The next second, a hand seized her shoulder and spun her body around.

It was the fair-haired man. "That was very foolish." He grasped both her shoulders and gave her a shake that set her teeth rattling. "Tell Longdon our employer wants his property."

"What property?"

Another savage shake. Her head whipped back and forth. Surely, it was going to fall off her neck?

"No more games. If Longdon and Zorkin try another double cross, first we'll carve you up so that your own mother will never recognize you. And then we'll get really creative."

A shudder rippled through her limbs. Her knees felt like water. Any second they would buckle beneath her.

"Oi," a male voice drifted on the air.

Her eyes widened, when she saw three toughs, all dressed in leather jackets and jeans bearing down on them. Their faces were partially shadowed, but they appeared to be in their early twenties. She swallowed hard, when she heard the soft *click*. Then, she caught a flash of steel.

Bloody hell. Gang members. Out of the frying pan and into the fire.

She felt panic swelling in her chest. No. She couldn't give in. She had to keep a clear head. It was the only way she would get out of this situation alive.

"Well, isn't it our lucky day, lads?" The one who appeared to be the leader demanded of her tormentors. He peered down at Emmeline. Up close, she saw the day's-worth of stubble shadowing his cheeks. His lips curled back to reveal crooked teeth stained yellow from smoking. "A pretty lady."

"Shove off," the fair-haired man said as he tightened his grip on her arm.

The gang leader brandished his knife and slapped the man's face. "Someone needs to teach you some manners."

Emmeline shrank back and raised her hand in a plea. "There's no need for violence." Her voice quavered. "Take our money and go."

"Shut up," the fair-haired man ordered.

The gang leader clucked his tongue and shook his head. "Rude again."

Without warning, he drew back his fist and landed a punch in the fair-haired man's solar plexus and his two friends started pummeling his colleague.

While both men were doubled over in pain, the gang leader snatched Emmeline's wrist. "Come on, love. Time to go."

He gave her a small shove. His two friends closed ranks and flanked her. She lashed out from side to side with her free hand, punching arms, chests, whatever she could.

"Help me," she yelled. "Help. I'm being kidnapped."

No one paid any attention to her. The trio merely chuckled and marched her forward.

The fair-haired man caught his breath and yelled after them. "Deliver the message to Longdon."

By this time, they were at the entrance to the Tube station.

"I don't think they'll be bothering you anymore tonight, love. Mind how you go, though," the leader advised.

He rubbed his hands together and stamped his feet to ward off the cold. He and his friends were grinning down at her.

Her eyes widened in disbelief. "Wh-hat?" Her gaze flitted to each one in turn. "I thought…I mean…Thank you very much."

"Off you go." The leader gestured with his chin toward the station. "We'll hang about to make sure those blokes don't follow you."

She murmured her thanks again and they parted ways.

The old saying was true: Never judge a book by its cover.

Her smile faded as her feet guided her by rote down the corridor toward the Jubilee line. Worry weighed on her mind.

The men who accosted her had to be Kozlov's lackeys. They were not the type to throw in the towel.

She and Gregory weren't safe.

Chapter 14

Emmeline breathed a deep sigh, as she shot the bolt into place. She rested her back against the door for a moment and squeezed her eyes shut.

She was home at last.

Her insides still trembled. On the walk from the Kensington High Street station, her nerves were a jittery tangle. Every few seconds, her eyes swept right and left like a pendulum. Her neck ached from craning it around. She couldn't shake the feeling that she was being watched. She eyed everyone who passed her along the pavement with suspicion. Every footfall, the wind's soft sobs, and the eerie shadows cast by bare tree branches seemed to be part of a sinister conspiracy and made her jump. Until she reached the corner with Stafford Terrace and saw their townhouse a few hundred feet ahead, she didn't dare let down her guard.

And here she was. The world's evils were locked on the other side of the door. But where was Gregory?

This disturbing question had barely escaped her consciousness, when the knot in the pit of her stomach uncoiled because a key rattled in the lock. The door swept open and all six feet of her husband was filling the hall.

She flung her arms around his waist and pressed her body tightly against his strong, solid frame. "Oh, thank goodness."

He caressed her hair before taking her face between his hands. He bent his head down and their lips met in an ardent kiss. When they drew apart, he said, "If that's the reception awaiting me, I'll make it a point of staying away from home more often."

She placed both hands on his chest and gave him a gentle shove. "Beast." He chuckled, but she glimpsed the wince that creased his features.

She frowned and cocked her head to one side. "What's wrong?" she asked warily, her gaze scouring the planes and angles of his face.

He turned away and unbuttoned his coat. His profile was toward her as he slipped it off and hung it on a peg. "Nothing is wrong."

Her eyes narrowed. "Liar," she snapped. "You forget that I know you. I will find out, so you might as well tell me. *Now*."

He threw his head back and laughed. "I married a hard-hearted woman. It's bad manners to bully your poor, defenseless husband. What I need is tender-loving care. Why don't we nip upstairs to our bedroom? After all, practice makes perfect."

She rolled her eyes at the ceiling. "Don't think you can distract me." She folded her arms over her chest. "Seduction will not work."

His playful manner evaporated in a weary sigh. He dropped an arm around her shoulders. "Let's go through to the living room."

She nodded and didn't utter another word as he guided

her to the sofa. Once they had settled down, side-by-side, he recounted his conversation with Villiers; Honeysett's unexpected appearance and his revelations about Colefax, Zorkin, the spy Snowdrop and the missing Fabergé egg. He reluctantly concluded with the encounter with the two thugs in Victoria Tower Gardens.

Her hand flew to her mouth. "Oh, darling." She started to tug at his shirt. "Let me see. You may be bleeding or have internal injuries." He shook his head and slapped her hand away. "Then, I'll go ring the doctor. You must see him straightaway."

She started to rise, but he pulled her back down. He laced his fingers through hers and gave her hand a reassuring squeeze. "Emmy, I'm fine. Really. I'll be sore for a few days, but that's all. No permanent damage."

She pursed her lips and held his gaze. She was unconvinced, but she could see that his mind was set. She nodded. "Right. You weren't the only who had an eventful day."

She hesitated for only a fraction of a second, before sharing what she had learned at Colefax's house and the subsequent discovery of Julie Brentford's body. He was far from pleased to hear that she had contrived to sneak a peek at the crime scene. He was even more upset when she told him about the two men who had threatened her.

"Why didn't you ring Oliver at once?" His tone was infused with a mixture of fury and alarm.

"Everything happened so fast, there wasn't time. Besides, he and Sergeant Finch have Julie Brentford's murder on their plates now. I probably used up all of the superintendent's goodwill for one day."

The air crackled with tension for several long minutes, while Gregory brooded and her own troubled thoughts swirled round and round her head.

Emmeline was the first to break the silence. "It's

obvious the two thugs who ambushed us are the same pair. They must be Kozlov's men."

Gregory grunted. "Or they work for the mysterious Snowdrop. I don't know which is worse."

"What frightens me even more is Nigel's behavior. He's hiding something about the murders. Superintendent Burnell is going to question him."

"Mmm. That's par for the course," he muttered.

"Perhaps"—she rested her hand on his thigh and arched an eyebrow—"someone should have a talk with Nigel. To bring him to his senses."

Gregory gave her a crooked smile. "Subtlety is not your strong suit, darling."

Emmeline pulled a face. "Well, he's your cousin. I tried reasoning with him, but his lips were closed tighter than a clam's shell. Nigel might be more willing to open up to a man."

"I don't like the fact that he's defending a man like Rossiter any more than you do. But that's his decision."

"So, that's it? You're just going to sit back and do nothing?" she bristled, her outrage marinating each word. "Nigel is drowning in quicksand."

"I am not the enemy," he retorted. "Nigel is a sensible chap. He doesn't have criminal tendencies. Things will work themselves out. We have to trust him. He'll resent us if we interfere."

"Huh," she grumbled. "Men are the most infuriating creatures on earth."

"Yes, we're completely inferior." He chuckled and nuzzled her neck, leaving a trail of kisses along the tender spot behind her ear.

"That is completely unfair." She half-heartedly tried to push him away.

He lifted his head and waggled his eyebrows. "But as a

tactic, it never fails."

In spite of herself, she laughed. "You have a one-track mind. We are *not* going upstairs. We have to come up with a plan of action."

Gregory sat up. The smile faded from his lips. "Plan of action? That sounds rather ominous."

She patted him on the arm. "I, for one, have to decide which thread to follow up on next. I will have to tackle Villiers, of course."

He brushed an invisible piece of lint from his trousers. "You know that's a nonstarter. It's also ill-advised."

"Since MI5 is now in charge of the Colefax case, as a good journalist, I *must* cover every angle to write a balanced story. I will simply have to wear Villiers down. He will eventually relent and talk to me. The trick is to be persistent. The public has a right to be kept informed."

"Hmph," he snorted. "You don't believe a word of what you're saying. Villiers will still be guarding his secrets jealously even when he's in his grave."

She tossed her chin in the air. "Yes, well. We each have a job to do. If he's his usual obstinate self, there are ways of getting around him." A smug smile tugged at the corners of her mouth.

"Philip will not be happy to find you on his doorstep *yet again* begging for a crumb of information."

"Philip's name did not cross my lips."

"It didn't have to. It's written all over your face."

She sniffed. "I *never* beg. Besides, Philip is a friend. Friends help one another. Through thick and thin."

"The day will come when he has you barred from entering the Foreign Office."

She pulled a face. "Ha. Ha. Maggie and the twins wouldn't allow such a thing. In any case, I'd like to interview Honeysett too. He's the only one with detailed knowledge about Colefax, Zorkin and the Galleon Egg.

And now, there's this juicy morsel about Snowdrop."

"Forget about Honeysett. Although he despises Villiers, they share the same opinion of the press: All journalists are indiscreet and not to be trusted."

"I don't accept that. Not only do we have two murderers, but a Russian spy as well. They pose a threat to society and the security of the realm. They all must be held to account. The only way to ensure that justice is served is if I ask questions to get to the truth. Other than the fact that's he's arrogant and secretive, what can you tell me about Honeysett?"

Gregory gave a reluctant sigh. "Apparently his father, who also had been a MI6 agent, became the target of a honeytrap. A treasure trove of sensitive intelligence fell into Russian hands because of him. Five agents were exposed and killed. From what I gathered, Honeysett has a spotless record. But he can't seem to shake off his father's sins. He feels he constantly has to prove himself and his loyalty. Zorkin and Snowdrop were his chance to finally shed the family stigma. But he lost focus and it exploded in his face. Or maybe that's precisely what the mole intended. To distract him.

"He's also haunted by demons. Villiers told me that Honeysett's wife and seven-year-old son were killed about a year and a half ago by a drunk driver, who was never caught. I think he feels guilty because his obsession with his job kept him from his family."

"How sad. The poor man," Emmeline murmured.

"Honeysett remarried about eight months ago. He became more animated when he spoke about his second wife. He said that she's a wedding planner."

She filed these details away in the back of her mind. "It's always best to know with whom one is dealing. I'll figure out a way to see Honeysett." She curled a hand into a fist and thumped it against her thigh. "Ooh, I wish Zorkin would resurface. He seems to be the key that will unlock all the answers."

"That makes him, and by extension anyone he comes into contact with, a target." Gregory kissed the tip of her nose. "Which is why you should drop this story. It is a matter for MI5 and Scotland Yard, and that fool Honeysett."

She smiled and pressed a hand to his cheek. "Think again."

Gregory dropped his chin to his chest and shook his head. It was always going to be a losing battle.

A sane woman would run at the first hint of danger. Not his Emmy. She charged headlong into the fray. This made him want to throttle her and wrap her in cotton wool at the same time.

Chapter 15

Although Emmeline had managed to track down Honeysett's phone number through one of her contacts, she had yet to actually speak to the MI6 agent. She had made four calls thus far that morning. Each time, a different clipped voice informed her that he was out in the field and had yet to return. She was encouraged to leave a message, which she didn't because she knew that it would go directly into the rubbish bin. Oh, well. Time to pay a visit to Vauxhall Cross to pin down the elusive Honeysett. It was his choice, after all.

She checked her watch. Ten-thirty. She judged that it had been a decent interval, since her last call. By now, Superintendent Burnell must have received at least some preliminary findings from Dr. Meadows, if not the full postmortem on Julie Brentford.

She was stretching out a hand for the phone, when it rang of its own accord. It was Jeremy Padgett, the editor-in-chief.

"Jeremy, good morning," she said cheerfully. "I'm hard at work following up on some leads on the Colefax and

Brentford murders. I should have some updates this afternoon." She crossed her fingers. *I hope.*

"That's precisely what I wanted to discuss with you."

Her brows knit together. "Oh, yes? It sounds as if I'm going to receive a rap on the knuckles. Whose feathers have I ruffled this time? Mind you, I consider it a badge of honor because it means I'm doing my job."

"Emmeline, you know how much the *Clarion*'s entire management team and I, personally, value your diligence and dedication. That's why you're editorial director of investigative features."

"Uh, huh. Stop dithering and tell me who's been whispering poison into your ear."

"The thing is I've just had MI5 Deputy Director Laurence Villiers on the phone."

She threw her head back and laughed. "Surprise, surprise. He can't be bothered to give me a five-minute interview and yet he can find the time to issue threats and ultimatums to you. How typical. Let me guess. He wants to lock me away in a jail cell for the rest of my life because I dare to report on things he'd rather not see the light of day. Secrets that are allowed to fester will only lead to corruption, or worse. It's called a free press for a reason."

"If I didn't believe that wholeheartedly, I wouldn't be in the news business. I'm on your side. I can't stand it when people in positions of power try to abuse it for their own purposes. I told Villiers he could go to the devil. Granted, it was in more diplomatic terms. He capitulated for today. However, I'm under no illusions that there won't be more battles in the near future. All I ask is that you try not to antagonize him too much. You're resourceful. Find the answers another way."

"Thanks for standing up for me. I know Villiers doesn't make it easy."

"I watch out for my correspondents. By the way, your

piece on the murders of Colefax and his goddaughter was terrific. The possible involvement of a Russian spy and a mafia boss are making papers fly off the newsstands and we're getting thousands of hits online. Keep digging."

"I intend to. I'm going to check with a friend at the Foreign Office. He might be able to give me some more insight. Matthew Honeysett, the MI6 agent, has been elusive, but I'll catch up with him. I'll ring Superintendent Burnell again about Julie Brentford's murder." She hesitated a moment. "As you know, Nigel is representing Damian Rossiter. Although a witness places Rossiter at the scene and Colefax's blood was found on his shirt, he continues to proclaim his innocence but refuses to provide an alibi. Perhaps, you can persuade Nigel to let me interview Rossiter."

"Nigel has hardly shown his face around the newsroom the past few days. Also, the fact that MI5 has taken over the case may put a spoke in the wheel. But I'll see what I can do. Off you go. Happy hunting."

ღღღ

Burnell was reading through Julie Brentford's postmortem report, when his phone pealed. *Please don't let it be Emmeline again.* She gave new meaning to the word tenacious. After yesterday's escapade to Colefax's house, she could wait for answers. However when he glanced up, he saw that it was not Emmeline. He swore fluently under his breath and grabbed the receiver, before it rang a third time.

"Yes, Sally, what do you want?" he snarled. "Make it brief. I'm up to my ears in murder."

And you'll find yourself on a table in the morgue, if

you're calling with your usual nonsense, he cautioned silently as he drummed his fingers on his desk.

Her sharp intake of breath made his mouth curve into a smile. One had to savor life's little victories.

She sniffed. "What a thoroughly boorish lout you are. It boggles the mind that you're still on the force. You should have been given the push a long time ago."

He groaned inwardly at this tired refrain. "If you like, instead of locking them away, I can give your number to all the baddies. You can invite them over for high tea to dissect my character flaws. Now, what is it?"

"Insufferable man," she muttered. "Assistant Commissioner Cruickshank wants to see you at once. He's quite upset."

"Why doesn't he just cry on your shoulder? I can't spare the time to play nanny. It would have been simpler, and faster, if he had rung me directly."

But no, the Boy Wonder relishes the drama of a dressing-down. It makes him feel superior to lord it over those under his command.

"We'll see what he says about your insubordination. Hold the line."

"Jolly good," he quipped with false good humor. "I'm waiting with bated breath."

The next instant, the assistant commissioner's pompous voice was echoing in his ear. "Really, Burnell, I don't know what you said, but Sally is nearly in tears."

Is she? Oh, good.

"Perhaps, she ate something that disagreed with her?" he asked innocently.

"Please don't insult my intelligence."

What intelligence? You're an incompetent prat.

"I thought I made it clear," the Boy Wonder droned on, "that you were to turn over the Colefax case to MI5."

"I followed your order to the letter. I personally gave all

the notes and statements, and the postmortem file to the MI5 agent who took Rossiter into custody."

"Then, why are you investigating the Brentford murder?"

"Ah, but sir," he pointed out as if he were speaking to a child, "Julie Brentford is a separate case altogether."

"I understand that she was Colefax's goddaughter."

"You are well informed, as always," Burnell replied. However, Cruickshank failed to detect the facetious inflection in his tone. "I'm not superstitious, so I wouldn't go so far as to say that the family appears cursed. But it is certainly a tragedy, wouldn't you agree?"

"What…Of course. Any murder is shocking, particularly if it's brutal. It's our duty to catch the culprit."

"I'm relieved to see we share the same point of view." *God forbid*, he thought. "Your stirring words always inspire the men and women of the Met to go out and do a good job. To make you proud. If there's nothing else, I'll be getting on with the Brentford case."

Burnell rung off before the Boy Wonder realized he had been hoodwinked by saccharine insincerity.

The superintendent put his glasses on his nose and flipped open the postmortem report again. He was skimming the last page, when there was a light tapping on his door.

"Come in, Finch," he called. "I wanted you to follow up—"

He broke off when he saw Nigel hovering on the threshold. He removed his glasses and steepled his fingers over his rounded stomach. His stare imprisoned the other man. "I see you've stopped playing hide-and-seek."

Nigel's back stiffened. A mixture of defiance and contrition was reflected in his eyes. "That's rather an exaggeration," he replied phlegmatically, as he pressed the door closed behind him. "I came about my client."

The superintendent motioned for him to sit down. "I have a great many questions to put to you."

Nigel shuffled over to the desk and lowered himself into the chair. He looked like a condemned man on the way to the gallows.

He cleared his throat. "I know you are no longer on the Colefax case, but I wanted to ask whether you could intervene with MI5. Damian has been taken to a safe house. They haven't informed me where he's being kept. He's been questioned without the benefit of legal counsel. This is highly irregular, to say nothing of the ethical ramifications. No one will tell me anything. I was hoping you could have a word with Villiers. He's refusing to accept my calls."

Burnell spread his hands wide and shook his head gravely. "I'm afraid I can't tread on MI5's patch. It would stir up a hornet's nest of interagency trouble."

"But Damian is entitled to a defense. This is not Russia. He can't simply be locked away for a crime he didn't commit."

The superintendent leaned forward and folded his hands on the desk. "By your own account, Rossiter isn't in a jail cell. Not yet at least. I must remind you that there is strong evidence pointing to his guilt." He paused for several seconds. "Rossiter baffles me."

"How so?"

"In my thirty years on the force, criminals always protest their innocence. Many provide a false alibi because they think we're stupid. Happily it doesn't stand up to good, solid detective work and they're put away for a long time to contemplate their sins. Rossiter is an anomaly. He has refused to provide any alibi at all."

Nigel crossed one leg over the other. He didn't flinch under the superintendent's unyielding stare. "He has placed his faith in the justice system."

Burnell snorted. "Pull the other one. He's a lying, scheming bastard with no respect for the law."

He let these words sink in before changing tack. "Although I'm no longer officially in charge of the investigation, I still feel as if I am. Would you like to know why?" Nigel held his tongue. "Because Emmeline and Longdon are running all over London. In fact, I hear that our intrepid reporter cajoled a visit to the crime scene." He raised an eyebrow. "Highly irregular."

Nigel gave a sheepish grin. "Superintendent, you of all people must realize she's a force of nature."

"I do indeed. But her enthusiasm must be curbed because it tends to place her in harm's way. As it did yet again."

Nigel sat up bolt upright, concern furrowing his brow. "What's happened to Emmeline?"

"Fortunately, nothing." Nigel slumped back, the tension easing from his shoulders. "Longdon called me this morning to say that a couple of thugs accosted her to put pressure on him. It's likely the same pair who roughed him up yesterday afternoon. However, he's all right too. The man has nine lives and always manages to extricate himself from sticky situations.

"No doubt you've read Emmeline's article in today's *Clarion*." Nigel gave a curt nod. "Then, you're aware that what was a straightforward murder case has spiraled into an international web of intrigue involving a notorious Russian mafia boss and a Russian spy. Villiers is probably spitting blood over these revelations, while MI6 has egg on its face in more ways than one. Thankfully, Emmeline has chosen to exhibit a modicum of discretion for the time being and has not mentioned that criminals of all stripes are desperate to get their hands on a lost Fabergé egg. We assume that Colefax was attempting to sell it and the red diamonds were the payoff, which he never received since they ended up in Longdon's possession. The egg went missing the night he was killed."

Burnell pinched the bridge of his nose and shook his head, before lifting his gaze once again to meet Nigel's. "It seems that was a particularly lethal night."

Nigel held himself very still. "Was it?" he asked, his voice hoarse.

"Yes, Julie Brentford, Alexander Colefax's goddaughter, was also murdered the same night."

"How…how shocking," Nigel stammered. "Only yesterday, Emmeline was talking about interviewing Miss Brentford."

Burnell's mouth curved into a smile that did not reach his eyes. "Apparently, she went directly to the victim's flat after her jaunt with you to Colefax's house. Emmeline ran into a neighbor who was concerned about Miss Brentford because she hadn't seen her in two days. The neighbor had overheard the victim arguing with a man."

"Really? Do…do you have any suspects?"

"Let's drop the pretense, shall we?" The detective's voice was edged in steel. "What do you know about the murder?"

Nigel scraped a hand over his jaw. "Which one?"

Burnell pounded his fist on the desk. "Stop wasting my time."

"I have the utmost respect for you and would never do so."

The superintendent's hard stare raked over his features. A blue vein pulsed along Nigel's jaw. "For an honorable man, you've garnered the dubious distinction of becoming an expert in the art of lying. How did you know Julie Brentford lived in Westbourne Terrace?"

"I didn't. Emmeline mentioned the address."

"She says she didn't. I believe her because just the other day you stood right here"—he tapped his finger on his desk—"in my office blathering on about how the Met was convinced your client was responsible for all the crimes in London. I quote, 'If a murder is reported in Bayswater tomorrow, for example, I *hope* you're not going accuse my client.' Now, a murder *has* been committed in Bayswater. Yet you sit there unmoved. News of Colefax's association with MI6, his ties to the Russian mob, and speculation about a Russian spy loose amid the corridors of power in Whitehall. None of it surprises you. I can only surmise that you already knew these worrisome details and chose to remain silent. That upsets my policeman's sense of order."

"Quite the contrary. I'm extremely surprised and appalled. As anyone with a shred of human decency would be. However, it merely reinforces my contention that someone other than my client murdered Colefax."

Burnell pursed his lips and regarded him steadily. "I can arrest you for perverting the course of justice."

"You have no grounds to take such action. I've cooperated with you to the best of my ability. We both revere the law but approach it from opposite directions. I have a duty to my client, while you have an obligation to find justice for the victims. To that end, you must review every scrap of evidence to uncover the truth. As a lawyer, I have told you everything that I can. My hands are tied." These words hung upon the air, as he rose to his feet. "I have complete confidence that you will fit all the puzzle pieces into the *right* place. All it requires is greater scrutiny and an open mind. Haven't you always said that criminals make mistakes because they're arrogant?"

"Just like Rossiter."

Nigel ignored this jibe and began buttoning his coat. "I would appreciate it if you could have a word with Villiers.

I must be allowed to counsel Damian."

Burnell sighed. It was pointless to press him further. "I'll ring Villiers, but he can be bloody-minded."

Nigel inclined his head. "That's all I can ask. Thank you."

Chapter 16

Emmeline dashed between the Corinthian columns and pushed through the doors of the Foreign Office's main entrance. She smiled and exchanged a few words with the guards on duty, as they glanced at her press badge. It was a mere formality. She was a familiar face in this bastion of diplomacy and power. Some ran in the opposite direction, when they saw her walking along the corridors armed with questions they would rather not answer.

The guards bid her good day and she crossed the elegant hall with its high, vaulted ceiling, gilded walls, and red-veined marble columns. She climbed the red-carpeted Grand Staircase to the gallery. At the top of the landing, she turned left and briskly strode down the corridor until she came to the office at the far end. She patted her curls into place, before opening the door into the antechamber of Philip's office.

She gave a silent cheer, when she saw that no one was waiting to see Philip.

Pamela, his secretary, glanced up from her computer

monitor. A smile spread over her face when she saw Emmeline. "Mrs. Longdon, how lovely to see you. I hope you enjoyed your trip to Madrid," she drawled politely.

Emmeline grimaced. "Well, yes and no."

Pamela nodded sagely. "Yes, I read your article about the Raven. It was fascinating. I'm sure there were details you weren't allowed to print." She jerked her head toward the closed door to Philip's office. "I suppose you'd like to speak to Mr. Acheson about the Alexander Colefax murder."

Emmeline gave her a conspiratorial grin. "How did you guess? Do you think Philip can spare five minutes?"

"Whatever it is. The answer is no. My diary is booked until well into the new year."

They looked up and were startled to find Philip standing in his doorway.

Pamela's eyes narrowed. "As I'm the keeper of your diary, I can attest to the fact that you have the next hour *completely* free."

He scowled at her. "Judas," he retorted.

But he wasn't fooling anyone. His tone was devoid of malice. Emmeline knew Philip considered Pamela a treasure. He couldn't have asked for a more resourceful, intelligent, and discreet secretary.

Pamela walked around the desk. "I'm certain you and Mrs. Longdon have important things to discuss." She flashed a smile at him. "Therefore, I will bring in a tray with tea." She inclined her head to Emmeline. "Please give my regards to your husband."

Philip folded his arms over his chest. "Don't think your efficiency makes you indispensable."

The secretary's soft chuckle floated upon the air for an instant before she closed the door behind her with a *click.*

Philip's blue gaze trailed back to Emmeline, who beamed and reached up to give him a peck on the cheek.

"You look better every time I see you."

He raised a blond eyebrow and grunted, "Hmph. Your husband is a corruptive influence. Flattery will get you nowhere." Despite this observation, he bent down and brushed her cheek with a kiss.

He sighed and assumed a martyred look. He jerked his chin toward the door and stood aside. "I suppose you had better come in, but"—he held up a hand—"I can only promise you ten minutes."

She squeezed his arm and hurried into his office. It was more like a gentleman's study than an office. The plush red wall-to-wall carpeting covering the floor muffled her footsteps. A graceful mahogany desk dominated the center of the room. In the corner to the right of the door, a Chesterfield sofa and two armchairs in the same claret leather were clustered around a highly polished oval coffee table made of cherry. The little area sat next to a large window that overlooked King Charles Street. On the opposite side of the room near the desk were two mahogany bookcases with glass doors, which contained leather-bound tomes.

She removed her coat, draping it over the arm of the sofa, and made herself comfortable in a corner. Philip settled in one of the chairs across from her and waited.

"Don't give me the evil eye," she remarked. "I don't have nefarious intentions."

"No, you're just hoping that your friendship with my wife and the adoration of my sons will be enough to pierce my armor so that you can charm sensitive information out of me for your article," he countered.

"You and I are friends in our own right," she pointed out primly. "And Gregory too."

He rolled his eyes toward the ceiling. "Don't bring Longdon into the conversation. I only have the strength to deal with one of you at a time."

"Very droll. Be honest. In the past few months, we've been thrown together on several occasions and you've come to realize that Gregory is a good man. As I, and Maggie I might add, have always told you."

He leaned back in his chair and propped his elbows on the armrests. "Longdon is an acquired taste. My wife, like all members of the female population, has fallen under his spell. Other than that she's perfectly rational."

She knew he didn't mean a word of it. His relationship with Gregory had thawed. Philip had come to respect Gregory and his abilities, even if he couldn't reconcile himself to her husband's criminal past. But Gregory wasn't stealing jewels anymore. He had promised that old life was behind him. He had a legitimate job as Symington's chief investigator. Philip would come to trust him implicitly, as she did.

She bit her lip, though. Guilt overwhelmed her when her thoughts strayed to his wife Maggie, her best friend since university. Maggie and Gran had been Gregory's staunchest champions through the ups and downs of their relationship. When she and Gregory were finally married two months ago, it was the culmination of all of Maggie and Gran's efforts to push them together. But that was a temporary respite. Now, the two of them couldn't stop dropping hints and giving not-so-subtle advice that it was time for a baby.

A baby. Emmeline sighed. She wanted a baby so much. And yet, it was too soon. In her heart of hearts she was afraid. The hollow ache and emptiness of the baby she'd lost two years ago never left her. At the beginning, she had wished she would simply die to put an end to the pain. The doctor said that she was perfectly healthy and there was nothing to prevent her from having children. But what if the doctor was wrong? Emmeline didn't know if she was strong enough to go through that a second time. That was why every time Gran and Maggie brought up the subject of a baby, a knife twisted in her chest.

These disconcerting ruminations were replaced by guilt once more as she regarded Philip. Maggie, like most people, thought he worked for the Foreign Office's Directorate of Defence and Intelligence. However, a small group, which included Emmeline, Gregory, Burnell and Finch, knew he really worked for MI5. Philip had sworn them to secrecy because he didn't want Maggie to worry. Although Emmeline had given her word, it stuck in her craw. She didn't like keeping Maggie, who was like a sister, in the dark. She kept hoping that Philip would tell his wife the truth one day soon.

"We should probably stop dancing around the elephant in the room." Philip's voice drew her back to the present. "You're here about Alexander Colefax."

She nodded. "No doubt Villiers has ordered you to plead ignorance and send me on my way."

A ghost of a smile played about his mouth.

She sniffed. "That man's contempt of the press borders on paranoia. I am not the enemy." She exhaled a long breath. "However, I will never change his mind. But you must know that I would never do anything to jeopardize the security of the realm. Nor would I ever jeopardize your position—"

"Not intentionally," he cut across her, "but I've felt the flames licking at my heels on too many occasions recently." He gave her a pointed look.

"Yes, well. Some things are out of my control. All I ask is for you to tell me whatever you can about Colefax, Bogdan Kozlov, Pyotr Zorkin and the Galleon Fabergé egg that everyone is willing to kill to possess. If you read my article today, you know that Colefax and his goddaughter were murdered the same night. Scotland Yard is going on the theory that the two deaths are connected. But I'm not so sure. I think there are two killers."

"Why?"

She told him about her visit to Colefax's house and what Mrs. Thorpe had said about the row Julie Brentford had with a man.

"The savagery behind Colefax's death indicates that his murderer was driven by desperation. Colefax posed a threat and had to be eliminated at all costs. It was horrid. There was so much blood at the scene." She swallowed the bile that rose in her throat and pushed the image aside. "Of course Superintendent Burnell and Sergeant Finch were being circumspect yesterday, and I haven't been able to find out anything yet about the postmortem's conclusions, but I have the impression that Julie's murder didn't involve such violence. This seems to suggest a crime of passion, which points to the boyfriend as the prime suspect."

Philip pursed his lips and nodded gravely. "That's sound reasoning. Unfortunately, I can't tell you very much about Colefax. He was an MI6 asset. In any event, it's far too dangerous for you and Longdon to be hunting down murderers and spies all across London. The mere mention of Bogdan Kozlov and Ilya Zorkin should prompt you to run as fast as you can in the opposite direction." He leaned forward, his features were pinched with concern. "Leave the investigating to Scotland Yard and MI5." As an afterthought, he added, "And MI6."

She threw her head back and laughed. "MI6? Really. From what I can see, Honeysett's incompetence set in motion this entire chain of tragic events. Now, he's scrambling to save face. Pyotr Zorkin has vanished and with him all of MI6's hopes of infiltrating the upper echelons of the Kremlin by turning his father. Then, we have Snowdrop, who is still burrowing deep into the agency and stealing its secrets. Finally, we come to the missing Galleon Egg and one hundred million pounds in red diamonds. Someone has to be held accountable. The truth, no matter how ugly, must be exposed. As a journalist, I can't stand idly by and allow longstanding interagency rivalries and mistrust, as well as political considerations, to impede the investigation. Gregory and I are of one mind on this point."

Philip snorted. "I very much doubt it. Longdon's past is as murky as sin." She opened her mouth to protest, but he gave a curt shake of his head. "No, you can't deny it." Her lips pressed into a thin line and she held her tongue. "To his credit and extreme good taste, your husband is besotted with you. He wants to ensure that no harm comes to you. Emmeline, you're not naïve. In fact, you're one of the most intelligent women I have the privilege of knowing. Use your common sense. Kozlov, papa Zorkin and Snowdrop are ruthless. Don't antagonize them. Your journalistic scruples mean nothing to them. They won't bat an eye at killing you."

She reached across and placed her hand on his. She looked him directly in the eye. "I'm fortunate to have so many people who care about me. But I'm perfectly capable of taking care of myself. I also love my job. It's important. I can't cower in a corner every time a criminal makes a threat. That's *precisely* when I must keep digging because it means I'm close to the truth."

She rose and slipped into her coat. "So I will do so without your help."

He was on his feet now too. He put his hands on her shoulders. "Has anyone ever told you that your stubbornness is a character defect?"

She chuckled. "I thought it was my short temper."

"The combination is lethal," he conceded. "Look, it

goes against my better judgment, not to mention Villiers's directive, but I'll have a discreet word with a couple of contacts at MI6 and see if I can discover anything useful."

Her eyes widened in mock surprise and she pressed a hand to her chest. "Oh, my. I didn't think MI5 and MI6 actually talk to one another. Isn't that considered treason?"

"I can change my mind."

"No, please. I was only joking, as you well know. I'd appreciate any lead you can provide. I was also wondering." She batted her eyelashes coyly. "Would you be able to arrange for me to interview Rossiter? Nigel said that MI5 has him squirreled away at a safe house, where agents are questioning him."

One blond eyebrow quirked upward. "That's not a wise idea."

She grinned at him. "Perhaps not, but it would make for great reading in tomorrow's *Clarion*. Rossiter is as dodgy as they come. He's an opportunist driven by greed. My theory is he stumbled upon Colefax's secret negotiations with Kozlov over the Fabergé egg and seized his chance to make a side deal of his own with the Russian. No doubt Kozlov was stringing Rossiter along with promises of riches. When the plan fell apart, Rossiter presented the ideal scapegoat for Colefax's murder. Mind you, Snowdrop could be the one playing puppet master behind the scenes. Or Rossiter was playing a dangerous game of pitting Colefax, Kozlov, and Snowdrop off one another. Obviously, Rossiter miscalculated badly. He's desperate. He's going to be charged with murder, unless he starts spilling what he knows. That's where I come in."

"Whether he's guilty or innocent," Philip observed, "why would Rossiter tell you anything, when blackmailing Kozlov or Snowdrop is far more lucrative?"

"That's what landed him in this mess in the first place. He has something in common with all criminals. His ego.

He wants everyone to know how clever he is. All I have to do is listen and just maybe it might lead to a bigger prize."

"The glint in your eye when you say prize makes me shudder. Do you mean the Fabergé egg, Kozlov or Snowdrop?"

"The ultimate prize is the truth. Someone has to fight for Colefax and Julie Brentford. And MI6's mole has to be unmasked."

"Opening Pandora's box is never advisable. You could very well wind up dead."

She flapped a hand dismissively. "You must learn to think positively." She turned and crossed to the door. She tossed over her shoulder. "It will do wonders for your outlook on life, while an exclusive interview with Rossiter will brighten mine."

She blew him a kiss and swept out of the office.

Chapter 17

Gregory strolled down Piccadilly until he reached Burlington Arcade, England's oldest and longest shopping promenade. The epitome of Regency architecture, the covered arcade was originally commissioned by Lord Cavendish in 1819 to prevent local residents from littering the gardens next to Burlington House. Today, it is a haven of refinement and opulence. Nestled beneath its elegant canopy are fine watch and jewelry boutiques, renowned parfumiers, and shops selling luxury leather-goods, knitwear, and Lalique crystal.

All the windows were brightly lit and their displays arranged to tempt the eye, and hopefully pry open the wallets of those who could afford to indulge their expensive caprices. His footfalls echoed off the gleaming gray marble floor and mingled with the low murmur of voices floating around him. He made a mental note to purchase a box of macarons for Emmy from Ladurée, when his present business was concluded. His pace slowed as he cast an admiring glance over the bounty of exquisite jewels and rare silver pieces winking at him from the windows as he passed.

He finally came to a halt in front of Roderick Trevelyan, a shop specializing in antique and vintage jewelry in Victorian, Edwardian, Art Deco styles. He smiled and indicated to the young woman behind the display case inside that he'd like to enter. A second later a muted buzz unlocked the door.

The corners of the woman's mellow brown eyes crinkled, as she offered him a warm smile. In her smartly tailored mauve coat dress, she exuded professionalism and sophistication. Not a single strand of her long chestnut locks was out of place. The shade of her lipstick matched her dress.

"Good afternoon, sir. Are you interested in anything in particular? Or would you like time to look around?" A perfectly manicured hand made an arc that encompassed the entire shop. "As you can see, we have some unique pieces."

Gregory flashed one of his most engaging smiles, which brought a pink flush to her cheeks. "You do indeed. Your shop is in a class by itself, when it comes to quality." He shot his cuff and removed his Patek Philippe watch. "Would it be possible for one of your jewelers to take a look at my watch?"

She extended a hand. "Certainly. I'll take it into the workshop. It shouldn't be long."

He inclined his head in thanks and casually said, "I was also hoping to speak with Mr. Trevelyan."

"You're in luck. He's in today. May I have your name?"

He reached into his inside breast pocket and drew out one of his business cards. Her brow furrowed, when she saw Symington's and chief investigator written upon it. He read the concern in her searching gaze. However, she merely murmured, "Mr. Trevelyan will be with you in a moment." Then, she disappeared through a door that led into the nether regions of the shop.

He was studying an antique Cartier sapphire and diamond brooch, when the door whispered open on its hinges. A man in his early fifties with a thick head of salt-and-pepper hair and dressed in a bespoke navy suit and dove gray silk tie sedately entered the shop. The woman was nowhere in sight.

His mellow brown eyes appraised Gregory from head to toe. He hesitated before extending a hand. "It's been a long time, Greg."

Gregory clasped his hand and gave it a brisk shake. "Hello, Rory."

His smile clashed with the other man's frosty stare.

"You shouldn't have come. Whatever it is, I can't help you."

"Can't or won't?"

Trevelyan shrugged. "Either way, the answer remains the same. You're too hot. And I don't want to get burned. I worked too hard to let you or anyone else destroy my business."

"All I want is some information. Then, I'll walk out that door."

Trevelyan thrust his hands in his pockets and shook his head. "As long as you have the diamonds and the Galleon Egg, I have nothing to say to you. I'm not foolish enough to double cross Kozlov. He's as nasty as they come. I don't want to wind up dead like Colefax."

Gregory balled his fists at his sides. "Scotland Yard has the diamonds," he replied through clenched teeth.

Trevelyan snorted. "You really expect me to believe that you turned over a fortune in red diamonds to the coppers? Pull the other one."

"It happens to be the truth. I'm assisting the police with their inquiries. As for the egg, Colefax's murderer likely stole it and is planning to sell it. I was wondering whether you've heard anything through the grapevine that might provide a clue."

The other man's eyes bulged wide in disbelief. "Do you take me for an imbecile?" He drew out Gregory's business card from his pocket and waved it in the air. "This is another one of your cons. You love the game too much to give it up. The only thing I know is that Kozlov is out for blood. It won't be long before he's knocking on your door. And another thing—"

He broke off and snapped his lips shut, when the door opened and the woman reemerged from the workshop area. She was smiling. "Here you are, Mr. Longdon. Our head jeweler made some minor adjustments."

She held out the watch to Gregory, but Trevelyan snatched it from her fingers. "Thank you, Allison. I'll deal with this. Please see to the invoices on my desk."

Her perplexed gaze flitted between Gregory and Trevelyan. "Yes, of course, Mr. Trevelyan. Right away," she murmured and left them alone again.

Gregory wordlessly took his watch. While he was fastening it on his wrist, Trevelyan ordered, "Don't come back. Everyone who comes near you becomes collateral damage."

Gregory lifted his eyes to meet the other man's hostile glare. "Your brother was too greedy. And arrogant. That's why he's in the nick for the rest of his life. He didn't have the skill to pull off that diamond heist in Paris."

Trevelyan pounded his fist against his open palm. "Bill was caught like a rat in a trap," he snarled, "because *someone* called in an anonymous tip to the police. Someone who needed a distraction so that he could steal the Devereaux collection on the other side of the city."

The angry words hurtled around the refined confines of

the shop, making the space suddenly feel claustrophobic.

Gregory stiffened. "Not me. Not my style," he replied stiffly. "Your brother bungled the job on his own and then put the nail in his coffin by killing that guard. Don't allow family loyalty to blind you to reality."

Trevelyan pressed the buzzer beneath the display case and jerked his chin at the door. "Get out. If you ever set foot in my shop again, I'll have you arrested for trespassing. In the meantime, I will content myself with the knowledge that one day Kozlov will catch up with you." His upper lip curled into a sneer. "I'm counting down the minutes."

−

Upon returning to her office, Emmeline began making some calls to her sources, as well as trawling through the paper's archives to find out more about Kozlov and Ilya Zorkin. Unsurprisingly, there was a plethora of information on Kozlov. His name had been cropping up with increasing frequency in recent years, as the tentacles of his criminal empire stretched out in ever-widening circles. Drugs, prostitution, and recently he'd entered the lucrative arena of arms-dealing.

She was making notes, when there was a tap at her door. Then, the paper's newest intern popped her head in.

"Hi, Emmeline. This was just delivered by messenger for you. I thought it might be important," the young woman said.

Emmeline stretched out a hand and waggled her fingers. "Thanks, Celia. How are things going today?"

"Brilliant. Frank took me to the press conference this morning on the government's new trade policies. It was fascinating. Jeremy said that he would allow me to sit in on the editorial meeting to discuss the stories for tomorrow's paper. I've only been at the *Clarion* for three weeks and already I've learned so much about the newspaper business."

"That's wonderful. If you have any questions, feel free to drop by anytime. I'd be glad to help you."

The younger woman smiled and gave a little wave. "Thanks. Well, I'd better get back to work."

Emmeline smiled. She liked to see her love of journalism mirrored in Celia's eyes.

She glanced down at the envelope in her hand and stuck her pinkie under one corner to tear it open. Inside were two tickets for a concert that evening at St. Martin's-in-the-Fields. Vivaldi's *Four Seasons*. She shook the envelope, but no note accompanied the tickets. Gregory probably bought them as a surprise. He knew how much she adored Vivaldi.

Her phone began to ring. She didn't recognize the number. Perhaps, one of her sources had found out something already. That was fast.

"Hello, Emmeline Kirby," she answered.

"Did you receive the tickets?" a man asked in crisp tones.

She frowned. "Who is this?"

"Peter will do. My surname doesn't matter for the moment. If you want to know the real story about Alexander Colefax and why he was murdered, you'll be at the concert tonight."

She sat up straighter in her chair. "How do I know that this isn't a practical joke?"

"You'll just have to take a chance. I'm taking a big risk contacting you. I'm putting my trust, and my life, in your hands. The least you can do is listen to what I have to say. Then, you can judge whether I'm on the level. Consider it a work outing. After we talk, you and your husband can enjoy the concert. I'll meet you in the Café in the Crypt before the performance begins."

He was about to hang up. "Wait. How will I recognize you?"

The line was silent for several seconds. "I'll find you."

With that, he severed the connection.

Her pulse raced. She should temper her excitement, in all likelihood it was nothing. Someone looking for publicity. The rational part of her brain knew that. And yet…Instinct told her that she had a break at last.

She began humming Spring from *The Four Seasons* as she called Gregory's mobile. They had a date tonight with Vivaldi and a mysterious stranger.

Chapter 18

Burnell swore under his breath as he slammed his phone back in the cradle. That had been the third time this afternoon that Villiers's secretary, more of a guard dog really, had refused to allow him to speak with deputy director because the great man was in yet another meeting.

"If MI5's leaders are sitting on their bums all day in meetings," he grumbled aloud to his office, "who's keeping the country safe from terrorists and assorted other criminals? I'll tell you who. It's overworked policemen."

He didn't need this aggravation. He was up to his neck in cases. He had kept his promise. Nigel would simply have to make his own arrangements to see his bloody client. If MI5 hadn't swept in, Rossiter would already have been charged with Colefax's murder.

He slumped back in his chair and pursed his lips.

I have complete confidence that you will fit all the puzzle pieces into the right *place,* Nigel had said. *All it requires is greater scrutiny and an open mind.*

What was Nigel trying to tell him? The evidence was

clear. Rossiter had a row with Colefax. He admitted they came to blows. The victim's blood on his shirt. Why was Nigel defending the man? And why did he push Emmeline to visit Westbourne Terrace?

Because he knew Julie Brentford was dead and wanted us to find her body.

The superintendent sat up straight. "Fit all the puzzle pieces into the right place," he murmured.

A kernel of an idea had rooted itself in the back of his mind.

He jammed his glasses on his nose and reached for the Brentford postmortem. He took his time. The findings hadn't changed. But he was looking at it through a different lens. When he had finished reading it, he nodded. Yes, of course. Emmeline saw it first, but she had it backward. And Nigel had told him everything and nothing.

All he needed was confirmation of his suspicions. He picked up the phone and called Dr. Meadows.

"Hello, Oliver" was his friend's cheerful greeting. Despite the unspeakable things John saw perpetrated by human hands on a daily basis, he somehow managed to retain his sanity and good humor.

"Hello, John. I'd like you to check something for me. It has to do with the Colefax and Brentford murders."

"I thought MI5 was in charge of the Colefax case now."

"They are, but I have a feeling I missed something, and if I'm correct it could have ramifications for both cases."

"All right. MI5 hasn't sent anyone around to collect the evidence yet."

A smile curled around the superintendent's mouth. "I was hoping you would say that. You discovered a second blood type on Rossiter's shirt that didn't match either him or Colefax. I'd like you to compare it to Julie Brentford's blood. I'm afraid it's a rush."

Meadows gave a low whistle. "Nothing ever changes.

It's always rush, rush, rush these days. Give me an hour. For the record, that's two pints you owe me on Friday."

Burnell chuckled. "That's a small price to pay. Thanks, John."

The hour ticked by agonizingly slowly. Burnell tried to bury himself in a stack of reports that he had not had a chance to review, but it was an exercise in futility. He kept reading the same sentence over and over because every few minutes his gaze strayed to his watch.

When his phone finally rang, his hand whipped out and grabbed the receiver.

"Sorry for the delay, Oliver," Meadows said. "But I wanted to be thorough, so I had the technicians check the unidentified fingerprints we found at the victim's flat against Rossiter's."

Burnell held his breath. "You were right. The blood on Rossiter's shirt is Julie Brentford's. And the fingerprints are a perfect match."

Burnell thumped his fist against his desk in triumph. "I have a killer to arrest."

"I'll send up the report."

Burnell thanked his friend and immediately called Finch to inform him of the new developments. As soon he spoke to Villiers, they would go and take custody of their suspect.

The superintendent should have known that even when one is on the side of justice, nothing is ever that simple.

❧❧

"No, it's out of the question," Villiers declared in his most condescending tone. "I can't turn over Rossiter to you, Superintendent."

The gloves were off. "Stop playing games," he growled. "I just told you. We have proof that directly ties Rossiter to Julie Brentford. His fingerprints were found in her flat and her blood was on his shirt. I sent my sergeant out to interview her neighbor again. She identified a photo of Rossiter as Brentford's boyfriend. We have a solid case. The Crown Prosecution Service will easily get a conviction."

"I seem to recall you saying the same thing about strong evidence when you arrested him for Colefax's murder."

Burnell curled one hand into a tight ball. He could picture the sneer engraved on Villiers's distinguished features.

"We didn't have all the facts. At the time, the coroner couldn't identify the second blood type on Rossiter's shirt. Now, he can conclusively. The Brentford woman was killed at the same time as Colefax. That rules out Rossiter as Colefax's murderer. My money is on Kozlov or MI6's mole."

"That Kirby woman and her bloody article," Villiers grumbled in his ear.

Burnell permitted himself a smile. It was good that he wasn't the only one to be irked by the situation. He decided to fan the flames. "That woman happens to be your daughter-in-law," he pointed out.

Villiers groaned. "Don't remind me. You can't honestly tell me that you're happy with the way she swans about as if she has a divine right to bombard everyone with reckless questions."

"I know she has a job to do—"

"Ha. She's a glorified gossip. Her specialty is poking and prying."

"I wouldn't go that far. We're not talking about Verena Penrose."

They both fell silent as their thoughts drifted to the blackmailing tabloid reporter, who had been at the heart of the recent case involving the Raven, an international assassin.

"She's just as bad as Verena. All journalists are a menace," Villiers griped.

"I agree Miss Kirby is reckless," Burnell said slowly, "but only when it comes to her own safety."

"And Toby's," Villiers mumbled.

"Longdon can take care of himself."

"How does that woman manage to dominate the conversation, even when she is not here," Villiers complained. "To get back to the purpose of your call, you can't take Rossiter into custody. It seems that two of my agents, who had him under guard at a safe house and now will be looking for employment elsewhere, didn't find it odd when an MI6 agent appeared unannounced on the doorstep and took him away for questioning. The same MI6 agent, I might add, who is responsible for the Colefax fiasco to begin with."

"Mmm" was Burnell's noncommittal response. After all, one couldn't very well say: *Better you than me.*

"Indeed. MI6 is trying to track down Honeysett. The bloody fool has gone dark. On our end, I've put Acheson in charge of the task. He's the only one I can rely on. This stunt will sabotage Honeysett's career, rather than save it. It's no wonder MI6 has a mole burrowed deep in its house, if they put such an inept man in charge of the search."

"Yes, well. About Rossiter," the superintendent prodded.

Villiers exhaled a long breath. "I'm sick of that man's name. You're welcome to him, as soon as we get our hands on him again. Check with Acheson."

He severed the connection without saying goodbye.

Burnell pursed his lips, as he replaced the receiver. Much as he disliked Villiers, he couldn't blame the man for his ill temper.

He slumped back in his chair, as thoughts chased themselves across his mind. It was odd, to say nothing of unusual, for MI6 to step on MI5's toes like that.

His policeman's nose smelled something else in the air. The stench was too offensive to ignore. He was surprised Villiers hadn't caught a whiff of the odor. Or maybe he had and he was holding his cards close to the vest, as usual. Either way, a storm was looming on the horizon.

Chapter 19

I'm not the criminal here," Honeysett asserted. His chest swelled and his mutinous gaze sliced Philip to pieces. "I was simply trying to carry out an interrogation. This was my case. I need to see it through."

They were standing toe-to-toe in an interview room at Vauxhall Cross, MI6's headquarters.

"You violated procedures. MI6 no longer has jurisdiction in the matter. In fact, he's not MI5's concern anymore either."

"I'm standing right here," Rossiter pointed out peevishly.

Philip and Honeysett continued to ignore him, instead channeling their antipathy toward one another.

"Superintendent Burnell of Scotland Yard is on his way to arrest Rossiter."

"That fat copper," Rossiter muttered. "Why? I didn't kill Colefax."

Philip permitted himself a smile. "Rest assured. He knows." He paused to heighten the tension. "Burnell is going to charge you with the murder of Colefax's goddaughter, Julie Brentford."

Rossiter drew in a sharp breath. His eyes bulged in shock. "*Goddaughter?*" he hissed through clenched teeth. "The conniving bastard. He set the bitch to spy on me. She was nothing. This is all the fault of that nosy reporter. Why did she have to go stirring up the pot? Someone needs to muzzle her."

This last comment set off alarm bells in Philip's head. "I'd have care what I say. You're in enough trouble already without threatening Emmeline Kirby," he rebuked sharply.

"That woman seems to be an expert at making a nuisance of herself," Honeysett complained. "She keeps calling for an interview. How she even got my name, I'll never know. Thus far, I've managed to avoid her."

Philip's gaze narrowed, but he bit back the tart barb on the tip of his tongue. It was more prudent to allow the subject of Emmeline to drop. The less attention focused on her the better.

"I'm *not* going to be sent down for Julie's murder," Rossiter declared. "I'm the victim here. Clearly, Alexander set me up. And Julie got what she deserved. I haven't lost any sleep over her. She deceived me. I demand to speak to my lawyer." He held out a hand and waggled his fingers impatiently. "Where's my mobile? I have a right to talk to Nigel. He'll sort this out."

"You can ring your lawyer, once you get to Scotland Yard."

Rossiter gave an emphatic shake of his head. "Oh, no. I have rights." His gaze was ablaze with fury as it trailed from Philip to Honeysett. "Someone is going to pay and it's not going to be me. I promise you that. I have friends in high places. My mobile. *Now.*"

Philip sighed. "Oh, very well." He acquiesced to shut the fellow up. Honeysett drew out the mobile from his inside breast pocket and handed it over.

"You have ten minutes," Philip said. He jerked his chin at the door. "Come along, Honeysett. Let's leave him."

The door had barely closed behind them, when Rossiter's mobile began to ring. He grimaced. The number sent an icy frisson slithering down his spine. He swallowed hard and tried to slow his racing pulse.

He pasted a smile on his face and pitched his voice low. "Mr. Kozlov, am I glad to hear from you."

"I am not happy, Damian," the Russian observed drily. "In fact, I am upset and extremely disappointed. We had a deal. I cleared your debts."

"Indeed, you did, Mr. Kozlov. I will be eternally grateful."

"Your gratitude is meaningless," the Russian sneered. "You have not lived up to your end of the bargain. I still do not have the Galleon Egg."

"Ah, there have been some complications. I've been arrested for murder. The police have the wrong end of the stick. As usual."

Kozlov laughed. "That is not my concern. I don't get involved in other people's petty problems. As a businessman, my only concern is my bottom line and a return on my investment, as you English say. I want my property. It would be unfortunate, if you had an accident."

"Now, now. There's no need to take on that tone. I have every intention of fulfilling my obligations. But I can't very well do so, if I'm locked away in a jail cell. You do see that, don't you?" He licked his lips. "If you could see your way to helping me—"

"*What?*" Kozlov exploded. "You have the nerve to ask for *more* help. I should have you killed right now."

"Then, say goodbye to the Galleon Egg forever," Rossiter shot back. "It's in your interest to help me. You can start by taking care of that bloody reporter, Emmeline Kirby. Her articles have as good as convicted me. I'm not going down for the murder of a bitch like Julie Brentford. Superintendent Burnell will be here any minute to collect me. An influential and clever man like you must be able to find a way to keep me out of prison. If you want to see the egg again."

These last words hung upon the air.

Kozlov exhaled a weary sigh. "I wanted to see what you had to say for yourself. Greed and desperation are such an ugly combination. Threatening me is a mistake. I don't like games. I find them tiresome. You, Zorkin, and Longdon will regret wasting my time and money."

"Wait, wait. You need me."

"Your arrogance is breathtaking. You're useless and not very intelligent, I might add. I have a reputation to uphold, therefore I should kill you," he remarked philosophically. "But this one time, I'll forgo that pleasure and leave your fate in the hands of the British legal system. I feel that would be poetic justice."

The line went dead.

"Bastard," Rossiter swore. "You can't do this to me."

The only person he was fooling was himself. Kozlov could do whatever he wanted.

Rossiter had one card left to play. He darted a glance at the door. He heard the muffled sound of male voices approaching.

With trembling fingers, he punched in a number. "It's in your interest to get me out of this mess," he whispered when his call was answered. "You'll have a great deal to lose, if I tell them that you murdered Alexander because he was going to expose you as a spy." He paused to listen for a few seconds. "What do you mean no one will believe me? Are you willing to take the gamble?"

Apparently, the answer was yes because the connection

was severed.

The walls were closing in around him. For the first time in his life, his lies had caught up with him. And he saw no way out.

The door flung open. "Well, well, Mr. Rossiter, I see we've come full circle," Burnell said as he entered the room. He couldn't hide the triumphant gleam in his eyes.

Finch was right on his heels. "We kept your cell warm for you," he offered cheerfully as he pulled out a pair of handcuffs and brandished them in the air. "Please stand up."

"I have to call Nigel. You can't take me in without my lawyer," Rossiter tossed back with a bravado that was fast ebbing.

The superintendent chuckled. "We informed Mr. Sanborn of your new predicament, before we left the station. Unfortunately, he has been forced to step down as your lawyer."

Rossiter surged to his feet. *"What?* He can't. That's…unethical."

"I'm afraid he can, and he did. Mr. Sanborn said that he was retained to defend you in the Alexander Colefax murder. Since you've been exonerated of that crime, he indicated that his many responsibilities in his role as corporate counsel for Sanborn Enterprises preclude him from representing you in the Brentford case. Therefore, you'll have to find a new lawyer. Of course, you have the right to free legal advice *at the station*." Burnell turned to the sergeant. "Finch, caution him."

Finch stepped forward. "Please turn around." He snapped the handcuffs on his wrists behind his back. "Damian Rossiter, you are under arrest for the murder of Julie Brentford. You do not have to say anything but it may harm your defense if you do not mention when questioned, something that you later rely on in court. Anything you do say may be given in evidence."

Rossiter's hot glare was full of spite and held an accusation, as it darted from the two detectives to the door where Philip and Honeysett were loitering in the corridor beyond.

His voice rose an octave. "You'll be sorry. I'll…I'll sue for wrongful arrest and false imprisonment. I *know* things."

"Yes, yes," Finch mumbled, as he placed an hand on Rossiter's shoulder and propelled him toward the door.

"Don't worry," Burnell said. "You'll have plenty of time to air your grievances and contemplate your poor choices in life, when you're tucked up in a cell."

He turned to Philip and addressed him formally. "Mr. Acheson, thank you for your assistance. Please convey my thanks to Mr. Villiers for MI5's cooperation."

Philip inclined his head. "Certainly," he murmured.

They started to walk away, when Honeysett called, "This woman's murder is tragic, of course. But you lot have lost sight of the fact that this man was Colefax's partner and has intimate knowledge about his business and his close ties to Pyotr Zorkin. I must find Zorkin. He's the only one who can identify the Russian mole. Every minute we waste, the spy wreaks more havoc at MI6. The country's security is at stake. Therefore, it's vital that I question Rossiter."

"Mr. Acheson is far more skilled in diplomacy than I am," Burnell replied tersely. "I'll leave it to him to explain the intricacies of agency jurisdiction." He gestured with his chin. "Let's go, Finch."

Chapter 20

Emmeline looped her arm through Gregory's as they wandered among the stalls of the Christmas market in Trafalgar Square. Bathed in light, the National Gallery kept watch from above over the square and the traffic beyond trundling down Whitehall. Slowly, they made their way to the northeast corner of the square. The clean lines of St. Martin's-in-the-Fields, the neoclassical Anglican church built of Portland stone, stood out against the indigo expanse of the evening sky. A thin scarf of gray clouds carried upon the chilly breeze drifted across the moon. Half of her pearlescent silhouette was cloaked in celestial shadows.

What secrets will be revealed tonight? Emmeline wondered, as the light changed and they crossed St. Martin's Place.

She shot a sidelong glance at Gregory's profile as they climbed the marble steps. His jaw was set in a hard line and his gaze was watchful. She knew he did not view tonight's foray into the unknown with the same level of exhilaration as she did. He must have sensed her scrutiny as they passed through the imposing Corinthian portico comprised of eight columns because he patted her hand and gave her one of those smiles that made her knees go weak.

She returned his smile. "No, we're not going home," she whispered, as they waited to show their tickets and enter the church.

"Did I say a word?" he murmured out of the corner of his mouth.

"I'm your wife. I know how your mind works."

They fell silent as a young man checked their tickets and wished them a pleasant evening.

Gregory drew her to the side and bent his head toward her once they crossed the threshold. His mustache tickled her ear. "On a chilly winter evening, Vivaldi and Bach cannot warm the heart, to say nothing of the rest of body, like an adoring husband's ardent embraces." His lips left a kiss on the tender spot behind her ear.

Her cheeks flamed and she gave him a gentle shove. "Behave yourself."

He straightened up, but one eyebrow arched up suggestively. "It's no shame to admit that our cozy bed is a more pleasing prospect than a drafty old church. After all, the heart wants what the heart wants."

She cleared her throat and looked directly into his eyes. "My heart wants answers about Alexander Colefax. Therefore, I'm staying. If you'd like to go home…" Her sentence trailed off.

He sighed and his playful manner evaporated. "We came against my better judgment, but I have no intention of leaving you here alone. You'll get up to all sorts of mischief."

"Ha. Ha. I'm surrounded by dozens of people. Nothing can happen to me in a church of all places."

He kissed the top of her head. "Unfortunately, darling,

evil lurks everywhere. It has a penchant of finding you."

"Don't be ridiculous," she reproached him. "The only way to fight evil and corruption is to shed light on the truth."

"The truth can be a double-edged sword."

She rolled her eyes at the ceiling. "Is that why you're still keeping so much of your past hidden from me?"

He pressed a hand to his chest and his eyes widened in feigned innocence. "Me? My life is an open book. You know everything that is important."

Her eyes narrowed. "Hmph. But not everything. I don't like double talk and evasion. It only makes me more curious and determined to discover the answers."

His mouth twitched into a smile. "Since you find me so intriguing, I can think of better ways to expend your restless energy."

She shook her head and glanced at her watch. "Come on. The concert starts in half an hour. Let's go down to the crypt and see what this Peter chap has to say about Colefax." She dropped her voice and cupped a hand over her mouth. "And the Russian spy."

They slowly descended the steep stone staircase that led to the café tucked away in the eighteenth-century crypt. Original exposed brick vaulted ceilings and walls, as well as the old tombstones and headstones lining the floor, gave the simple space a unique cachet. Rather than being sinister, the ambiance was a pleasing mixture of ancient and modern. The café was set up as a self-service canteen.

The tinkle of cutlery against plates mingled with the hushed ripple of conversation as they took a turn around the café. No one made eye contact or attempted to approach them.

Gregory sighed. "I fear that Peter was having you on."

She had a feeling that he was right, but she wasn't

willing to give up quite yet.

"Perhaps, he's running late."

He cocked his head to one side and gave her a pointed look.

"Well, he could be. London traffic is notorious. There could be a problem on the Underground. Shall I go on?" she asked with a touch of asperity, daring him to contradict her.

"How about a glass of wine," he suggested, "while you fume about being stood up by a stranger?"

She pulled a face. "At times, you can be insufferable."

He gave her cheeky wink. "Only sometimes. I must work harder."

She swatted his arm. "Oh, go on. I'd like a Sauvignon Blanc."

"Yes, my lady." And he sauntered toward the counter.

She wandered between the columns and tables, but the patrons were either eating, drinking or chatting. No one showed a particular interest in her.

A reluctant sigh escaped her lips. Damn. It wasn't the first time a potential source had gotten cold feet. But it was especially galling because she had been so sure that "Peter" had been legitimate. Although their conversation had lasted no more than a couple of minutes, there had been something sincere and urgent in his tone. She also had detected a note of fear. She stopped short, an icy tendril slithering down her spine. What if Peter had had an accident or worse because he contacted her?

Her brain didn't have time to take this unsettling thought further.

"Oof," a woman exclaimed, as she collided into her.

She was tall and slender with long, honey-colored hair that was swept up and fastened with two tortoise shell combs. Her hazel eyes went wide with embarrassment. "Oh, dear." She clutched Emmeline's arm. "Are you all right? I'm terribly sorry."

Emmeline smiled. "I'm fine. Really."

Relief washed over the woman's strained features. Upon closer scrutiny, Emmeline saw that her eyes were red-rimmed. She had been crying.

"Good," the woman said, as she rummaged in her handbag. She pulled out a handkerchief and waved it in the air. "Wouldn't you know it? It managed to bury itself at the bottom of my bag. It was my fault entirely. I wasn't looking where I was going."

"It happens. Forgive me if I'm prying, but you seem upset," Emmeline probed gently.

The woman gave her a watery smile, but her voice cracked when she responded. "Yes, of course." She dabbed at the corners of eyes. "It's merely my mascara running. I must look a mess."

Emmeline pursed her lips. The woman wasn't wearing mascara.

An awkward silence filled the space between them.

The woman glanced around and then back at Emmeline. "My husband went to get us some wine. We share a passion for classical music, you know. This is the first time we've been out in…in a couple of months." Her fingers nervously twisted and crumpled the handkerchief. "Classical music is what brought us together."

Emmeline nodded politely and murmured, "Oh, really." Clearly, the woman needed to talk. Sometimes it was easier to unburden oneself to a stranger.

"Yes. We've only been married a few months. I suppose it was Fate the way we met. A friend of mine is an artist and was having a showing at local gallery. I don't particularly like her work." She grimaced. "It's too abstract, but I went for moral support. My husband was at the showing too. He was dragged there by a colleague from work. He was trying to make a good impression. You know how it is." Emmeline inclined her head in assent. "We were both bored out of our minds and trying to find a way of sneaking off without offending anyone. We began chatting and realized we had other things in common. At the end of the evening, he asked me out for dinner the following night. Then, it was a concert here at St. Martin's-in-the-Fields and we began seeing each other regularly. We were married about a month later."

"A true whirlwind romance."

"Yes. I fell head over heels in love with my husband at first sight." She gave a sheepish grin. "I know it sounds cliché, but it's true. I thought it was the same for him. Everything was absolute bliss the first couple of months." Her voice trailed off and she cast a sideways glance at the queue of customers waiting to pay the cashier.

Emmeline felt sorry for this poor woman. Her eyes were bright with a sheen of unshed tears, which threatened to cascade from her eyes again.

The woman cleared her throat and sought to regain her composure. "Tonight is meant to be a nice, relaxing evening. I thought we could recapture some of that happiness we had at the beginning. Music has always given me such joy. When I was a little girl, my dream was to become a violinist. But life intervened and took me down a different path. I run my own business these days. But music is still my refuge. Especially now." Her breath caught in her throat. "I've been so terribly lonely these past couple of months. My husband is rarely home. When he is, he broods and drinks far too much." Her voice dipped to a hoarse whisper. "I'm afraid he regrets marrying me. He can't bear to look at me anymore. He was married before, but his wife died." She covered her mouth with a hand. Her chest swelled with a sob. "And…and I think he's still in love with his first wife."

Oh, dear. Emmeline patted her arm reassuringly. "Perhaps, your husband is preoccupied with work. You know how men are. They keep things bottled up inside because it's been drilled into them that showing emotion is a sign of weakness."

The woman's head snapped up. "Do you really think it's as simple as that?" She was desperate to clutch at the tiniest strand of hope.

"I'm certain of it."

"Meredith, there you are," called a male voice tinged with irritation.

The woman turned her head away and edged closer to one of the columns. She swiped at her eyes with the back of one hand. "God, that's my husband. Please, please, don't say anything."

Emmeline nodded. "My lips are sealed." She gave her a conspiratorial smile.

"A full-bodied Cabernet for you." The dark-haired man handed a glass to his wife and then seemed to notice Emmeline. "Oh, hello." He extended a hand. "I'm Matthew. Are you a friend of Meredith's?"

His handshake was firm and cool. He was a head taller than she was. Emmeline took the opportunity to study him. He was about five years older than his wife. His temples were touched with a few silver strands. She guessed he must be in his early forties. He was attractive, but there were purple smudges beneath his green-gray eyes. Something was keeping this man up at night.

His wife laughed. "Actually, we bumped into each other. Literally. My fault entirely." She turned to Emmeline. "I didn't have a chance to introduce myself properly. I'm Meredith. This is my husband, Matthew."

"I'm delighted to meet you both. I'm Emmeline Kirby. My husband will be along in a minute with our wine." She smiled at each of them in turn.

Matthew stiffened. She felt the full force of his glacial stare. "Emmeline Kirby from *The Clarion*?"

"Yes, that's right. I'm the editorial director of investigative features."

"You're the bloody reporter, who's been ringing the office all day. Don't you ever give up? Now, you've followed me *here*. This is outrageous." He wagged an accusatory finger at her. "I'm going give your paper an earful in the morning."

Emmeline blinked in confusion. "I beg your pardon?"

Meredith tugged at his sleeve, her nervous glance darting from side to side. "Matthew, you're making a scene."

He shook off her grasp. "I don't care. This woman shouldn't go around invading people's privacy," he retorted acidly.

Emmeline bristled. "I do not 'invade people's privacy.' My job is to uncover the truth."

"At what cost?" he hurled back at her.

"I don't even know you, Mr…"

"Honeysett," he snarled. "Matthew Honeysett. And I don't appreciate being hounded."

Ah, the MI6 agent. "Mr. Honeysett," she replied tartly, "you're under a misconception. I was trying to give you an opportunity to tell your side. To provide a balanced story so that readers understand and can make up their own minds."

He snorted. "Zorkin is in the wind because of you."

"Who's Zorkin?" Meredith asked.

He ignored his wife and went on, "You're a loose cannon."

Emmeline felt a hot surge of anger swelling in her chest. "I can well understand your embarrassment at bungling the Colefax affair. After all, his safety as well as that of Zorkin were your responsibility. But don't try to assuage your ego by making this debacle my fault. I'm an outside observer."

He took a step closer, looming to try to intimidate her. *Good luck with that*, she thought. The more he protested, the more she was going to keep digging. Because beneath all the bluster she caught a glimpse of fear and unease.

She opened her mouth to fire off some questions, but they lodged in her throat when Gregory materialized at her elbow.

"Emmy, is everything all right?"

Before she could answer, Honeysett interjected, "Longdon, what the devil are *you* doing here?"

Although Gregory's tone was light, she saw a flicker of annoyance in his eyes. "Honeysett, I'd say it was a pleasure to see you again, but I would be lying."

"Has Laurence set you to spy on me?"

Gregory handed Emmeline her glass of wine. "Not that it's any of your business, my wife and I are here for the concert."

The other man's brows shot up nearly to his hairline. "Wife? Do you mean *she*"—he jerked a thumb at Emmeline—"is your wife?"

Gregory beamed at her and lifted her hand to his lips, grazing her knuckles with a kiss. "Indeed, she is. In another week, it will be two months since we were married."

"You're still newlyweds," Meredith murmured. "How lovely, isn't it, Matthew?"

Emmeline gave her a weak smile, but her husband was in no mood to wish them happiness. From the thunderous look on his face, it was exactly the opposite.

"I can see it all clearly. It's a plot to trap me." His nostrils flared and his jaw hardened into a tight line. "You take it in turns. I see Laurence's hand all over this. He's the puppet master and will stop at nothing to bring me down."

Meredith snatched her husband's sleeve, as her bewildered gaze searched his face. "Matthew, you're not making any sense. No one is trying to destroy you. You're just tired. Why don't we go home?"

"Listen to your wife," Gregory suggested. "Before you embarrass yourself any further."

"I'm sorry" Meredith mouthed and tugged at her husband's arm.

Honeysett dropped his voice to a dangerous hiss. "Two can play at that game. You think you've pulled the wool over the old man's eyes, but I've looked into your past." The menacing words hung upon the air, as his gaze latched onto Emmeline. "I'll wager you haven't the courage to share all your dirty secrets with your wife. Despite her fondness for the truth, I don't think even she would be quite as open-minded if everything came to light. Stay out of my way. Both of you."

"That's enough." Meredith gave him a shove.

He threw his hands up in the air and stalked off, leaving her to hurry after him. She tossed an apologetic glance over her shoulder.

"What a brute," Emmeline mumbled. She bit her lip as she watched Honeysett disappear up the stairs. "Do you think he's violent?"

On impulse, she chased after Meredith. "Wait."

The other woman spun around startled. "I'm sorry you had to see Matthew like that, but now you understand why I've been so concerned."

Emmeline fumbled in her bag and drew out one of her business cards. She pressed it into Meredith's hand. "Here. Call me if you need anything."

Meredith tried to give it back to her, but then appeared to change her mind. She stuffed it in her handbag and turned toward the staircase without another word.

Gregory came up behind Emmeline and put an arm around her shoulder. "Darling, I can hardly wait to see what you have planned for an encore, if that was the main entertainment."

She leaned into him. "The evening's been an utter disaster. I don't think Peter is going to show up, if he had any intention to do so in the first place. And Honeysett"— she gnashed her teeth and balled her fists at her side— "Ooh, that man. Beneath the heated rhetoric, he's worried. That means I'm getting too close. But to what?" Her frown deepened. "Colefax's killer? Snowdrop? I feel more lost than I did this morning. It's as if I'm trapped in the center of one of those garden mazes and no matter which way I turn it's a dead end."

"You can take comfort in the fact that Julie Brentford's murderer has been apprehended," he pointed out.

She nodded and felt a surge of pride. "Yes, that's the one bright spot today."

People were starting to make their way up the stairs.

"The concert's about to start. At least, we can salvage part of the evening with the soothing sounds of Vivaldi and Bach."

Gregory kissed the top of her head. "That's my Emmy. Always looking on the positive side. Come on."

Upstairs, they showed their tickets to one of the ushers. "D22 and D23. Just along this side toward the front," he pointed out.

The rectangular church was airy, with a five-bay nave divided from the aisles by arcades of Corinthian columns. Galleries extended over both aisles and at the west end.

The low buzz of conversation drifted around them. They found their seats and settled into the pew. A piano and a handful of music stands were arranged in a cluster in the nave. The soft glow from the chandeliers was reflected in the leaded glass window.

While Gregory perused the program, Emmeline tipped her head back to admire the elegant details on the barrel-vaulted ceiling. The creamy, ribbed stucco panels were decorated with cherubim, clouds, shells, gilded scroll work and a royal escutcheon. She craned her neck around to cast a glance at the magnificent Walker organ. With its 3,000 pipes, it was considered the finest organ in London.

It was a wonderful setting for a musical interlude, she thought as the performers entered and began tuning their instruments.

"Excuse miss," a man whispered just over her left shoulder. "You dropped your program."

She frowned because she was staring at her program in her lap.

"I'm afraid you've made a mistake—" But an arm brushed her shoulder and thrust a program into her hand.

Both she and Gregory turned around to face the stranger.

He was about forty with an oval face and ash-blond hair. His pale blue gaze was shrewd and intense.

"You're being watched," he hissed. "If you're not careful, you're going to get all of us killed." He flapped the program. "Here take it."

Emmeline's eyes went wide with realization. She pitched her voice low. "Peter?"

He gave an infinitesimal nod and waved the program again. "Tomorrow."

Then, he quietly slipped out of the pew as the music began.

Emmeline glanced down at the program.

Scrawled in the top left corner was one line.

The Clermont Victoria Hotel. 5 p.m.

Chapter 21

The Clermont Victoria, designed by architect and editor Sir James Thomas Knowles who was an intimate friend of poet Alfred, Lord Tennyson, opened in 1862. It was London's first railway hotel. The graceful, Grade II listed building sits next to bustling Victoria Station and is a mere two blocks from Buckingham Palace and St. James's Park.

At precisely five o'clock the next afternoon, Emmeline and Gregory pushed through the revolving door and stepped into the lobby's welcoming embrace. The sparkling facets of the chandelier caught the light and made the white marble floor, with an alternating pattern of black diamonds, gleam. A table in the center with a huge vase with fresh flowers drew the eye to the moss-green carpeted, marble staircase with a gray and beige balustrade beyond that branched off to the right and left, leading to the arcaded first-floor gallery above. At the foot of the staircase nestled on either side was a nook. A mirror covered one wall and gave the impression of depth. And yet, the plush gold velvet loveseat, the pair of charcoal velvet chairs and a standing lamp with a fringed burnt umber shade to mute the light that were clustered together offered privacy and an inviting spot to share confidences watched over by two Victorian ladies in the painting hanging on the opposite wall.

At the moment, both nooks were devoid of a human presence. In fact, Emmeline and Gregory were the only ones loitering in the lobby.

"Peter's game of hide-and-seek is becoming tiresome," Gregory muttered out of the corner of his mouth.

Emmeline glanced at her watch. "It's only a few minutes after five. Let's give him a chance."

His lips pressed into a thin line. "Mmm" was his noncommittal response.

"May I help you?" a young woman asked from one the reception desks.

Gregory flashed one of his most engaging smiles. "We're meeting a friend. He seems to be running a bit late. Is it all right if we wait?" He motioned to one of the nooks.

The receptionist nodded. "Certainly," she said politely and turned her attention back to her computer screen.

He took Emmeline's elbow and guided her to the nook on the left side, where they would have perfect view of the doors.

There was an ebb and flow of activity. The concierge called taxis for guests on their way out for the evening. New guests arrived, checked in, collected their keys and drifted toward the bank of lifts. Half an hour ticked by and still Peter did not appear.

"Right." Gregory rose and extended a hand to Emmeline. "Peter can go to the devil. We're leaving."

She took his hand, but she remained seated. "You can go. I'll stay a bit longer."

He gave a curt shake of his head. "That's a nonstarter. Not with Kozlov and his band of merry thugs on walkabout and that nutter Honeysett." He waggled his fingers impatiently. "Come on, Emmy."

"Honeysett can't arrest for me writing an article. That would cause a scandal at a time when he least needs it. As for Kozlov, he wouldn't dare come after us again. He must know Superintendent Burnell is on the lookout."

"Kozlov didn't reach the rarified ranks of Russian mob circles by cowering from the police," he sneered. "Either they're in his pocket or they meet with an unfortunate accident if they choose the high moral ground. It's a crude and simple business practice that he has honed over the years."

"I don't argue with that. But what if we have it wrong and Snowdrop is the one who murdered Colefax and is now trying to hunt down the Fabergé egg."

Gregory lifted an eyebrow. "Well, that makes all the difference," he replied facetiously. "You've put my mind at ease. We're leaving."

"I can't blame you." The crisp tones of a familiar voice floated to their ears.

They looked up in unison to find Peter leaning against the banister with his arms folded over his chest.

Emmeline surged to her feet. "Peter, where have you been? You kept us waiting for half an hour."

He pushed away from the stairs and walked over to them. He extended a hand first to her and then to Gregory. They both hesitated before shaking it.

"Forgive me. I've been here the entire time. I've been watching from up there." He pointed to the first-floor gallery, which overlooked the lobby. "I had to be sure you were alone. I couldn't risk you bringing unwanted shadows, albeit unintentionally, to my doorstep like you did last night."

"Enough of all the cloak-and-dagger nonsense,"

Gregory commanded. "I don't know who you are or how you're mixed up in all this, and frankly I don't care. My only concern is for my wife."

Peter shot an apologetic glance at Emmeline. "You have no reason to believe me, but I'm truly sorry that you stumbled into this nightmare. Unfortunately, Alexander was a master of leaving collateral damage in his wake." He sighed. "Don't waste your sympathy on him, though. He was the architect of his own death."

She cocked her head to one side and studied him. His pale blue gaze was at once armored and haunted. "How do you know Colefax?"

His eyes widened in surprise. "I thought you knew." He pressed a hand to his chest and in the most plummy of British tones said, "I'm Pyotr Zorkin. But please, I prefer the English version. Peter is much less stuffy, don't you think?"

She and Gregory traded a stunned glance.

"Of course, I should have realized," she mumbled.

His mouth quivered in a bemused smile. "Now that the formal introductions have been exchanged, shall we go into the bar? We won't be as conspicuous in there. I'd invite you up to my room, but I don't think you would feel comfortable. After all, we are strangers."

"Your room?" Gregory asked suspiciously. "Are you staying at the hotel?"

"Yes, I booked in two nights ago."

Gregory's eyes narrowed. "Why? You own the five-story, three-bedroom penthouse in The Tower at One St. George Wharf. The most exclusive and prestigious address in central London."

Peter pitched his voice low. "Actually, my father owns the apartment. It's merely a *pied-à-terre*, when I'm in London."

Gregory gave a derisive laugh. "Oh, I'm glad you

clarified that point."

"To answer your question, I've taken up residence here temporarily because someone left a bomb in my apartment the other day. The authorities say that the damage was concentrated in my bedroom. Tragically, the cleaning lady set it off. They tell me she was killed instantly and didn't feel any pain. I sincerely hope that was the case. I have a strong aversion to dying, so I thought it would be prudent to take up residence in a place where I have no connections until I figure out my next move. Money has become a bit of a problem because Her Majesty's government's sanctions have frozen many of my father's assets and bank accounts. If I've satisfied your curiosity, let's go into the bar to talk."

The trio retreated into their own thoughts as they walked down the short corridor to The Soak, the Clermont's bar lounge where one could also have a starter or a light meal. The oval-shaped bar, with its white marble top counter, was plunked in the middle and split the space into two halves. The door from the lobby led into a section, where high-top tables stood with tall stools.

Peter stopped at the bar and asked them what they would like to drink. Gregory opted for his usual tipple, a single-malt Scotch, and Emmeline a glass of Sauvignon Blanc.

Peter nodded. After giving their order and telling the barman to charge the drinks to Peter Smith in Room 541, they drifted toward the front area, where there was an entrance from the side next to Victoria Station.

They settled into the powder-blue velvet bucket chairs at a low table tucked in a corner. It was quiet. There were only a handful of patrons in the lounge. It was still early.

Emmeline waited until their drinks appeared and they had taken a few sips, before venturing, "Peter, after your friend's murder and the subsequent attempt on your own life, I can see why you felt it necessary to drop out of sight. But surely, you would be safer if you went to the authorities. They can protect you."

"I'm not safe anywhere. My days are numbered," he scoffed, bitterness rolling off his tongue. "Alexander saw to that."

She slumped back in her chair. "I'm confused. The way you talk, one would think Alexander Colefax was an enemy rather than a trusted friend."

"Trust and Alexander were a contradiction in terms. How can you trust a man whose only loyalty is to money? Alexander enjoyed manipulating people to do his bidding. If you could benefit him, then you were his bosom mate. When you outlived your usefulness, he turned his back on you. You were as good as a stranger.

"I had no illusions about Alexander. Yes, he could be great fun, but he had a dark side. Winning was always important to him. He didn't care who he hurt or how he achieved his goal, as long as he achieved what he wanted in the end. I've always known that he murdered his cousin on that skiing holiday in Gstaad all those years ago just so that he could become indispensable to his uncle and get his hands on the company. Alexander was brilliant. His hotel empire is a testament to his business acumen, but only a ruthless man resorts to murder."

Emmeline's fingers gripped the stem of her glass tighter. She shot a glance at Gregory and saw her own shock reflected in his eyes.

Peter gulped down his vodka in one swallow. "I only have myself to blame. I knew, but I chose to turn a blind eye because Alexander's charm was hypnotic and made you forget that a viper lurked beneath the surface. I allowed him to persuade me to collude with MI6 against my father and steal the Galleon Egg. It sounded perfectly reasonable when Alexander suggested I turn over the egg to him for safekeeping until I could disappear and reinvent myself as someone else. And since he was the liaison with the MI6 agent, it was logical that I hand over everything on Snowdrop to Alexander. Now, I have nothing. I'm hunted by Kozlov because he hates my father. Alexander made a secret deal offering me up as a sacrificial lamb. Worst of all, Snowdrop is after me. Snowdrop's mask of respectability is so convincing that even the seasoned spy can't see what's in front of him."

"While I appreciate you taking us into your confidence," Emmeline said, "and I don't doubt what you've told us, I fail to see what we can do. You haven't told us who Snowdrop is."

He continued to hedge. "You have a reputation for never giving up on a story. I'm a dead man walking. I'm passing the baton to you. You're the only one with the fire and tenacity to bring down Snowdrop and Kozlov. Please don't let me down."

"Your trust in me won't be misplaced, but you must tell me Snowdrop's identity. I intend to follow the story to the end."

Gregory slammed his tumbler down, sloshing some of the amber liquid onto the table. He leaned forward and snarled, "You won't." Then, he turned to Zorkin. "I won't allow you to make my wife a target. You made this unholy bed. Now, you can lie in it *alone*."

He stood up and pulled Emmeline to her feet. "We're leaving."

The look on his face prohibited any argument.

Peter gave a reluctant nod. "You're right, of course. It was an unreasonable request."

Chapter 22

The conversation over the breakfast table that morning had been strained. Neither she nor Gregory had been willing to relent. She knew he loved her and was concerned for her safety. However, that did not give him the right to drag her out of the Clermont. She was not a child who required scolding. Her job was to report the news, good *and* bad. That was a responsibility she took seriously. If she didn't abide by the highest tenets of journalism, it would give a murderer and a spy license to continue tearing at the fabric of civilized society. To ensure that law and order reigned, the truth must come out. Secrets and lies were an insidious threat. Eventually, Gregory would see that. Or would he? She bit her lip. She could hear his voice in her head.

My life is an open book. You know everything that is important.

But not everything. And that was what scared her.

A sigh escaped her lips. She would *not* go down that road. She trusted her husband.

She grunted. It was time to pour her energies into

rattling cages. That was what she did best. She began flipping through her notebook. The flutter in the pit of her stomach told her that she knew the answer, but it was just out of reach. She stopped and stared out of the window. It was something Peter had said about the church and being watched. Watched by Kozlov or Snowdrop?

She closed her eyes and replayed in her mind the night at St. Martin's-in-the-Fields. What marred the evening was their contretemps with Honeysett and his wife in the crypt before the concert. Honeysett had accused her and Gregory of following him. Was he feeling paranoid and insecure because reprisals were looming in the wake of Colefax's murder and Peter's disappearance? Or was there more to it?

Honeysett's rhetoric had been too vehement. She had the impression then that his outrage was hiding something. She was even more certain of it now.

Snowdrop's mask of respectability is so convincing, Peter had told them, *that even the seasoned spy can't see what's in front of him.*

Her hand flew to her mouth. "Oh, my God." The words slipped out on a sharp breath.

The seasoned spy could only refer to Villiers. If Snowdrop was cunning enough to fool the shrewd and calculating Villiers, whose brain was always ten moves ahead of everyone else, then that could only mean that Snowdrop was Honeysett.

Treason ran in the family. His father had passed sensitive information to the Russians. What if Honeysett shared his father's sympathies and had bided his time until he was well-positioned to offer his services? Or maybe the Russians had groomed him as a sleeper? The boys in the Kremlin must have been patting themselves on the back when Honeysett was placed in charge of finding the elusive Snowdrop. He could have gone on draining intelligence from MI6 for years. But what if his superiors started to take notice when all the supposed leads on the mole turned out to be dead ends? Honeysett had to quell these rumblings, so he devised a dazzling alternative to divert attention from Snowdrop.

What better way to elevate his standing at the agency than to propose turning Ilya Zorkin. He came up with a bold plan and overnight he became the golden boy with his superiors. After all, Zorkin would be a major coup for MI6. Honeysett was taking a risk, though. If Moscow found out that he was willing to sacrifice one of its elite to save his own skin, his life would be over in an instant. He couldn't attract attention by overtly going after Zorkin. That's why he approached his old mate Colefax, whom he knew was maneuvering to open a hotel in Russia. He pressured Colefax to use his business contacts as well as play on his friendship with Peter to compromise Ilya Zorkin. With Colefax as the intermediary, Peter would never know that Honeysett was behind the plot.

Emmeline nodded and pushed herself to her feet. She started to pace back and forth. She became more certain by the second that her speculations were correct. Peter was a playboy. He enjoyed the privileges of being the powerful Ilya Zorkin's son, but he had no money of his own. He had told them last night that he wanted to start a new life somewhere no one would know him. When Colefax came to him with MI6's proposition of a new identity and more importantly money, he jumped at the chance. And all he had to do was to steal the Galleon Egg and provide some information to MI6 to break free of his father's suffocating control. That was not so bad.

She gave a disapproving shake of her head. She could not condone such scheming. Was it any wonder that Peter was a marked man?

Meanwhile, Colefax must have decided to double cross both Peter and MI6 by throwing in his lot with Kozlov. Another thought struck her. What if Kozlov discovered that Colefax had murdered his cousin to take the helm of the family's hotel business? If the truth were to leak out, the empire he had painstakingly built over the past two decades would be worthless overnight. He'd be a pariah. Seeing the writing on the wall, he agreed to turn over the Fabergé egg to Kozlov. But as an astute and practical man, Colefax knew he would never be free of Kozlov. So did he make a deal to sell the egg to a third party? That would explain the red diamonds. That still left the problem of Kozlov. Unless Colefax planned to murder him. After all, he had killed before. With Kozlov out of the way, it would be business as usual. That only left Snowdrop. Peter likely told him Snowdrop's identity and Colefax embarked on his own blackmailing campaign.

"Oh, what a tangled web we weave," she muttered.

She couldn't decide who had the stronger motive to murder Colefax—Kozlov or Snowdrop? Both were willing to do anything to possess the Galleon Egg. The fact that Kozlov's men had threatened her and Gregory indicated that he didn't have the bejeweled treasure. On the other hand, Honeysett's efforts to retain MI6 jurisdiction over the Colefax case and Rossiter seemed to suggest that he didn't have the egg either. The police didn't find the egg in Colefax's house. Therefore, the logical conclusion was that he had hidden it. But where?

Adrenaline coursed through her veins as she crossed to her desk.

She snatched up her phone. She couldn't keep her theories to herself. However before she could tell either MI5 or the police, she had to talk to Peter. She needed confirmation that Honeysett was Snowdrop.

She punched in the number for the Clermont Victoria Hotel. Her call was answered immediately. "Good afternoon, Clermont Victoria."

"Hello. May I speak to Peter Smith in Room 541. This is Emmeline Kirby."

"Just a moment, madam."

She tapped her fingers on her desk, as she waited to be connected. She prayed he hadn't gone out. But would he risk exposure?

"Hello." His voice echoed in her ear.

"Peter, thank goodness. It's Emmeline. I need to know who Snowdrop is."

"You already know. You were talking to Snowdrop in the church the other night. I couldn't believe my eyes. I almost bolted because I thought it may have been a trap to lure me out into the open."

I knew it, she told herself. "So just to confirm the mole is Hon—"

He cut her off. "Sorry, someone's at the door. Why don't you pop by the hotel in an hour? I have an idea where Alexander may have taken the egg. He has a chalet in Switzerland on Lake Thun. He called it his 'little Alpine flower.' He went there when he wanted to escape London. He gave me a spare key. We can discuss everything when you get here." Then to whoever was knocking, he said, "Just a moment, I'm coming."

There was a click and the line went dead.

Chapter 23

Emmeline was in her element when she was in the thick of things. The more pressure she was under, the more she was able to accomplish. First, she rang Gregory and shared her theories, which he agreed were sound. He was far from pleased to hear that Peter had confirmed Snowdrop's identity. Naturally, he didn't want her going to the hotel alone. Rather than have another row, she comprised and suggested that he meet her there. In the interim, he would stop by Scotland Yard to have a word with Superintendent Burnell. If they couldn't persuade Peter to go to the authorities, perhaps Burnell could put the hotel under surveillance.

Her next call was not as successful. Villiers's secretary refused to allow her to speak to him. "The deputy director has no comment" was her snide response.

Although unsurprising, it still left a bitter taste in her mouth. *Bloody woman*, Emmeline swore. This was a matter of national security.

There was one person who would take her seriously.

"Hello, Mrs. Longdon," Pamela's mellifluous voice

said, when she rang Philip's office. "Of course, Mr. Acheson is always delighted to take your calls. I'll put you straight through."

A smile touched her lips. She didn't know how true that was, but at least Philip did her the courtesy of at least listening. "Emmeline, as usual, you've been a very busy bee."

"It keeps the mind agile."

"Mmm. And everyone else tries to run for cover because they can't keep pace."

"Very droll. If I hadn't been persistent and pursued all the leads, who knows how long it would have taken to discover poor Julie Brentford."

"When the human body decomposes, it begins to smell. I think that may have given someone a clue that things weren't all tickety-boo."

"Ugh. Don't be horrid."

"It's a matter of biology. Now, what do you want?"

"It has to do with Colefax's murder. I know who the MI6 mole is. I tried to inform Villiers, but he wouldn't even give me five minutes. Snowdrop is Matthew Honeysett."

He had seen first-hand the lengths to which Honeysett had gone to interview Rossiter and keep Colefax's murder within MI6's purview. She explained that this was all part of an elaborate ruse to cover Snowdrop's tracks and disappear with the Galleon Egg. "But Colefax threw a spanner in the works by playing footsie with Kozlov. Everyone wants the Fabergé egg and Pyotr Zorkin has become a pawn. Honeysett wants him dead because he can identify Snowdrop, while it's a matter of retaliation for Kozlov. Killing Peter would be the latest volley in his high-stakes tit-for-tat with Ilya Zorkin. Peter has been staying at the Clermont Victoria Hotel because someone set off a bomb in his penthouse the other night. He's not a saint, but I can't sit back and allow him to be murdered. Peter is a sitting duck. On the other hand, he doesn't trust the police or MI5. I can't really blame him.

"Philip, you're the only one who can make Villiers understand the seriousness of the situation. He'll listen to you. In the meantime, I'm going to meet with Peter at the hotel. He has an idea about where Colefax could have hidden the Fabergé egg for safekeeping. I'm going to try again to persuade him to allow the authorities to place him in protective custody."

"I will speak to Villiers. I don't like the idea of you going to see Zorkin alone, though. Kozlov's men or Honeysett could be watching."

"You needn't worry about me. Gregory is going to meet me there, after he sees Superintendent Burnell. Besides, a hotel is a bustling hive of activity. People are always coming and going."

Philip was only slightly mollified. But there was nothing he could do to prevent her meeting with Zorkin.

⁓⁓⁓

"Longdon, why are you roaming the corridors of the Met?" Assistant Commissioner Cruickshank demanded in clipped tones.

Since when did they let the prat loose on walkabout? Gregory thought. *I really don't have time for his nonsense.*

He plastered a smile on his lips and spun around on his heel to face Cruickshank. "Assistant Commissioner, how good to see you."

Cruickshank eyed him suspiciously. "The feeling is far from mutual. I can't think why you're here."

Well, try not to think too hard, old chap. You'll do

yourself an injury.

Gregory wagged a finger. "Ah, there's that charming sense of humor. You're famous for it the length and breadth of the Met. Laughter is always echoing down these hallowed corridors thanks to you."

Cruickshank straightened his shoulders and preened. "As a senior officer, one does one's best to keep up the morale of the junior ranks."

Lord, help us all.

"You do an admirable job," Gregory observed ironically. "I'm glad we had this inspiring little chat. I must be off."

He started to walk away.

"Just a moment," the assistant commissioner intoned. "You still haven't explained what you're doing here."

Gregory turned slowly. "Haven't I? There really is no need for concern." He lowered his voice conspiratorially. "I'm doing my duty as a law-abiding citizen. I'm here on police business. Consulting on an important matter." He shot his cuff and glanced at his watch. "I'm afraid I must dash."

Cruickshank's forehead puckered in a frown. "What police business? Why was I not informed?"

Gregory caught a glimpse of Burnell at the other end of the corridor.

"Ah, Superintendent Burnell, there you are," he called, leaving the detective with no choice but to join them.

"Burnell, Longdon tells me he's consulting on a case. Why I'm only now hearing about this?"

Burnell's annoyed glare clashed with Gregory bemused grin.

The superintendent cleared his throat, but Gregory spoke before he could offer a response. "Assistant Commissioner, an officer of your vast experience"— Burnell rolled his eyes at the ceiling—"knows that things can break in a case in a flash and time is of the essence, if the criminal is to be caught. This is just such a moment. So, you'll appreciate the fact that Superintendent Burnell and I have a good deal to discuss to ensure that order is restored." He clapped Cruickshank on the shoulder. "You can take great pride in the fact that you have a detective of the superintendent's caliber under your command. After all, a leader is a reflection of his subordinates."

A pained expression pinched Burnell's features, but Cruickshank nodded in agreement. "Yes, well. One doesn't like to boast."

Gregory and Burnell murmured in unison, "Certainly not."

The assistant commissioner waved a hand. "Carry on. I'll expect an update tomorrow." And off he went without ever finding out what case Gregory was "consulting" on.

"Yes, sir," Burnell murmured. He waited until Cruickshank had disappeared into the lift and then rounded on Gregory. "What do you want?'

Gregory batted his eyelashes. "To see you, of course, Oliver."

"Longdon," he growled.

Gregory's mood sobered. This was no time to indulge in verbal sparring. He had to meet Emmy at the hotel.

He pitched his voice low and threw an arm around Burnell's shoulders. "There have been developments in the Colefax case."

The superintendent raised an eyebrow. "That's a MI5 matter now. Talk to Villiers. The Boy Wonder will have my guts for garters, if I stick my nose in."

"Villiers is incommunicado. Acheson is going to brief him, but things are moving rather quickly. Emmy is on her way to meet Pyotr Zorkin."

"What?" The word rumbled from Burnell's throat

attracting curious glances from those passing by. "My office. Now," he ordered.

Once the door had closed behind them, Gregory briefed Burnell on Emmeline's theories about the murky labyrinth that ensnared Honeysett, Colefax, and Kozlov and the mad hunt for the Galleon Egg. "What worries me the most," Gregory concluded, "is that Pyotr Zorkin confirmed to Emmy that Honeysett is the MI6 mole, Snowdrop. Either Honeysett or Kozlov could have been responsible for the failed attempt on Zorkin's life. Both men are ruthless and will not stop until the job is done. That's why I'd feel a great deal better, if you came with me to the hotel. Oliver, you're the only one who can make Zorkin see the gravity of the situation."

Burnell snorted. "He's already well aware of it. Otherwise, he wouldn't be in self-imposed exile in the hotel."

"For Emmy's sake then," Gregory pleaded.

Burnell sighed wearily. "Yes, well. Emmeline is a different matter entirely." His tone had softened. "Your wife's crusading spirit is noble. It also makes my ulcer do somersaults." He leveled a pointed gaze at Gregory. "As do your illicit antics."

Gregory's eyes widened in mock innocence. He pressed a hand to his chest. "Oliver, my heart is pure as that of a dove."

"Hmph. You may have been able to fool your wife, but I *know* that you haven't retired from the game. It's too much of a temptation for you to stop. Stand warned. I will catch you one day. I pity Emmeline, but that's the way things must be."

Gregory's mouth curved into a wry smile. "You're welcome to try, but you're doomed to fail, Oliver."

"We'll see. And I needn't have to remind you that it's *Superintendent Burnell.*" Gregory merely chuckled, grating on his nerves as he reached for his phone. "I want to apprise Finch of the situation with Zorkin. I'm going to have him come along with us. I'll also send a couple of plainclothes officers to watch the hotel for any sign of Honeysett or Kozlov's thugs. In a perfect world, Acheson or MI6 would have captured Honeysett by now to prevent him from inflicting anymore damage. As we both know, this is not a perfect world."

Gregory clucked his tongue. "Really, *Oliver*. What's happened to that sunny disposition we all know and love?"

"Put a cork in it." He did his best to ignore the mischievous gleam in Gregory's eyes, as he barked his orders.

Burnell had barely returned the receiver to the cradle, when Finch burst in. The look on the sergeant's face did not bode well.

"What is it, Finch?"

Finch hesitated for a second, his gaze snaking a glance at Gregory. Then, he directed his full attention to his boss. "Sir, you're not going to like this."

The superintendent waggled his fingers. "Well, don't drag it out."

Finch swallowed hard. "Sir, the red diamonds were stolen from the evidence store."

Burnell surged to his feet. "How is that possible?"

"It's all right, though. All of them have been recovered."

The tension in the superintendent's shoulders eased slightly. "Where?" He held his breath, steeling himself for the answer because his ulcer was already rumbling in protest.

"In the boot of Longdon's car."

Chapter 24

The brilliant, golden sunshine and blue skies of that morning were a distant memory. Ominous charcoal clouds had started gathering, when Emmeline had left the *Clarion*. Now as she emerged from Victoria Station, the heavens had been torn asunder and rain was bucketing down. She didn't bother opening her umbrella, though. The hotel was just around the corner on Buckingham Palace Road. She clutched her handbag tightly to her side and made a mad dash. A queue of people at the bus stop clogged up the pavement in front of the hotel, delaying her progress. Finally, she bounded up the steps and plunged through the revolving door, which decanted her soggy and bedraggled form into the lobby.

She patted her wet curls into place and hitched her handbag higher on her shoulder. She walked over to one of the reception desks. "Hello. My name's Emmeline Kirby. Can you ring Mr. Peter Smith in Room 541 and let him know I'm waiting for him here in the lobby."

The young man smiled and picked up the receiver. "Just a moment, madam." He let it ring and then returned it to cradle. "I'm afraid Mr. Smith is not answering."

Emmeline frowned and then remembered that Peter had said he had been watching her and Gregory from the first floor gallery the other night. She stepped back to the center of the lobby and craned her neck around. Her gaze swept over the gallery. Peter was nowhere in sight.

She crossed to the reception desk again. "I don't understand. I spoke to Mr. Smith only an hour ago. We arranged to meet."

"I'll try his room again." He smiled at her, while he waited. Then, he shook his head. "I'm sorry. There's still no response. Let me check the computer." He tapped away for a few seconds. "Ah," he mumbled and then looked up at her. "It seems Mr. Smith has checked out."

"What? That's impossible."

"There's no mistake. His bill is paid in full. According to the computer, he checked out an hour ago."

She frowned. "That makes no sense. Why would he ask to meet me here, if he was going to leave?" He raised his hands and shrugged his shoulders helplessly. "Are you sure that he checked out? Perhaps, one of your colleagues entered the information for a different room into the computer."

He pursed his lips. "I rather doubt that, but I could send one of the maids to knock on his door."

"Would you? I'd appreciate that."

He inclined his head and proceeded to call Housekeeping. She hovered by the desk, while they waited. It felt like an eternity before his phone rang. He murmured a few words and then hung up.

"I'm afraid Mr. Smith has indeed checked out. However, it seems he left a large hold all behind."

"That's rather odd."

"He must have forgotten it in his rush," the man

suggested.

She gave him a pointed look. "How does one forget one's bag?"

"It's not unusual. Guests forget things all the time. In any event, one of the porters is bringing it down. Don't worry, madam. We'll put it in storage, until Mr. Smith calls to have it collected. Your friend's bag will be quite safe, I assure you."

Although he took the matter in stride, the hairs on the back of her neck prickled. Peter would *not* vanish without leaving word for her.

The receptionist continued with his business, while Emmeline stood off to the side where she kept her eyes glued on the bank of lifts. Ten long minutes later, the car doors slid open and a porter emerged, pushing a luggage trolley with a single bag upon it.

The receptionist looked up from his computer, when he rolled up to the desk. "Ah, there you are Roy. Is that the bag from Room 541? The occupant was a friend of hers."

Roy dipped his head deferentially.

"Did Mr. Smith leave a note for me? Emmeline Kirby."

Roy shook his head. "The only thing in the room was the bag." He made a sweeping gesture with his hand toward the trolley. "It's no wonder your friend left it behind. It weighs a ton of bricks." He turned to the receptionist. "Here, Tom, give us a hand."

Tom shot him a look that said, *It's not my responsibility*. However, he came around the desk to help the porter to remove the bag. They huffed and grunted as they lifted it off.

A damp, dark spot was left in the center of the trolley.

Emmeline squinted. "Something's leaking from the bag."

"Brilliant," the receptionist complained. "Mr. Fitzsimmons will get his knickers in a twist, if we make a mess in the lobby. Roy, let's put the bag against the wall. I'll ring Housekeeping to mop up whatever the bloody stuff is." He glanced up suddenly remembering Emmeline. "Pardon the language, madam."

She waved off his apology. She couldn't tear her eyes from the cherry-red trail the bag made against the pristine polished white marble floor. She took a step closer. Bile rose in her throat.

Her hand trembled as she pointed. "Look, it's…it's blood." The words came out as a hoarse croak.

The two men stopped and stood upright. They stared at one another, uncertain what to do. Their complexions were suddenly ashen.

"I…I suppose we should open it," Tom said.

Roy nodded. "Right. Go ahead."

"Me? Why me?"

"You're the face of guest relations."

"You're a porter," Tom shot back.

"Oh, for heaven's sake," Emmeline remarked with more than a touch of asperity. "One of you open it. We have to find out what's inside."

Tom swallowed hard and gingerly unzipped the bag.

Emmeline's hand flew to her mouth. Beads of sweat broke out across her brow and the lobby began to spin.

Pyotr Zorkin was crumpled like a pretzel in the bag. The last thing she saw before she sank into oblivion was the accusation in his unseeing eyes.

❦

"Emmeline," a muffled male voice called from far, far away.

Leave me alone.

But the annoying twit didn't seem to get the message because he kept repeating her name over and over, as if he were chanting. To make matters worse, he began shaking her.

How rude. Leave…Me…Alone.

Where was she? She couldn't see. It was plunged in pitch blackness. Her body shuddered. And it was cold. Very cold.

"Emmeline, wake up. Open your eyes," the fellow demanded. "Come on."

You deserve a punch on the nose.

But her brain tingled with a jolt of awareness. With a tremendous effort, she cracked open one eye and then the other. She blinked for a few seconds and then Philip's concerned face came into focus.

She sat bolt upright. "Philip. What happened?"

"You fainted," he replied gently. He smiled and put an arm around her shoulders. "Here sit back." He made her more comfortable on the loveseat in one of the nooks next to the staircase.

He cast a glance at the gaggle of police officers gathered in the center of the lobby. Their voices fused together. They only caught the occasional word.

And then she remembered. "Zorkin is dead," she whispered.

"Yes," Philip muttered. "He…committed suicide."

Her head whipped round and she stared at him. At first, she couldn't turn her thoughts into a sentence.

"Suicide? That's ridiculous. How does a man commit suicide and then seal himself up in his hold all?"

His gaze darted to the officers and then back to her. "Nevertheless, that's the *official* determination. Open and shut." He lifted a blond eyebrow to emphasize this point.

She folded her arms across her chest and tossed her chin in the air. "Only a gullible fool will believe it," she said mulishly. She scooted closer to him and lowered her voice. "This has Kozlov written all over it. He was sending a message to Ilya Zorkin and we both know it."

"Emmeline." His tone held a warning.

"Hmph. It's preposterous. MI5 and Scotland Yard will be a laughingstock. Speaking of Scotland Yard. Where's Gregory?"

"Ah, there's been a spot of bother."

Chapter 25

I'm a shrewd judge of character. When I caught this man skulking in the corridor, I knew he was up to no good," Assistant Commissioner Cruickshank declared, as he paced back and forth in one of the interview rooms.

"I was hardly skulking," Gregory drawled dispassionately, as he crossed one leg over the other.

Burnell glared at him. "You're not helping."

"My dear, *Superintendent* Burnell," Gregory replied with a smile, "I'm merely trying to set the record straight."

"Sir, I think—"

"What is patently clear," Cruickshank prattled on without allowing Burnell to inject a word, "is you came to the station on a false pretext to steal the diamonds."

"You're entitled to believe what you like. Mind you, your theories don't have even a nodding acquaintance with the truth."

Cruickshank halted his perambulations and spun around on his heel. "Do you take me for a fool?"

Gregory smoothed down the corners of his mustache and offered him a wry smile. "I'm afraid I don't know you well enough to form a proper opinion, so I'll reserve judgment."

Burnell and Finch both rolled their eyes toward the ceiling.

The assistant commissioner's jaw clenched. "Longdon, it will go much easier for you if you start talking. Who paid you to steal the diamonds?"

Gregory's gaze snaked from Cruickshank to Burnell, who were both staring at him intently.

He propped his elbows on the table and leaned in. "Although the Met's hospitality leaves a great deal to be desired, I'll take pity and tell you chaps everything."

The assistant commissioner's brown eyes gleamed with triumph. On the other hand, Burnell oozed skepticism from his pursed lips to his furrowed brow.

Gregory enjoyed dragging out the moment and being the center of attention. After all, anticipation is half the fun, isn't it? "No one paid me because I didn't steal the diamonds."

Cruickshank threw his hands up in the air and groaned. His face crumpled into a crestfallen expression.

"Where's my husband?" Emmeline's voice seeped through the door. She was arguing with an officer outside in the squad room. "I don't care what you found. Someone is trying to frame him. I demand to see my husband."

Cruickshank and the detectives exchanged a wary look. The conversation dipped to a muffled murmur.

Gregory shook his head. "You poor sods. My Emmy has lost her temper. I'm afraid you're in for it now."

"Stuff it," Burnell snarled.

"Does Superintendent Burnell know that you are detaining my husband? I'd like to speak to the superintendent."

"Please, Mrs. Longdon. Please calm down," the hapless

officer implored.

Then, they heard Philip's voice. "Emmeline, getting upset will not help matters. Cooler heads must prevail."

"Upset? I'm not upset. I'm outraged. I'm going to write an article about police incompetence and miscarriages of justice. It will be the leader in tomorrow's *Clarion*."

"Sir," Burnell urged Cruickshank. "I think it would be prudent for someone to explain the situation to Mrs. Longdon."

The assistant commissioner clapped him on shoulder. "Sound idea, Burnell. I'll leave the matter in your capable hands." He glanced at his watch. "I…I have a meeting."

He bolted out of the room, nearly colliding with Emmeline. She stalked after him, hurling questions at his retreating back. He ignored her and scurried off like a fox who had a pack of hounds nipping at its heels.

Gregory hooked an elbow around the back of his chair. "It stirs the soul to see such an intrepid leader. The Met must be bursting with pride."

"Coward," Burnell muttered under his breath.

Emmeline saw her husband through the open doorway. "Gregory."

"Mrs. Longdon," the constable called, as he hurried after her. "You are not permitted in the interview room."

Burnell waved him off. "It's all right, Harris. You can go back to your duties."

The constable shot him a grateful look and was gone.

Emmeline threw her arms around Gregory's neck. "Are you all right?"

He caressed her hair and pressed a kiss to her cheek. "Steady on, darling. I'm fine."

She drew back, her dark gaze searching his face to ascertain whether this was truly the case. Once she was satisfied, she rounded on Burnell and Finch. "This is utter nonsense. You know Gregory is being framed. He surrendered the diamonds to you of his own volition. Why would he then come back to steal them? And from the evidence store no less. It boggles the mind." Her chest heaved with fury. "He's not a thief."

Burnell and Finch traded a doubtful look, but wisely chose not to argue the point in her present mood.

"Emmeline, be reasonable," Philip counseled. "Superintendent Burnell and Sergeant Finch are just as baffled as we are. We must allow them to do their jobs."

Belatedly, Gregory extended a hand to Philip. "Thank you for bringing Emmy." Philip inclined his head.

Emmeline took a deep breath. "I'm sorry, Superintendent, and Sergeant Finch. My nerves are a bit raw. I'm still shaken by what happened at the hotel."

Two vertical lines appeared between Gregory's brow as he studied her more closely. "How did you get that bruise on your temple? What happened with Zorkin?"

She cast a glance at Philip out of the corner of her eye and he nodded. She turned back to confront the expectant gazes of her husband and the two detectives.

Her fingers lightly touched her temple. "I must have hit my head when I fainted."

"Since when do you faint? I'll throttle Zorkin, if he laid a hand on you."

She gave a sad smile. "You don't have to defend my honor. He didn't molest me. In fact, I didn't speak to him at all. Zorkin was murdered."

"Ahem." Philip cleared his throat. "Zorkin committed suicide."

Burnell raised an eyebrow.

"Oh, for heaven's sake," she groused. "It's only us now. We don't have to maintain the charade."

Philip sighed and went to shut the door. She gave a nod of approval and proceeded to tell them everything that occurred from the instant she entered the Clermont, culminating in the gruesome discovery of Zorkin's body stuffed into his hold all.

"A rational person would say this was Kozlov leaving his calling card. But no, MI5 in its infinite wisdom has determined that Zorkin committed suicide." Her gaze raked over the faces of her captive audience. "Can anyone tell me how a man commits suicide and then manages to zip himself into a bag? Perhaps if Houdini were still alive, he could enlighten us."

"Emmeline, this is the way it has to be," Philip asserted. "You can't print a word to the contrary. Our relations with the Russians are already strained. The last thing we need is an international incident. If Ilya Zorkin wants to exact revenge on Kozlov, that's his paternal prerogative. But he can do so on Russian soil."

"Hmph" was her dissatisfied retort.

"Acheson is right," Gregory pointed out. "The ongoing feud between Zorkin and Kozlov is not the UK's concern."

Burnell and Finch nodded their agreement.

"Now to get back to our current problem," the superintendent remarked. He fixed his stare on Gregory.

"Oliver, I didn't steal the diamonds."

"No, I don't believe you did. The whole thing was too clumsy."

"You're far too cunning to leave one hundred million pounds in gems in the boot of your car," Finch chimed in. "We were meant to find the diamonds. Someone needs a distraction and decided the best way was to throw suspicion on you."

"Then, it must be Honeysett," Emmeline ventured. "Snowdrop has been exposed. It's pointless to hide anymore. His only option is to abandon his life here in the UK and run. He needs money, though. Enter the Galleon Egg. If he can sell it, he'll have wealth beyond his wildest dreams. But first, he has to get his hands on it. While the police are focused on Gregory and the diamonds, Honeysett has all the time in the world to retrieve the Fabergé egg without having to look over his shoulder."

"That's all quite plausible," Philip observed, "but it doesn't help us. We have no idea where Colefax hid the egg."

Her mouth curled into a Cheshire cat grin. "But *I* do. Peter told me that Colefax has a chalet in Switzerland on Lake Thun. Peter said it was his sanctuary. I'd wager the Crown Jewels that's where the egg is."

"I think Her Majesty would take umbrage at you gambling with the nation's treasure," Philip countered.

Her smile broadened. "The end justifies the means. Peter said that Colefax gave him a key to the house. Philip, since MI5 is overseeing the case, perhaps you can get the key. Then Gregory and I can pop over to—"

"You and Longdon are not going anywhere," Burnell intoned.

Emmeline's molten scowl would have left a weaker man charred beyond recognition. The superintendent was made of sterner stuff. His glacial air of command doused her fiery protest before the first ember had a chance to kindle.

He raised a finger. "No." The single word ricocheted around the room like a bullet. "First of all, you are civilians with no legal authority. Honeysett is desperate, which makes him irrational and dangerous. Who knows what you would be walking into. And second, Longdon is suspected of a crime. In the eyes of the law, he is a flight risk. Therefore, he remains here under the Met's watchful eye until we can sort this mess. Do I make myself clear?"

She drew a ragged breath and made a supreme effort to tamp down her anger. "Gregory did not commit any crime.

We *all* agreed a few minutes ago that Honeysett framed him."

"That is mere conjecture at this stage. The evidence tells a different story. I must follow the law. I can't make exceptions."

"But—"

"Emmy," Gregory admonished softly. "You know Oliver is right. How would it look?"

"That means Honeysett has won. He's ensured that we're stuck here, while he jets off to Switzerland. He's going to get away scot free. Doesn't that bother any of you?"

"We're only guessing that Colefax took the Fabergé egg to Switzerland. Zorkin could have been wrong."

"Well, we won't know for certain unless we go to Switzerland."

"It's out of the question. Longdon stays."

She opened her mouth to say something and then snapped it shut. Her livid expression transformed into one of sly smugness before their eyes, filling their hearts with trepidation. Her temper they could handle. Her wild imagination was terrifying to behold.

"Superintendent Burnell, I apologize for my outburst. I do see that you are bound by the law." Burnell inclined his head, but he was not fooled by her *volte-face*. "Anger pushed reason aside for a moment. However now that I've had time to reflect upon the matter, I understand that the proper authorities must pursue Honeysett. Therefore, I have come up with a solution." She paused for a beat. "Philip could come with me to Switzerland, since Gregory must remain in custody *temporarily*. It's the perfect compromise. Don't you agree?"

Chapter 26

No one agreed with her practical solution. *Hmph, men.* Did she really expect a different reaction? No, not really. But it had been worth a try.

Ooh, why were they tying her hands? She had done some digging and found out that Colefax had returned from Switzerland two days before his death. He was there one night. Who goes to Switzerland and stays only one day? The logical deduction was that he went to hide the Galleon Egg, until he could make arrangements to sell it.

The one spot of good news was that Burnell had released Gregory that morning. Further investigation had revealed that Honeysett had been at the station yesterday afternoon on the pretext of trying to interview Rossiter again. He was shown the door. However shortly afterward, CCTV cameras had caught him breaking into Gregory's Jaguar. That was sufficient evidence for the Met to offer Gregory its profound apology and to happily see him on his way.

She was relieved. She had made herself sick with worry and consequently hadn't slept a wink all night. Her stomach was still churning, but that was likely because she had been so consumed with the problem of Honeysett that she hadn't eaten anything again. She didn't need food, though. Another stiff cup of coffee would sustain her. It would also stimulate her brain cells.

Where was Honeysett? She had rung MI6 pretending to seek an interview. She was advised that neither the agency nor Honeysett would be issuing a statement to the press at this time or in the near future. All inquiries must be directed to MI5, which, of course, had in place the same noncommittal policy. The typical runaround.

Well, two can play at the game. She snatched up the phone to call Philip. She intended to wheedle as much information out of him as she could. Then, she would come up with a plan of attack and sod off to anyone who disapproved.

The phone rang once. "Good morning, Mr. Acheson's office." Pamela had answered, although it was Philip's direct line.

"Hello, Pamela. It's Emmeline Kirby. May I speak to Philip?"

"I'm afraid not. Mr. Acheson cleared his diary. He will be out of town for the next few days. He was asked to accompany the Foreign Secretary on his European mission to discuss further Russian sanctions."

Emmeline tapped her fingers on her desk. *I'll kill him.*

"This is rather unexpected. Where are the talks being held?" *As if I didn't know.*

"I'm not at liberty to disclose that information because of the delicate nature of the matter. Mr. Acheson gave me strict instructions not to speak to the press."

"Uh, huh. The entire Fourth Estate or just me?" Then, she softened her tone. It was not Pamela's fault. "I'm sorry. It's unfair to place you in an untenable position."

"Thank you for understanding. If I can help in any other

way…" Her sentence trailed off.

"No, that's all right. Bye."

She dropped the receiver back in the cradle. After seething for several seconds, she grabbed the phone again and called the political editor.

"Sam, hi. I seem to have misplaced the press release on the Foreign Secretary's European trip. If I recall correctly, the talks are being held in Switzerland."

"Yes, Bern. I have Arthur covering it. Is there a problem?"

"Bern, that's right. No problem. Thanks very much." She hung up before he became too curious about her sudden interest.

Bern validated her suspicions. Peter had said Colefax's chalet was located on Lake Thun, a train ride away from Bern. Unfortunately, he didn't have a chance to tell her which town. So what did she know about Colefax? He was the sporty type and loved skiing. A frisson slithered down her spine, when she remembered Peter's story about Colefax engineering his cousin's skiing accident. She shook her head as if to physically dispel that disturbing image.

When she had accompanied Nigel to Colefax's house, there had been a wall covered with photographs. She remembered one was of a chalet at the edge of a wood. A meadow swept down to a turquoise lake that sparkled at sunset. That must be it. But *where* precisely was it located? It could be in any of a dozen towns between Thun and Interlaken. Of course, the photo didn't have a caption with the name of the chalet. That would have been far too easy. And now with MI5 in charge of Colefax's murder, she had no way of getting back into Colefax's house to look through his papers.

She suddenly recalled her last conversation with Peter.

He called it his 'little Alpine flower.' He went there when he wanted to escape London.

"Little Alpine flower," she repeated aloud. "I wonder."

Edelweiss was the Swiss national flower. It grew in the mountains. Could Colefax's hideaway be called the Chalet Edelweiss?

She tapped away at her keyboard and held her breath. She wanted to scream for joy, when her search unearthed a magazine article from 2007 that featured a three-page color spread entitled, "The Charming Chalets of the Swiss Alps." There was a photo of a Chalet Edelweiss on Lake Thun. It was taken from a different angle, but it was indeed the same chalet. The article said that it was in the town of Merligen, which was near Interlaken. The owner was listed as the Lashbrook Corporation. But that didn't mean anything. It could be an offshore shell company that Colefax used to conceal his investments.

Did Honeysett know about the chalet?

The insistent peal of the phone jarred her from these speculations. She didn't recognize the number. Perhaps, it was someone calling with a tip for a story.

"Hello, Emmeline Kirby. *The Clarion.*"

"You said…I need…help," a raspy female voice stammered. The words were slurred as if the woman were drunk.

"Madam, this is the *Clarion* newspaper. I suggest you dial Nine Nine Nine, if this is an emergency."

She was about to hang up, but the woman pleaded with her, "Em-meline, please…help me. He's in the loo…but he'll be…back in a minute. I think…he drugged me."

Emmeline sat up straight in her chair. "Who is this?"

The silence stretched for so long, she thought they had been disconnected. "Meredith… Honeysett. We met…"

Blood thundered in her ears. "Yes, yes, I remember, Meredith. Has your husband hurt you?"

"No, just…drugged my coffee. I didn't realize. He's very angry. Not making sense. I'm…frightened. Cleared out our bank account. He said…said that they wouldn't look for a married couple. Left last night…Eurostar."

Another excruciating pause.

"Meredith, are you in Paris?"

"My head feels heavy." She gave a great yawn. "So sleepy. Have to switch soon. Going to…Oh, he's coming back…He threw my mobile in the…rubbish bin. Didn't want the police to trace us, he said. Nice man let me call…Shh, secret…have to go…"

"Train to where?" Emmeline shouted.

She strained to listen because the other woman had neglected to end the call. Meredith was definitely in Paris. In the background, she heard an announcement about an arriving train. Meredith was at Gare de Lyon. The mobile's owner must have realized that the line was still open and terminated the call.

Honeysett was on the run and he had dragged his wife along as cover. Gare de Lyon. Trains to and from Switzerland, Italy, Germany, and Spain passed through the station. She checked the timetables. A train was leaving at seven-fifteen that evening and its final destination was…*Bern, Switzerland*. It would arrive at ten twenty-six in Basel, where a change was required. That train was scheduled to depart half an hour later and would reach Bern just before midnight.

She leaped from her chair. This gave them a narrow window.

Since Philip was on the ground in Bern, she called to warn him about Honeysett. In his official capacity, he could alert his counterparts at the Federal Intelligence Service (FIS), Switzerland's main intelligence agency, as well as the local police and Interpol.

Damn. It went straight to voicemail. She had no choice but to leave a message and hope he would have enough time to act.

Next, she rang Jeremy, the editor-in-chief, and told him that she had a hot lead on the Colefax story and would have to go to Switzerland. Time was of the essence, and she couldn't go into detail. He'd have to trust her. She said that she'd likely be back by the end of the week. "I'll call you tomorrow with an update. Save the leader on the front page. I promise it will be explosive."

"I expect brilliant copy."

"Have I ever disappointed you?" was her parting rejoinder.

The only thing left was Gregory. She took a deep breath and steeled herself. Her husband was not going to like what she proposed to do.

She sighed and picked up her mobile. Best to have it done with.

"Hello, darling," she greeted him, injecting an extra dose of heartiness into her voice. "I hope you're not the worse for wear, after the unpleasant episode at Scotland Yard."

"The Met's accommodations fell far short of five-star, but a shower and change of clothes erased any lingering traces. Oliver was a brick. However, I told you all this earlier."

"Yes, of course you did. I was merely checking to see—"

He cut across her. "Emmy, whatever you're plotting, forget it."

"Why would you think I'm plotting anything?"

"Because your imagination is a vast landscape of alarming ideas."

"That's highly insulting. I should divorce you."

"Never. You'd miss me too much. Admit that I'm right. Now, out with it."

"I admit nothing. We can have a proper row later. Just listen."

In a breathless rush, she proceeded to explain that Colefax had made a quick jaunt to Switzerland days before his death and how she had determined that he owned Chalet Edelweiss. She concluded with the disturbing call from Meredith.

"Gregory, she's in trouble. Even if Honeysett hasn't resorted to physical violence, he's irrational. He must be stopped. If he's pushed too far, he won't hesitate to kill again. The Galleon Egg must be at the chalet. He'll vanish, if he gets his hands on it. We can't allow that to happen."

"*We* don't have to do anything. I'm glad you had the presence of mind to call Acheson. Let the authorities handle it."

"It may be hours before Philip has an opportunity to listen to my message. After all, he's in Bern with the diplomatic delegation. The discussions could take hours. By then, it may be too late to mobilize. We have to see this through to end. Besides, I'm the only one who knows where Colefax's chalet is," she pointed out triumphantly.

"That's easily remedied. I'll inform Villiers and he'll pass it on to the Swiss."

She curled her hand into a fist. "After Honeysett's attempt to frame you, I would think you'd want to be there when he is arrested."

"Emmy, this is dangerous."

"Precisely. But we know what we're walking into. I could never forgive myself if something happened to Meredith."

"We may be too late anyway. They're halfway to Switzerland. It would take us at least a day to get there."

This gave her a glimmer of hope. Because she knew that in his heart of hearts Gregory was as keen as she was to see Honeysett pay for his crimes as well as recover the Fabergé egg.

She crossed her fingers, allowing the silence to stretch out for several minutes.

"You've flipped your lid. You're absolutely crackers."

She smiled. She had won.

He sighed. "I'll ring Villiers."

"And I've reconsidered the divorce. I'll keep you. For the time being."

"That's just as well as," he observed cheekily. "There isn't another man on earth who has the courage or the stamina to do battle with Boudica of the Fourth Estate."

Chapter 27

In the end, Gregory's powers of persuasion and charm chipped away, brick by brick, at Villiers's wall of intractability. The deputy director of MI5 reluctantly agreed to allow Gregory and Emmeline to go to Switzerland. He would have his secretary make their travel arrangements. They would fly to Bern and then take the train to Interlaken. She would book a hotel in Interlaken for them. However—with Villiers there was always a however, nothing was ever straightforward—they were to remain in Interlaken until Acheson arrived. They were not, under *any* circumstance, to go to Colefax's chalet *alone*. Acheson and the Federal Intelligence Service (FIS) would place the chalet under surveillance. If Honeysett or his wife made contact, they were to immediately inform Acheson. Either husband and wife abided by these conditions or Villiers would have them taken to a safe house, where they would be placed under twenty-four-hour guard, until Honeysett was apprehended. Thus, Emmeline would lose her scoop.

Gregory readily acceded to all these directives,

although he had other plans to catch their prey.

Meanwhile, Fortune was smiling upon them because French rail workers, perpetually disgruntled and seeking a wage increase, had decided to launch a forty-eight-hour strike. It had been set to start at midnight, but trains came to a halt all over France at ten o'clock. Consequently, Honeysett and Meredith were stuck in Paris until the strike ended because the airports were a nightmare. In any event, Honeysett risked greater exposure if he opted to fly to Bern. Therefore, Emmeline and Gregory would already be in Switzerland, waiting.

℘℘℘

Emmeline and Gregory's flight had arrived in Bern at six o'clock the next morning. They hadn't checked any baggage, so they went directly to passport control. As it was early, the queue was relatively short and they were outside hailing a taxi within half an hour. The morning traffic was light. The trip to the train station took only seventeen minutes. Before they left London, they had spoken to Philip. He had purchased tickets for them on the 8:04 SBB, or the Swiss Federal Railways, double-decker train to Interlaken. They could collect them at the ticket office. However, he wouldn't be able to join them until the following day. He was already coordinating with FIS. He also had alerted the Sûreté, the French national police, and Direction générale de la sécurité extérieure, or DGSE, the French foreign intelligence service. They were conducting raids across Paris and its suburbs, but thus far Honeysett remained a ghost.

Philip's plea for Emmeline and Gregory to return home fell on deaf ears, so here they were comfortably ensconced in their seats on the train. Soon after they left Bern, the train was rolling past the picturesque countryside. Undulating meadows, which must be a lush emerald green in summer, now wore an alabaster gown of snow stained with red claret as the sun's feathery lashes fluttered opened and woke the world to a new day with endless possibilities. Emmeline pressed her cheek to the window and imagined the wind was scattering sweet-nothings in the sooty half-gloom of the sleep-swollen hills. Low-lying clouds dallied over chalets and farmland like the smoldering ashes of last night's dreams. As they approached the town of Thun where they would make a short stop, the wind at last nudged away the pristine wisps of mist to reveal the rugged, snow-capped Alps. The train runs along Lake Thun, whose cobalt waters shimmered. The views became even more dramatic, leaving Emmeline breathless the closer they drew to Interlaken, which meant "between the lakes." The town sits on the narrow strip of land separating Lake Thun from Lake Brienz. She could see that the enchanting vistas had made as deep an impression on Gregory as it did her.

When they pulled into the station in Interlaken, husband and wife were eager to explore the town. It was ironic that murder and espionage had brought them to this serene haven. She sighed. Sadly, in beauty there was danger.

She pushed this thought aside on the short walk from the station to Hotel Chalet Swiss, which was set several streets back up a slight slope from Hoheweg Boulevard, the main street, in the center of the town. The hotel was a traditional alpine chalet. A small garden flanked the entrance on either side. In summer, roses would be in bloom. Now, they enjoyed their winter slumber. She tilted her head back to gaze at the building. She imagined the flower boxes on the three balconies above the door brimming with scarlet, white, pink, and magenta geraniums and petunias in the summer months.

The neatly dressed receptionist greeted them politely, if a bit stiffly. Everything was in order with their reservation. Although it was early, their room was ready and they could go up immediately. She handed Gregory the key and an envelope.

"Mr. Longdon, a gentleman left this for you."

Emmeline craned to see the envelope.

Longdon was printed across the front in neat block capitals.

He murmured his thanks, tucked the envelope in his inside breast pocket, and they climbed the stairs to their room. Emmeline dropped her bag beside the bed and crossed to the window to savor the view of the majestic snowy peaks of the Eiger, Mönch, and Jungfrau, a vast limestone mountain wall where glaciers and frozen lakes cling to the ridged slopes. She couldn't tear her gaze away.

"Emmy," Gregory called.

Reluctantly, she turned her back on Mother Nature's chef d'oeuvre and came to his side.

He flapped a piece of paper in the air. "This is from Hans Troxler. He's with the FIS, Swiss intelligence. Troxler will be overseeing things until Acheson arrives. He warns us to be on our guard because most likely we're being watched."

She grimaced. "Mmm. Somehow I don't feel flattered when our choice of admirers is between the Kremlin's minions and Kozlov."

Gregory grasped her shoulders and looked her directly in the eye. "We can go home right now. There's no shame."

She placed her hands on his chest and held his gaze. "And miss all the fun? Certainly not. We've come this far. I'm going to see this story through to the end."

He kissed the tip of her nose and then rested his chin on

top of her head. "I was merely checking. But I knew once you had set your mind to something, there's no turning back." He broke their embrace and looked at the paper again. "Troxler wants to meet with us somewhere public. He suggests that we take a boat ride to Thun tomorrow. He says we can catch the boat at the docks in Interlaken West. The first boat in the morning leaves at 10:40. The trip takes about two hours. He'll make contact on the boat or in Thun, once he determines that it's safe."

"I can't think of a more delightful way to kill two birds with one stone."

He gave her a pointed look. "A poor choice of words for a journalist. Hopefully no more killing will be involved from this point on."

"Well, no. We've seen far too much of that in the past week. But there's no harm in wishing for a dash of excitement to add some spice to our daily routine."

He slipped his arms around her waist and drew her against his body. "Mrs. Longdon, are you saying that you find married life dull?"

She arched an eyebrow. "One should always strive for improvement."

"Oh, I see." He dipped his head closer and whispered in her ear. "Since I appear to be woefully deficient, perhaps you can instruct me in the finer arts of marital relations."

Her lips parted, but the playful rejoinder she prepared to toss back was smothered by his ardent kiss. They tumbled onto the bed and soon all thoughts of spies, murder, diamonds, and a priceless Fabergé egg were a distant memory. There was plenty of time for trouble tomorrow.

❧❧

After enjoying a late lunch at a restaurant in a rustic wooden chalet tucked off a side street, Gregory said that he would go purchase their boat tickets for the next day. When Emmeline offered to go with him, he suggested that she do some shopping along Hoheweg Boulevard because he had to take care of some Symington's business as well and she'd be bored to tears watching him make calls. He assured her it would only take a couple of hours. Then, he gave her a peck on the cheek and sauntered off.

He's up to something, she mused. But she couldn't figure out what it could be. Although she longed to follow him, she wouldn't. Aside from love, a marriage must have trust as its foundation otherwise it would crumble. He would tell her, eventually. She hoped.

Chapter 28

The next day as they stepped onto the steamship, white-gold strands of sunlight dangled from the cerulean sky and stirred the frigid marrow of the air. Emmeline and Gregory were among the handful of brave souls who chose to remain on the outer deck for the entire journey up Lake Thun. It would have been a crime to miss the quaint fishing villages and historic castles rolling past, or the romantic bay of Spiez. They watched shadows tumble down gleaming slopes and chase one another into valleys carved out long ago by the glaciers. Their senses surrendered to the sensual beauty of the snow-capped Alps reflected in the aquamarine waters of the sleeping lake.

The keep and lake tower of Oberhofen Castle came into view. The impressive castle sits right at the shore in Thun and was built in the thirteenth century. One of the towers is literally in the water. Emmeline had read that some of the rooms in the castle are in the Gothic and Baroque styles. The castle is a museum today, but unfortunately it was closed during the winter. She would have liked to have visited it.

They would soon be disembarking and still Troxler had not approached them.

Gregory saw Emmeline's frown and threw his arm around her shoulders. "Don't worry, darling. His note said that he'd either make contact on the boat or in the town. He's probably being cautious."

"What if something happened to him?"

"He's a trained intelligence officer. He's prepared for all eventualities." He drew her closer and gave her shoulders a reassuring squeeze. "Let's just enjoy Thun, shall we?"

She nodded, although she remained uneasy. What if Honeysett had somehow managed to elude the French authorities and was here in Switzerland?

As the boat drew up to the dock, she cast a surreptitious glance around the boat, as well as toward the shore. Nothing seemed odd. In fact, they soon lost themselves among the romantic cobblestone streets and raised promenades of the Old Town, which was in a festive mood. Thun Castle, with its four white towers high up on a hill, loomed over the town. They wandered through the Christmas market on Waisenhausplatz and browsed at the myriad small shops on different levels. They admired the traditional rows of old houses along the embankment. After a leisurely lunch at a café, they wended their way back to the dock weighed down with some gifts for Emmeline's grandmother, Maggie and Philip and their sons, as well as Pamela.

With her elbows leaning on the railing and her face turned to the brisk wind, Emmeline ventured, "I wonder if this was a test by Troxler to see whether he could trust us."

Gregory pressed his shoulder against hers, as he stared out over the water. "That's quite possible. Villiers let slip that Switzerland has become a haven for espionage activity in recent years. Apparently, Russian agents are running rampant after a series of expulsions in Europe. Villiers said that many are what's known in intelligence circles as covert source handlers, who are trained to recruit, exploit, and manipulate targets working in organizations of interest to garner sensitive information."

Her head whipped round. "Ooh, do tell. This will be the focus of my next article. One of these covert source handlers probably recruited Honeysett, unless he was so disillusioned he offered his services to the Russians."

He rolled his eyes toward the heavens. "I should have kept my mouth shut," he muttered under his breath. "Why did I have to marry a woman whose blood begins to race at the mere mention of crime and espionage?"

She swatted his arm. "I'm a Renaissance woman. I have many interests. To be a well-rounded individual, I must keep abreast of current events. It's my job, after all. And this juicy little nugget of information is screaming to be explored in greater detail."

A resigned sigh escaped his lips. His gaze snaked back to the riparian landscape, where the silvery-white embers of the afternoon sun became caught in the aquamarine netting of liquid silk.

"Beautiful isn't it?" a man beside him asked. He had a German accent, but his English was flawless. "It is hard to believe that these waters hold a secret."

He was a tall, slim man with chestnut hair threaded with silver and watchful brown eyes. Emmeline guessed he must be in his late forties.

Her curiosity was piqued. "I'm fascinated by secrets." She waved a hand at the water. "Tell me what hers are?"

The corners of the man's eyes crinkled, when he smiled. "I don't usually have such an eager audience. Most of my friends tell me I talk too much." His gaze strayed to the water. "Although Switzerland was neutral during the Second World War, it accumulated munitions, artillery shells, hand grenades, ordinary bullets and other ordnance in the event of an invasion by Germany or Fascist Italy. Thankfully, this never came to pass. Some caches included matériel seized from trains crossing from Germany into Italy in violation of neutrality agreements. Well until 1964, we disposed of the munitions by dumping them into at least four Alpine lakes. Lake Thun is 700 feet deep in places and provides a watery grave for over 9,000 tons of munitions."

Emmeline's eyes widened. "I wasn't aware of that fact. I've always been interested in history," she said, "because it's important to know the past so that we can understand how things evolved to the way they are today."

"Very true, Mrs. Longdon. Or should I say Miss Kirby?"

Gregory stiffened and placed his body so that he blocked her from this stranger.

The man put his hands in the air. "Please don't be alarmed. I'm Hans Troxler. I had to be sure you were who say you are." He extended a hand toward Gregory.

Gregory clasped it. "Yes, of course. I said as much to my wife. You can't be too careful."

Emmeline stepped around Gregory. Troxler gave her an apologetic look, as he proffered his hand. His handshake was firm and confident.

"To business." He cast a glance around the deck, but they didn't have to be concerned about anyone overhearing their conversation. The biting wind had sent the other passengers scurrying for the warmth of the cabin. "Honeysett remains at large. I must warn you there was a report this morning of a man and a woman in Bern fitting the descriptions of Honeysett and his wife."

Emmeline clutched Gregory's sleeve. "How did he

manage to avoid detection and leave Paris?"

One of Troxler's shoulders twitched in a resigned shrug. "Sadly, the only conclusion is that he had help either from someone in the Sûreté or DGSE. I checked with my colleagues. There have been no sightings of Honeysett in Interlaken. Yet." The word was carried off by the wind but seemed to echo ominously in the space between them. "As you can imagine, the situation is rather fluid. However, we still have time to plan. Although my superiors briefed me before I left Bern, I would appreciate it if you could provide all the details so that I know what to expect."

Emmeline and Gregory took it in turns to recount the long, twisting saga that began in Madrid with the red diamonds, meandered to London and the murders of Colefax and Zorkin, and now found them in this fairytale landscape waiting for a traitor and killer.

Troxler scraped a hand over his jaw, when they had finished. His angular features were pinched with concern. "Honeysett's wife complicates matters." He looked them both directly in the eye. "To be honest, I am not happy with your involvement either. Your presence here is ill-advised. Honeysett is a dangerous man with nothing lose."

Emmeline tossed her chin in the air. "We have no intention of leaving. We are an integral part of this investigation, if you think about it. We continued to dig and pieced together the evidence, while Scotland Yard, MI5. and MI6 chose to waste time bickering with one another over jurisdiction."

Gregory gave a disapproving shake of his head because he was far from enamored with the prospect of her being in the throes of peril yet again. However, they had vowed to stand by one another through better or worse and thick and thin. That's why he would follow her to the ends of the earth no matter how vexing her ideas because she was his life.

"Naturally, my wife and I will not do anything to jeopardize the hunt for Honeysett. But we are staying to ensure that justice is served and will help in any way possible."

Emmeline beamed at him. He couldn't help but return her smile. Her adoring look meant the world to him.

Troxler blinked. He was momentarily speechless. At last, he said, "I have never met a couple like you. I can't decide whether you are noble or reckless."

"Consider us like a good single-malt Scotch. Once one acquires the taste, one can appreciate its finer notes," Gregory retorted.

Troxler threw his head back and laughed.

By the time they arrived back in Interlaken, he had given them his card with his mobile number and extracted a promise that they would not chase after Honeysett on their own. They were to ring him *at once*. If Meredith contacted Emmeline again, she was to ring him *at once*. If Honeysett approached them, they were to ring him *at once*. He prided himself on his professionalism and spotless career, therefore he refused to have the lives of two civilians on his conscience. They murmured solemn pledges not to do anything without apprising him, which left him far from reassured.

His brows knit together. Did that mean that they would do so before or after the fact?

As the crew tied up the boat to the jetty, Troxler informed them that he had Chalet Edelweiss under surveillance. "No one can enter or leave the premises without being seen."

His parting words were "Be on your guard." Then, he strode toward the gangway without a backward glance. They had agreed to disembark separately to keep up the pretense that they were strangers, who happened to strike up a casual conversation on the boat.

Although they couldn't have asked for a more idyllic day on the lake and in Thun, Honeysett's ghost trailed in their footsteps. A flutter in the pit of her stomach told Emmeline that he was here in Interlaken. Watching and waiting.

Her suspicion was confirmed when they opened the door to their room and found it had been ransacked.

⁊⊃⁊⊃

"You have what I want," Honeysett's hoarse voice growled in Gregory's ear. He put the call on speakerphone and held his mobile so that Emmeline could hear as well. "No one else has to die. Colefax was a bastard. He had it coming. Just give me the egg and I'll disappear for good. You're the only one who could have stolen it, Longdon."

Emmeline couldn't restrain her tongue any longer. "You'll never get away with this, Honeysett. The Swiss police know you're here. The noose is tightening around you. Let Meredith go and give yourself up."

"Don't shed a tear about my wife. She's fine," he sneered. "On the other hand, Villiers's boy Acheson is not as pretty as he was when he left London. I wonder if his wife knows he has a soft spot for you. All it took was a desperate message from you and he was bolting out of his conference. He's been our passport thus far. It would be a pity to kill him, after he's been so useful. But that's up to you."

She drew in a sharp breath and her gaze shot to Gregory's face. A muscle in his jaw pulsed with tension.

Honeysett was chuckling. "I thought that might capture your attention. Now if you'd like him to return home in one piece, I suggest you turn over the egg.”

"I must say your decorating talents leave a great deal to be desired,” Gregory quipped. *“Chacun à son goût* is all well and good, but our room is in quite a state. I have a good mind to ask for our money back.”

Emmeline punched his arm and mouthed, “Don’t antagonize him.”

"Put a sock in it, Longdon,” Honeysett snarled.

"You needn’t get shirty about it. I believe you were about to issue an ultimatum. It probably ends in ‘or else.’ These things generally do.”

She gave him a pointed look and he patted her arm, but she was far from soothed.

The silence stretched out for several long seconds. Then, Meredith’s voice came on the line. “Please do as Matthew demands,” she implored. There was a tremor in her voice. “I’m…frightened. He’s liable to do…anything. Don’t upset him anymore.”

"Are you all right, Meredith?” Emmeline asked.

Honeysett was the one who answered instead. “You’ve wasted enough time. I want the egg. Or someone gets hurt. I’ll start with your friend.”

"You win,” Gregory conceded. “It was too dangerous to bring the egg here to the hotel. It’s still hidden at Chalet Edelweiss in Merligen. I was planning to go back tomorrow to retrieve it. Why don’t you meet me at the house at midnight and we’ll make the exchange: the Galleon Egg for Acheson and your wife?”

"I’ll be there.”

Then, Honeysett severed the connection.

The tension in Emmeline’s muscles uncoiled slightly, as Gregory called Troxler.

She admired how he had cleverly maneuvered Honeysett into a trap. Troxler’s men were already in place. At midnight, their prey would be ensnared and they could all breathe easy once more.

Of course, nothing in life was ever that simple.

Chapter 29

The Moon's voluptuous golden form dozed in her celestial bed of cobalt cloud as Gregory guided the hired car along the curving Seestrasse, which took them along the Aare River to Merligen. It was a short drive from Interlaken. The plan was for them to arrive an hour before the rendezvous at Chalet Edelweiss, where Colefax had stashed all the secrets that were responsible for his death.

An icy tendril slithered down Emmeline's spine. What were they going to find?

She cast a sideways glance at Gregory, who hadn't uttered a word since they left their hotel. His profile was half in shadow and his eyes were fixed on the road. His fingers were gripped tightly around the steering wheel, stretching the fine leather of his gloves across his knuckles.

He must have sensed her scrutiny because he turned his head and gave her a wink. "Nearly there. Acheson is fine. Don't worry."

"You can't be sure of that. What if—"

"No, Emmy. No what ifs. Nothing can happen.

Troxler's men are watching. They will spring into action the instant he gives them the word."

She slumped back. "But we don't know where Colefax hid the Fabergé egg."

He reached out and blindly patted her hand. "All we have to do is stall."

Weighed down by the silence filling the car, questions swirled round her head.

"Why was Honeysett so convinced that you had the egg?"

"Hmm," he grunted distractedly, as he turned off the highway onto a local road.

"You didn't answer my question."

"What? No idea." He cut the ignition. "Oh, look. We're here."

Her eyes narrowed. She couldn't see the expression on his face, but she could feel him smiling.

He had his door open and one foot on the ground. "Come along, darling."

He had parked the car by the surrounding woods, which were plunged in a pool of onyx darkness. She squinted into the trees as she stepped out of the car and quietly pressed the door closed. She couldn't see Troxler's men. Her ears strained to listen for the sound of any human presence, but only the wind's sibilant sighs rustled the icy branches. Well, the whole point was for them not to be seen. Still, it made her uneasy. She tossed a last glance at the forlorn woods and hurried round the car to Gregory.

Silvered by the moon's caress, cobalt shadows flirted and danced upon the frosty air as they coaxed Emmeline and Gregory toward the chalet. It was not what she would have expected one of Britain's wealthiest men to own. Small and rustic, the wooden house seemed to be embedded in the landscape.

Gregory unlocked the door, whether it was with a key or by some other means, she didn't want to know. He went in and fumbled for a light switch and flicked it on. They found themselves in the living room, which had bare hardwood floors. The only furniture were a sofa bed nestled against one wall, a functional, square wooden table and chairs across from it, and a standing lamp tucked in the corner. A sliding glass door opened onto the balcony. The compact kitchen opened onto the living room.

Emmeline crossed to the sliding door and stepped out onto the balcony. It overlooked a meadow covered in an opalescent crust of ice that sloped down to Lake Thun. The untrammeled whiteness against the blue-black waters beyond made her feel as if she were suspended somewhere in time. She wished she could stay lost here forever. She reluctantly turned away from the view and stepped back inside to wait for a spy and murderer. She and Gregory conducted a quick search of the chalet, noting potential means of escape.

They were exploring the basement, where Colefax had built some shelves into one wall and created a rudimentary wine cellar, when they heard the floorboards on the balcony above creak.

They froze and held their breath. Another creak. Damn Honeysett. He was early.

Gregory grabbed Emmeline's arm and motioned with his chin for her to go out the sliding door. "Run around the house and go lock yourself in the car," he whispered. "Don't move until this over."

She stood on tiptoe and brought her lips close to his ear. "I'm not leaving you."

He shook her arm. "*Go.*"

"No, we do this together," she hissed.

He groaned inwardly at the wall of stubbornness that was his wife.

"Aren't you a bit old for hide-and-seek, Longdon?" Honeysett's voice floated down to them. "Stop being rude and come out to say hello."

Gregory pointed at the sliding door one last time, but Emmeline refused to budge.

He threw his hands in the air in resignation. "Fine. At the first sign of trouble, run as far and as fast as you can into the woods. Don't look back. Just run."

She hesitated for a fraction of a second before nodding in assent.

Slowly, they climbed the stairs. They found Honeysett standing in the middle of the living room, a nine-millimeter Beretta dangling from one hand while the other was clamped around Meredith's arm. Her hazel eyes darted around wildly. What sent a shudder through Emmeline's body was the fact that Philip was nowhere in sight.

"Ah, a family affair," Honeysett remarked facetiously. "I see we both can't leave home without the little woman."

Emmeline ignored this condescending comment and demanded, "Where's Philip?"

"One thing at a time." He took off the safety catch on his gun and leveled it at Gregory.

"The Galleon Egg."

"The deal was the egg for your wife and Acheson," Gregory replied calmly.

"Acheson is insurance until I can get out of the country. As for my loving wife"—his words were laced with venom as he flung her onto the sofa bed—"You're welcome to her. I have no use for her."

"You're a hunted man," Gregory pointed out. "How far do you think you'll get?"

"That's none of your concern. If you and your wife want to live to see another day, you'll get the egg *now*. I can't hang about here all night. After what I've been through, I deserve the egg." He huffed a bitter laugh. "It's my consolation prize."

"What you've been through?" Emmeline bristled. "You murdered two men to cover up the fact that you betrayed your country. And now, you've come here to claim the Galleon Egg as your reward? You're a cold-blooded thug."

Honeysett swung his arm in an arc to point the gun at her chest. "I thought you were in love with the truth." His hand trembled. "I can sue you for slander because you have your facts wrong, Miss Nosey Parker."

Gregory pushed Emmeline behind him, shielding her with his body. But she was having none of it and stepped around him.

"What do you mean?"

Honeysett laughed again. It was a harsh sound that scraped the ears. "Curiosity is like a disease with you, isn't it? Always poking your nose everywhere. Well, I wouldn't want you to *die* of curiosity. So, I'll tell you the sordid truth."

He lowered his voice conspiratorially and said, "I only killed Colefax. You want to know why?" It was a rhetorical question that did not require an answer. "Because he was sleeping with my wife."

Emmeline flicked a glance at Meredith, but Honeysett's voice drew her back. "That's right. Peas in a pod, those two. Both conniving, ruthless opportunists. He enjoyed rubbing it in my face, when I confronted him that night. He said that MI6 must be truly desperate to have recruited someone as woefully lacking in intelligence and competence. I wanted to wipe that smug smile off his face. All Colefax cared about was building his bloody hotel in Moscow. I told him I would do everything in my power to make sure that never happened. Then, he threatened to expose Snowdrop.

"And you couldn't have that, could you?" Gregory prodded.

"The shadow of Dad's betrayal has hounded me for most of my career. You don't know what it's like to have to live with something like that. To have to prove yourself day after day. It took years, but I had. Colefax would have ruined me because of Snowdrop." His voice dropped to barely a whisper. It was as if he was speaking to himself. "So many secrets had fallen into Russian hands because of Snowdrop and now it was going to come crashing down around my ears."

"You committed treason," Emmeline pointed out. "A double agent lives on borrowed time. It was bound to come out that you were spying for the Russians."

A pained expression clouded his eyes. "No, I wasn't. Snowdrop is the spy. My faithless wife, who stole intelligence and made it look as if I'm the traitor."

Emmeline's jaw dropped, as she gaped at Meredith.

The other woman smirked. "It was child's play."

She really should keep her mouth shut, Emmeline thought as her gaze strayed to Honeysett, whose jaw clenched.

A vein throbbed at his temples and a crimson flush crept up his cheeks, but he ignored her and went on with his story. "Colefax was sleeping with a spy, but he didn't care. He thought her Moscow connections could secure him permission to build his grand hotel. She was using him to keep an eye on her childhood friend Zorkin, who had the misfortune of bumping into her one day in Hatchards. Somewhere along the way, Colefax realized that she was never going to help him. As a practical businessman, he cut his losses and turned to someone who could get him what he wanted."

"Kozlov," Gregory murmured.

"Got it in one. Since he no longer needed sweet little Meredith anymore, Colefax said that he would see to it that Zorkin's evidence on Snowdrop reached my superiors at MI6. He pointed out that I was the unwitting leak and no one would ever believe that she and I weren't working together from the outset. He took great pleasure in stressing that it would take years, if ever, for the truth to come out. I wanted to destroy him. I hit him, and kept hitting him, until he wasn't laughing anymore. I have no remorse for what I did. Colefax deserved to die. Everyone was a commodity to him. He even served up his bosom mate Zorkin as an incentive to seal his odious deal with Kozlov. But Meredith is the one who signed Zorkin's death warrant. She made sure that whispers reached Kozlov that Zorkin was in hiding at the Clermont Victoria. One less problem she had to worry about. And here we are now in Colefax's cozy chalet."

The raw truth hung heavy upon the air, filling their lungs and suffocating them with its malevolence.

Gregory was the first to break the silence. "You have to turn yourself in, Honeysett. Let Acheson go and the authorities will be more lenient with you. I can have a quiet word with Villiers. You know that he wields tremendous influence in the corridors of Whitehall."

"We both know no one will risk their careers to help me. They don't want to be painted with the same brush of scandal. Give me the egg." He took a step closer and waved the gun in Gregory's face.

"No one else needs to get hurt." Gregory deliberately made his tone soft, cajoling.

The disgraced MI6 agent leered. "Oh, but you're wrong. Someone always gets hurt and someone always has to pay."

Without warning, his arm whipped out and he shot Meredith.

Chapter 30

eredith slumped back against the wall, her eyes wide with shock. A sinister red stain was spreading from hershoulder. She glanced down and put a hand to the wound. Blood was dribbling through her fingers.

Bile rose in Emmeline's throat and her stomach revolted. She was feeling lightheaded. She willed herself not to faint again. Gregory caught her arm and pulled her toward him. It was just as well. Her legs felt like water.

He put a hand up. "Let my wife go and we can discuss things calmly."

"No more talking," Honeysett snapped. "Give me the egg."

"I'm afraid that's out of the question," Troxler informed him matter-of-factly.

No one had heard him enter the chalet. He must have come up from the basement.

Emmeline squeezed her eyes shut and sagged against Gregory. "Oh, thank goodness."

Troxler strode into the living room, a gun gripped

tightly in his hand. His assessing gaze swept over Meredith's ashen face. "How bad?"

"I'm losing blood. I need a doctor." Her voice was hoarse.

Troxler grunted and then turned to Honeysett. "You've caused an awful lot of trouble."

The bullet found its target and pierced Honeysett's chest with a soft *thud*. He was dead before he hit the floor.

Emmeline drew in a sharp breath.

"Meredith, go to the car," Troxler ordered. "Longdon and I have some unfinished business."

The infamous Snowdrop lumbered to her feet and shuffled out of the chalet, one hand pressed to her wounded shoulder.

"No one was ever coming tonight, were they?" Gregory asked, although they all knew the answer. "Your mission was to extract her." His chin gestured to the door. "Are you even an FIS officer?"

Troxler shrugged nonchalantly. "Oh, yes, but I report to Moscow. Now, the Galleon Egg. It's part of Russia's cultural heritage and must be returned. I know you have it. I followed you here yesterday. It wasn't in your hotel room, so where did you hide it?"

Without taking his eyes off the spy, Gregory murmured out of the corner of his mouth, "Emmy, remember what I told you earlier in the basement? It's time."

He gave her a rough shove and then his fist whipped around, catching Troxler off guard and landing a hard blow to his jaw.

Another part of her brain took over and she plunged down the stairs to the basement, nearly tumbling as the groans of the grappling men drifted to her ears. The sliding door was stuck and she had to rattle it. Finally, it opened and she burst outside. Without a coat, the wind's gelid breath set her teeth chattering within seconds. Terror and worry about what was happening to Gregory almost made her turn back. But then, Troxler would have two of them. If she ran, she stood a chance of summoning help. So, she clambered the crumbling wooden fence. She slipped once or twice on the icy crust, but managed to keep herself upright as she dashed across the meadow toward the woods. The snow was deeper in a few spots, slowing her progress because she sank to her knees.

Her lungs burned and her breath was snatched from her in smoky wisps upon the air. A few more steps and she would be in the safety of the woods. Just a few more steps.

A strong hand clamped down on her shoulder, yanking her back. She landed awkwardly and it took a few seconds to catch her breath again. When she turned over, she found herself staring up at Troxler. Although half in shadow, his eyes glinted with naked rage. His nostrils flared with the exertion of the chase, puffing like a dragon in a children's story. Only this was cold, hard reality.

Tears pricked her eyelids. *Where was Gregory?*

She didn't have time to dwell on the disturbing possibilities because Troxler pulled her to her feet, nearly wrenching her arm out of its socket.

"Get up." His tone thrummed with savage ferocity.

He began dragging her across the snow. She couldn't keep pace and stumbled, falling face down and choking on a mouth full of snow. That didn't stop him. He grabbed the collar of her turtleneck and continued trudging forward heedless of the bumps to her body.

Finally, he stopped and drew her to her feet. They were at a boathouse at the edge of the lake. He took the gun from his waist and shoved into her ribs as he pushed her inside. Holding onto her arm, he found some heavy rope in a corner. He lashed her wrists together.

"It is rare for someone to have such pure appreciation

of nature. I saw it yesterday on the boat," he commented in a remarkably conversational tone, as he gathered some more rope and pulled over a heavy wooden crate, "Therefore, what could be a more appropriate final resting place, a watery grave with the sunken munitions to keep you company. No one will ever find your body."

Unbidden, her gaze shot to the lake, which she glimpsed through the open doorway. The lapping blue-black waters taunted her. He couldn't intend to toss her in? To leave her to die?

When she looked at Troxler again, his lips were drawn back in a lupine leer.

"You're mad. You'll never get away with this."

He snorted and pushed her down to the floor so that he could bind her legs.

No, a voice screamed inside her head.

One leg swung up, startling him off balance. She leaped up and tried to run, but he grabbed one ankle and she fell forward. She groaned as she landed hard on her right side. For a moment, she couldn't move. She wondered if she had broken a rib. He was tugging her by the ankle towards him inch by inch. She kicked out wildly and was satisfied when she heard the crunch of bone as her foot made contact with his nose. Troxler let out a howl and immediately released her leg.

She clumsily struggled to her knees, and then her feet, and bolted out the door. She barely had time to feel the crisp air on her cheeks, when he was on her. His large hands went around her throat, as he dragged her to the water's edge. She pummeled his chest with her bound fists and tried to catch her breath. He was trying to lift her. To throw her in the water. The tips of her fingers clutched at his arm. She thrashed with every ounce strength.

And then suddenly, the world tilted upside down and they were falling. The glacier waters were covering her head, filling her mouth and lungs. Gurgling, bubbling. She couldn't free her hands. She was sinking. Troxler was pushing her down, down, down.

Lake Thun is 700 feet deep in places.

She wanted to laugh hysterically. That was not a comforting fact.

Gregory.

She tried to claw her way back from the blackness enveloping her. Alas, oblivion's seductive embrace was too tempting to resist.

Chapter 31

Emmeline heard the murmur of male voices as if she were at the other end of a very, very long tunnel. Why did they insist on talking so loudly? Honestly, men could be so inconsiderate at times.

Where was she? She had no idea. Why was everything so dark? It took a while for this question to reach her brain. Ever so slowly, she came to the realization that her eyes were closed. Thank heavens for that. She was beginning to worry that she had suddenly gone blind. She concentrated, hard—beads of perspiration formed on her brow with the effort—and finally managed to open her eyes a tiny sliver.

She blinked several times to clear her vision. Everything started to sharpen into focus, both mentally and visually. She was on the sofa bed in Colefax's chalet. She had been bundled in several blankets, but she was still shivering. A wave of nausea washed over her and she retched all over the hardwood floor.

She put a hand to her mouth in embarrassment, as a balding man in his mid-sixties rushed over to her. "I'm sorry," she mumbled.

"Never mind," he instructed in French-accented English. "Can you sit up?"

She nodded. "*Bon.*" He helped her to rise.

"I am Dr. Darroze. Now please let me examine you." He poked and prodded, and listened to her heart with his stethoscope. He grunted. "Good news. No broken bones, but you may have some internal bleeding. You were also in the water for some time. I want to run some tests at the hospital."

"Is that really necessary? I feel all right."

The disapproving expression etched into the lines of his face told her that she had no choice in the matter. She dropped her chin to her chest and gave a resigned nod.

She put out a hand and clutched his wrist. "My…my husband." The words hung upon the air.

The doctor's features softened, and he patted her hand reassuringly. "Your husband is fine, madam. Only a few bruises."

A tear escaped the corner of her eye. "Thank goodness. Where—"

"Emmy." Gregory rushed to her side and dropped down beside her. "Darling." He raised an eyebrow at the doctor. "She's all right?"

Dr. Darozze nodded. "My preliminary examination reveals nothing broken, but I want to take her to the hospital for some tests. She was exposed to the cold and the water. There is a possibility she may develop pneumonia or bronchitis. I also want to make certain that there is no internal bleeding."

"I told the doctor I feel perfectly fine."

"You go," Gregory ordered.

"Listen to your husband." The doctor rose. "I will arrange for the ambulance. You have a few moments."

Gregory stood and extended a hand, murmuring his

thanks. Then, he sat down again and draped his arm around her shoulders. He pushed an errant curl away from her face.

She watched a swarm of uniformed and plainclothes officers huddled together. "Troxler?" she whispered.

"He's dead. He drowned. The FIS men arrived just as the two of you went into the water. Two dived in and pulled you out. Another five minutes and you would have met the same fate as Troxler." He pressed a kiss to her temple. "He knocked me out and left me for dead. That's why he came after you. For the rest of my life, I'll never forgive myself for putting you through that."

She rested her head against his chest. "And Meredith?"

He sighed. "She escaped. The Swiss issued an alert. They notified Interpol as well."

She waved a hand at the officers across the room. "How did the authorities get here so quickly?"

Gregory smiled. "They had a tip from a friend."

She tilted her head to look him in the eye. "What friend?"

"Ahem." A man cleared his throat as he sidled up to them. "Shame, Emmeline. That dip in the lake must have given you amnesia."

Her head whipped round at the familiar voice. "Philip." She assessed him from head to foot. "You're all right."

He bent down and gave her a peck on the cheek. "I was never in any danger. Honeysett told a tissue of lies to lure the two of you out. And it worked. I don't know whether to be flattered or have Burnell lock you in a cell."

He went on to explain that although he had been stuck at the conference in Bern. He was coordinating with FIS and Villiers. "Longdon had the foresight to ring Villiers and tell him about your meeting with Troxler on the boat and tonight's plans. As you've surmised, I never made any arrangements to have Troxler contact you. I knew immediately that something was amiss and hastily left Bern. My only regret is that FIS and I didn't arrive here in time to prevent this tragedy."

"Enough talking, gentlemen," Dr. Darozze declared. "It is time to take this young woman to the hospital."

Gregory assisted Emmeline to her feet. "I'm coming too."

"I'm afraid FIS and I have a few questions for you, Longdon," he said. "Primarily, where is the Galleon Egg?"

Gregory's lips quivered in a smile. "You mean it's not here?" he asked innocently. "I guess we were all wrong about Colefax's hiding place."

"Uh, huh," Philip replied. "Still, we have other questions about Honeysett and his wife. As Emmeline is not fit at the moment—"

"I'm perfectly fit. Just a bit soggy."

Philip arched a blond eyebrow. "As Emmeline has a date with the doctor, you will have to do."

Gregory inclined his head. He patted Emmeline on the arm. "It's all right, darling. I'll come to the hospital, as soon as I've finished assisting Acheson and the brave officers of FIS."

☙❧

It was mid-morning, when Dr. Darozze came to visit Emmeline on his rounds. He promised she would only have to stay one day. She had been dozing. She blinked awake, when she sensed the air stirring beside her bed.

"Ah, good. Sleep is good for you after your adventures." Although his words were solicitous, the expression on his face was stern.

She pushed herself up on the pillows. "Is something

wrong?"

"The test results came back." He pursed his lips. "I suggest you consult your doctor as soon as you return home."

She felt the blood drain from her face. "If…if I'm ill don't spare me, I'm strong. I want to know the truth. Please, doctor, you must tell me everything."

So he did.

An hour later, Gregory found her staring out the window. Her fingers were pleating the sheets.

"Emmy," he called softly as he approached the bed.

The expression in her dark eyes was guarded. He couldn't read what thoughts were stirring in her head. Cold dread clutched at his chest.

"Darling, what's the matter?" He tried to keep his tone level and calm.

She patted the bed and he sat down on the edge. She was quiet for a long moment. Then, she pressed a hand to his cheek. "In the excitement, I forgot to wish you a Happy Birthday."

He kissed her palm. "That's all right. Plenty of time to celebrate, when we get back to London. Is there something else?"

A tear seeped from the corner of her eye. "Dr. Darozze was here a little while ago."

He held his breath.

"He ticked me off for putting myself…us in danger. He said…" Her voice dropped. "I'm pregnant. About three weeks."

Gregory stared at her. For instant, he thought he hadn't heard her properly. "Pregnant? A baby."

She nodded her head.

He crushed her in his arms. Then, he took her face between his hands and kissed her tenderly. "Oh, darling, this is the best birthday present I could have asked for."

She giggled. "I can't believe it. I've been feeling a little off, but it never crossed my mind. That's why I became nauseous when Nigel and I visited Colefax's house and the reason I fainted at the Clermont Victoria."

He was beaming as he pulled out his mobile. "We must ring Helen this instant. Your grandmother would never forgive us, if we waited until we returned home. It goes without saying that Maggie is next."

She nodded. His excitement was infectious. She placed a hand on top of his on her abdomen. She swallowed hard and pushed away her fears. By this time next year, they would have a beautiful baby to cuddle and love.

A beautiful baby. She hoped with all her heart.

☙❧

Emmeline filed her story from Interlaken, but they decided to spend a few more days in Switzerland to celebrate their wonderful news. On pain of death, Helen and Maggie made them promise to be back before New Year's Eve. They did so solemnly.

On their last day, they took a tour of the Lauterbrunnen Valley, often called the valley of seventy-two waterfalls. The highlight of the trip was a visit to the Trümmelbach Falls, which is a UNESCO World Heritage site and Europe's largest subterranean falls. Ten waterfalls twist and roar inside a mountain. The waterfalls are accessed through an innovative network of walkways, tunnels, galleries, and overlooks. They are the only waterfalls in the world that can be viewed this way. Meltwater from the glaciers atop the Jungfrau, Mönck, and the Eiger mountains rushes onwards into the valley below. At some points, the waterfalls form an underground river. The violent crashing and sluicing of water has chiseled away layers of stone, creating breathtaking rock formations.

Emmeline could feel the tremendous force of the water and droplets of froth on her cheeks, as she and Gregory carefully wandered along a walkway. They stopped at a particularly dramatic spot and were gazing over the railing, when they became aware of a woman bundled in a thick wool coat with the hood obscuring her face. There was little doubt she was following them.

"Keep calm. You have the baby to think about now," Gregory warned. "Walk on. I'll catch up with you."

"Be careful," she whispered. But her words were drowned out by the thundering water.

Reluctantly, she did as he said. But she kept glancing over her shoulder.

Gregory whirled around and caught the woman by the arm. "What do you want?" he demanded.

She laughed and threw off her hood.

"Meredith," he hissed. "Or whatever your name is."

"Meredith will do. I want the Galleon Egg, Longdon." She peered over his shoulder at Emmeline, who was staring wide-eyed at her a few hundred feet down the walkway. "I don't care about you and your wife. I won't hurt you. You have no reason to believe that, but it's true." She plunged her hand into her pocket and took a step closer to him. "I carry a gun because self-preservation has drilled into me that surprises could be lethal. You're an intelligent man. I know you won't do anything foolish that will force me to use it." He could feel the solid bulk of the gun through her coat, as she looped her arm through his elbow.

"Now, all I want is the egg. Honeysett was more trouble than he was worth. I want a bit of comfort when I'm old and gray. If I ever get to be old and gray. A spy's life does not provide much security. The egg is not too much to ask."

"Why do you think I have the egg?"

She laughed again. "Please, Longdon. Your reputation precedes you."

He cast a quick glance at Emmeline and smiled. He gestured with a hand that everything was fine.

Meredith dug the gun deeper into his side. "Shall we have your wife join us?"

"No, leave her out of this. I'll take you to the Galleon Egg. It's in a box in the fireplace in the garden of Chalet Edelweiss. I had to hide it quickly. I was planning to go back this afternoon to retrieve it."

She leaned in closer. "There's no time like the present. I have a car."

"Give me a moment to tell Emmeline to return to the hotel on her own."

"We'll go together. I wouldn't want you getting lost in this underground watery maze."

He gave a reluctant sigh.

When Emmeline saw them walking toward her, she hurried to meet them. Gregory put up a hand to wave her back.

"Emmy, it's all right." He arched an eyebrow and gave her a pointed look. "We're going for a little drive along the Aare River. I'll meet you later at the hotel."

Her gaze flitted between his face and the spy. "You can't be serious."

"Do as your husband says. He has your best interests at heart. I promise to bring him back in one piece."

"You're a spy. That makes you a born liar. Your promises are worthless," Emmeline spat back.

"Emmy, go back to the hotel," Gregory ordered.

She opened her mouth to say something else and then snapped her lips shut.

They left her standing there fuming. He could feel his wife's gaze boring into his back. He just prayed that she remained calm and had understood the message he had tried to telegraph to her.

Meredith made Gregory drive so that she could keep an eye on him. An hour later, they arrived at Colefax's chalet. Everything appeared deserted. With the gun trained on him, they exited the car and followed the side path to the fireplace in the garden.

She gave him an impatient shove. "Stop stalling. Get the Galleon Egg."

Gregory moved forward and started to dig it out of its hiding place, when a phalanx of FIS officers materialized from all directions. They were surrounded. The lead officer told them not to move.

Meredith snarled at Gregory, who sketched a little bow. He left her to the tender ministrations of the officers, who were extremely keen to make her acquaintance.

His lips quirked into a smile. He should never have doubted Emmy, despite her temper and her tendency to worry.

And the Galleon Egg's fate? A private collector had made him a generous offer he couldn't refuse.

All in all, it was a delightful way to end their escapade in Switzerland.

Epilogue

London April 29, 2011

Nurses and doctors in blue scrubs were scurrying in all directions in the Accidents & Emergency department at St. Thomas's Hospital, where Emmeline and Gregory sat waiting.

"All of London is on the streets watching Prince William marry Kate Middleton, while I'm stuck here in A and E waiting to be taken for some tests," Emmeline complained.

Gregory read the fear in her eyes. He pressed a kiss to her temple. "Emmy, everything will be fine. The nurse said it was a routine test."

"It's not all right. If everything were all right, I wouldn't be spotting. Something's wrong with the baby." A lump rose in her throat. "I'm sorry. I was careful. So careful."

He took her face in his hands. "Darling, you won't lose the baby. The doctor merely wants to run some tests to see what's going on."

"Then, why does he want to keep me here overnight?"

"It's a precaution. That's all." He took her hand and intertwined their fingers.

She nodded, but a spasm of fear rippled across her face.

He found an *Evening Standard* next to him and flipped through the pages to find something to distract her. "How about if I read the classifieds to you? Some are quite interesting. Take this one for instance: 'Woman seeking puppy for a band' or 'Leaving for Australia, willing to sell restaurant for one pound.'"

She swatted his arm. "You're making this up."

He poked the paper. "Truly, I'm not. Here's another one: 'Wishing to trace'…" He stopped reading abruptly and stared at the page. He crumpled the paper in his hand. "You're right, darling. This is silly."

He pushed himself to his feet. She frowned at him. "Is something the matter?"

"No, of course not. Everything is fine." He bent down and pressed his forehead against hers. "You must know that you are my world. And now little poppet"—he pressed a hand to her abdomen—"will make our lives even happier." He gave her a soft kiss. "The nurse mentioned something about some forms that needed signing. I'll go see about them and then I'll pop home to get a bag with some of your things."

She snatched his hand.

He smiled. "I won't be long. I promise."

She nodded. "All right." But as she watched him disappear down the corridor, she suddenly felt uneasy.

Once Gregory was in the lift, he pulled out his mobile and punched in a number.

Without offering a greeting, he plunged in, "Did you see the advert in the *Evening Standard*?" He listened for a few seconds and glanced at his watch. "It's Bedlam today because of the royal wedding, but I'll meet you at Waterloo station in an hour."

He severed the connection and immediately made another call.

He couldn't help but smile when he heard Maggie's voice. "Maggie darling."

"How's Emmeline? What did the doctor say?"

"She's fine. She's still in A and E. They are going to do some tests and then the doctor wants to keep her overnight as a precaution. Look, I was wondering whether you could do me a favor."

"For you, anything."

"Can you pop over to the house and put some of Emmy's things in a bag and bring them to the hospital?"

"Of course. The boys are playing with some friends. Philip and I will go straightaway."

"Thanks, love."

He ended the call before she could ask any questions.

༄༅༄

Emmeline was tucked up in a hospital bed, when Maggie and Philip entered the room. Maggie flopped down on the edge of the bed and gave her a tight hug. Philip bent down to give her a peck on the cheek.

Maggie dropped the bag on the floor. "Gregory asked us to bring you a few things."

Emmeline frowned. "I don't understand. He said he was going home."

Maggie gave a nonchalant shrug. "He didn't say."

"Mrs. Longdon, the doctor says you're…Oh, hello. I didn't realize you had visitors."

A nurse entered and nodded at Maggie and Philip.

Emmeline waved a hand. "These are our closest friends. Maggie Roth and her husband Philip Acheson." She glanced at the door and then looked back at the nurse. "Has my husband finished filling out the forms?"

The nurse blinked and stared at her uncertainly. "Pardon. Your husband left the hospital two hours ago. I was in the lift, when he made a call. He was going to meet someone at Waterloo station."

Emmeline slumped back against the pillows. "Yes, of course. Silly me. How could I forget?"

"Now, you must get some rest." To Maggie and Philip, the nurse said, "Please don't stay long."

When she'd gone, Emmeline looked at Maggie and Philip. "Where's Gregory?"

Maggie took her hand. "Don't worry. There's a reasonable explanation." Then, she shot a pointed look at Philip.

"Let me make some calls. We'll get it all sorted." He patted her arm and stepped into the corridor.

For twenty minutes, her eyes were glued to the corridor. The hushed murmur of Philip's voice floated to her ears, but she couldn't hear what he was saying.

His face was grim, when he came back into the room.

"Emmeline, I'm sorry to have to tell you Longdon's missing."

Her brows knit together. "What do you mean missing?"

"He's disappeared, vanished. The last CCTV image was of him leaving the hospital."

They say what you're most afraid of comes true.

Gregory wouldn't leave me, she rebuked herself. *Not again.* She placed a hand on the growing bulge of her belly. *He wouldn't leave me. Not now.*

℘℘℘

"Excuse me, sir, would you have the time?"

Gregory turned around to answer the man. But the words died in his throat.

Something came crashing down against back of his neck, sending a white-hot jolt to rattle the top of his skull. He was falling. Falling. Faster and faster. His bones juddered when he hit the pavement. A second blow landed against his kidney, stealing the air from his lungs and sending searing daggers of pain across every sinew of his body. He saw a white van. Some men leaped out and started to roll him up in a carpet.

"Emmy," he mumbled.

The darkness swallowed him.

And then there was nothing.

Author's Note

For those readers who are history buffs, the Galleon Egg is not among the missing Fabergé treasures. It is purely my creation. Only forty-three of the fifty bejeweled Easter eggs that Tsar Alexander III and Nicholas II commissioned between 1885 and 1917 are believed to exist today.

I also would like to set your minds at ease. There has *never* been a murder at the Clermont Victoria Hotel in London. The hotel and staff are lovely. However the minute I stepped into the gleaming lobby, I simply had to feature the Clermont in my story. It would have been a crime not to do so.

One last note, you cannot visit the Trümmelbach Falls during the winter. But as setting plays a vital role in my stories, I thought what more dramatic place for Emmeline and Gregory to have a final encounter with a spy. I hope you agree.

About the Author

Daniella Bernett is a member of the International Thriller Writers, Mystery Writers of America and the Crime Writers Association. She graduated summa cum laude with a B.S. in Journalism from St. John's University. *Lead Me Into Danger*, *Deadly Legacy*, *From Beyond The Grave*, *A Checkered Past*, *When Blood Runs Cold*, *Old Sins Never Die*, *Viper's Nest of Lies* and *A Mind To Murder* are the books in the Emmeline Kirby-Gregory Longdon mystery series. She also is the author of two poetry collections, *Timeless Allure* and *Silken Reflections*. In her professional life, she is the research manager for a nationally prominent engineering, architectural and construction management firm. Daniella is currently working on Emmeline and Gregory's next adventure. Visit www.daniellabernett.com or follow her on Facebook at https://www.facebook.com/profile.php?id=10000880231 8282

and on Goodreads https://www.goodreads.com/user/show/40690254-daniella-bernett.

www.ingramcontent.com/pod-product-compliance
Lightning Source LLC
Chambersburg PA
CBHW071425200726
48294CB00002B/523